Praise for *The Joshua Files*

"A gripping survival story ... a fantasy of
pyramids, caves and tunnels"
Daily Telegraph

"Fast-paced and exciting, this is one for
fans of Alex Rider and Young Bond"
The Bookseller

"A splendid adventure story"
Mail on Sunday

"It's the Mexican and Mayan flavourings that give Harris's
adventure yarn that bit of extra bite as she weaves a
satisfyingly twisty plot around the science fiction
staples of UFOs and time travel"
Financial Times

"A gripping read"
Sunday Express

Also by M.G. Harris

The Joshua Files
Ice Shock
Zero Moment

M.G. HARRIS

THE JOSHUA FILES

INVISIBLE CITY

■SCHOLASTIC

For Josie and Lilia

First published in the UK in 2008 by Scholastic Children's Books.
This edition published by Scholastic Children's Books, 2010.
An imprint of Scholastic Ltd
Euston House, 24 Eversholt Street
London, NW1 1DB, UK
Registered office: Westfield Road, Southam, Warwickshire, CV47 0RA
SCHOLASTIC and associated logos are trademarks and/or registered
trademarks of Scholastic Inc.

Text copyright © M.G. Harris, 2008
The right of M.G. Harris to be identified as the author of this work
has been asserted by her.

ISBN 978 1 4071 2421 6

Printed in the UK by CPI Bookmarque, Croydon, Surrey
Papers used by Scholastic Children's Books are
made from wood grown in sustainable forests.

1 3 5 7 9 10 8 6 4 2

www.scholastic.co.uk/zone

www.thejoshuafiles.com

Any life is made up of a single moment:
the moment in which a man finds out,
once and for all, who he is.

Jorge Luis Borges

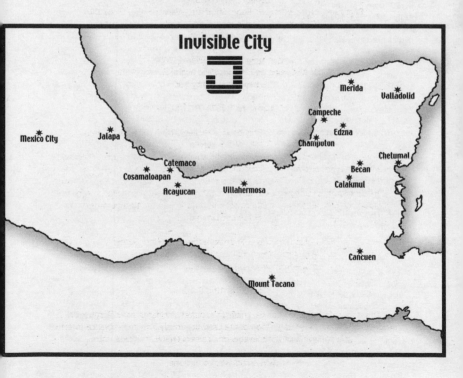

Doomsday 2012?

At least it's after the Olympics…

An ancient prophecy that the world will end on Dec 22, 2012, was on the minds of visitors to an archaeology exhibition in Mexico this week. Visitors to the Museum of Anthropology in Jalapa, Veracruz, Mexico, were astonished by a display that claimed to be part of an ancient Mayan machine.

"It was just incredible," said Angela Winstone, a schoolteacher from Brownsville, Texas. "I always suspected that the Maya were more technologically advanced than we've given them credit for. This totally confirmed that for me. And it really makes you take that 2012 prophecy a whole lot more seriously."

The exhibition, which closed just two days after opening, included two large fragments of metallic material inscribed with Mayan hieroglyphic writing.

"The Maya weren't supposed to have developed such advanced metalworking," added a British visitor, anthropology student Marcus Tennant. "This is either a very clever hoax, or else there's a lot more to the Maya than we ever knew."

Photographs of the exhibits have not been made available. Deputy Director Dr Adriana Velasquez commented, "It's not clear at this time how the pieces came to be included in the exhibition, which was meant only to display artefacts found in the Orizaba region of Mexico. The Mayan kingdom didn't even stretch as far as Orizaba, here in Veracruz. Obviously, this is someone's idea of a joke."

We weren't able to speak to the museum's director as, in a rather unusual move, comments from Dr Xavier Bernal have been embargoed under an order from the Mexican government.

Oxford University professor Andres Garcia, a renowned Mayan scholar, told this paper, "From what I've heard within the museum, staff simply took material from the relevant storeroom and put it on display without checking. Nobody knows how those metal objects got there. I haven't seen the alleged artefacts, so can't say whether they're real or not. It seems unlikely, though. I'm certainly surprised that the Mexican government has become involved."

The ancient Maya, whose empire of pyramids and stone-built cities stretched from Mexico to Guatemala, Belize and Honduras, reached the height of their civilization around 900 AD … and then disappeared mysteriously, abandoning their grand cities, falling back into the jungle.

Their "Long Count" calendar ends on 22 December 2012.

Is this the Mayan date for the end of the world?

Some within the "new age" community disagree. "22/12/12 is about rebirth, the dawning of a new era of consciousness," claims Gabe Goodge, author of *2012 - Preparing For Rebirth.*

Hoax or not, should the worst happen … at least we'll still get to enjoy the London Olympics, which take place in July 2012!

If w
will s
aside o
nately
my r
to get
include
by yo
furbis
tion.
from

If w
will
aside
nately
my rec
to get
included
by your
furbish
tion. I r
from m

you have wandered into a conspiracy-theory zone

This blog belongs to:
Josh Garcia

What's it all about?
This is a record of my search for the truth behind my father's death.

Age:
Thirteen

Location:
Oxford, UK

About me:
Me, I'm the son of a Mexican archaeologist (Dad) and a British history teacher (Mum).

Favourite bands:
Green Day, Arctic Monkeys, Nirvana

Favourite books:
His Dark Materials

Favourite sports:
Capoeira – it's a Brazilian martial art.
Erm . . . that's about it!

If eight out of ten cat owners prefer M&Ms, what do the other two like?
They live on a pure diet of orange Smarties.

Visit http://www.thejoshuafiles.com/blog

BLOG ENTRY: WALKING CONTRADICTION

∇○⊘◐○⬡△⬠⟊⬠

I need a place where I can get rid of all these things going on in my head. Things you don't want to talk about. Things your friends, your family don't want you to talk about.

Hence this blog.

I didn't use to be like this, mooching around on my own, writing down my deepest, darkest thoughts. It wasn't even that long ago that it happened – a couple of weeks back, I was just another guy at school. OK, probably not the cleverest or strongest, definitely not the best-looking or most popular, but apart from that I don't think I had a single complaint in the world.

The thing was, I didn't know it. I thought my problems were a big deal.

Well . . . I had no idea.

There was this phone call and people are telling me I need to go home early. So I'm on my skateboard and down the road.

Never thinking it through. Never guessing that somewhere up the street, a storm was brewing. I sailed towards it, practically singing.

Innocent.

Stupid.

It's capoeira night. Capoeira is this cool Brazilian martial art that I've been learning for almost two years. Our teacher, "Mestre" Ricardo, takes a call on his mobile and calls me out of the *roda* – a circle we make around the two players who "fight". He tells me to get my stuff, to go straight home. At the time I don't really notice, but later I remember something about the look in his eyes.

Mestre Ricardo is a former soldier. Not an easy guy to worry would be my guess. The way he looks at me is something I've never seen from him, never dreamed I'd see: pity.

I remember every detail about the skateboard ride home, over the bridge, the college towers behind me, big puffs of marshmallow cloud in a blue sky reflected in the lead-paned windows. It's the last memory I have where I'm really happy.

I arrive home to find my mother perched on the living-room sofa. Jackie from next door, she's there too, holding Mum's hand. As soon as Mum stands up, I can tell she's been crying. Her face is a colour closer to grey than her normal

English-rose pink. There's a smile of affection on her lips – it looks forced. The ends of her hair are wet, like she's just washed her face. She tries to kiss me, and I shrink from her touch, pull back to look into her eyes.

She's actually shaking, won't even look at me.

She can't.

A chill seeps into my blood. Dread floods through me. A suspicion grows, a tiny seed of horror in the deepest recesses of my mind. It's such a heart-stopping idea that I can't even bring myself to take it seriously.

Mum begins. "Josh, sit down; there's some bad news, I'm afraid. Terrible, terrible news."

She doesn't get any further, though; she's overwhelmed by tears. Her palms go up to her face, cover her eyes. She sinks back down on to the sofa. Jackie takes hold of both my hands, which feel rough, cold and huge in her small fingers.

Between Mum's sobs I make out, "The Cessna plane your dad was renting in Mexico. It went down. And . . . Josh, I'm so sorry. So sorry, but . . . he's dead."

Then it's like I'm disconnected from the moment. Bodily I'm still there, holding hands with my middle-aged neighbour, nodding slightly. But somewhere deep inside I begin a scream of rage and disbelief. I can hear that Jackie is talking, but she seems distant, remote. Mum's face is nothing but a blur as I struggle to grasp what I'm hearing.

Then the screams in my head finally catch up with my mouth. It's as though I'm possessed. I start shouting: *"What? What?!"*

Both women try to hug me, but I shake them off. I can't take it in. Then I'm punching the living room door, yelling at them, "No, no, no, no, no." For an instant I catch the fear in Mum's eyes at my sudden violence.

But within seconds I've stopped, already exhausted. I feel sick. My legs actually buckle slightly underneath me. I slump on to the couch. When I glance up, I notice a shimmering haze around Mum and Jackie. I'm shocked, trembling, numb. Mum grabs hold of me, holds on tight, but all I can think is how her arms aren't long enough for a proper hug. And I wonder: how it would have been if Mum, not Dad, had died? Would Dad's arms be long enough? At the thought of losing Mum too, I burst into tears.

Yet there's this hard little kernel of me that's still ticking over. Still able to look on the bright side.

Wait a bit . . . what if it isn't him?

I'm full of questions. How can they be sure it's my dad? Maybe Dad changed his mind about hiring that plane. Maybe it's some other bloke.

"No, Josh, no," Mum murmurs. "The detective who came round – DI Barratt – says the Mexican police are sure it's him. Your dad hadn't been seen for three days, since he hired this plane."

I shake my head, thinking furiously. Trying to find any loophole. "No. Not Dad. Just cos he's gone missing . . . he could be camping near some ruins. They can't be sure without proof. Have they got proof? What is it they do – they look at dental records, don't they? Yeah, I've seen it a million times in films. I bet the dental records will show it's not my dad."

"I'm sorry, love," Jackie explains kindly. "It wasn't that simple. Wish it was, poppet."

"What . . . why not?"

Mum holds my hand. They exchange a look. Mum nods at Jackie. Very slightly.

"Your dad's plane hit a tree. A branch. Would have shot through the windscreen at God knows what speed. He had no chance, Josh. No chance at all."

"What?! Just tell me," I insist, through my tears. "What aren't you telling me?"

Jackie straightens up; her voice steels, becomes faint, distant, cold.

"He was decapitated," she says. "In the plane crash. There is no head. Just your poor dad's burned, broken body."

I take a few moments to absorb that. I'm already beginning to join Jackie in that remote place.

That's where I need to be now. Somewhere else. Anywhere.

Death would have been instantaneous, she's quick to assure me. *Better hope so.* The thought of something like that happening slowly is unbearable.

There was no sign of foul play. No severed fluid lines, nothing suspicious. The best guess from the Mexican police is that he fell asleep at the controls, lost altitude, plunged to his doom.

My emotions start to shut down. Movements become purely mechanical. Would I like some tea? I'm nodding, asking for milk and two sugars.

Like it matters.

I wish I could stop the TV scenes that begin to play through my head. Two sympathetic policemen at the door, the phone call from the hospital, the phone call from abroad. On TV, I've seen bad news delivered lots of ways. Now it's my turn.

Jackie seems to know just what to do. She has nerve; in the midst of our little storm, she holds firm. She's all gentle Irish humour as she makes us hot buttered toast. She serves us thick slices with mugs of sweet, milky tea. She turns on the TV. We watch a whole film, but later I don't remember a single detail. I keep glancing at Mum, wondering what we do now. Am I supposed to hug her? Or what?

I know what Dad would say: *Son, you take care of your mother, you got that?*

Mum's eyes look glazed, staring. After my initial outburst, things are calm. We take it quietly then.

Later, when I go to bed, I get to thinking. I can't stop wondering about something Jackie said; something I hardly noticed at the time.

So far, the Mexican police haven't actually found his head. The rest of his body was burned beyond recognition. They are sure of two things: it was the plane Professor Andres Garcia rented, and his luggage was found thrown clear of the crash.

That's where it begins, that's the root of the matter. Call it what you like: doubt, suspicion, a hunch.

I don't believe it. Not "can't". I'm pretty sure that I could if it only felt true. But something doesn't feel right. Dad has only been flying for three years. I know he's still cautious, plans every detail.

There's no way he'd fall asleep at the controls.

There has to have been some horrendous, monumental mistake.

BLOG ENTRY: THE JOSHUA FILES

ΛƆЯ؟ᴨᴑΔƎᴜя

So here's the thing – everyone thinks I'm crazy.

Well, it's weird. When people reckon you're going a bit barmy, they don't actually use words like *barmy*, *crazy*, or even *psycho*. They say things like *normal grief response* and *therapy*.

What's really baffling my mum and her friends is that I'm not even getting "barmy" right. Maybe she'd prefer it if I were crying loads, or just sitting staring into space. But it's like there's a sign taped to my forehead: *Does not fit the textbooks.*

All I'm doing is looking at the circumstances of this plane crash and asking a few questions that don't seem to interest anyone else.

1. Dad told Mum and me that he was going to Cancuen in Guatamela. Some Mayan king was murdered there hundreds of years ago. So . . . why was Dad's plane found hundreds of miles from where he'd rented it *and* hundreds of miles from Cancuen?

2. Why did the local newspaper not have a single witness who saw the plane come down?

3. Why did that same local newspaper carry eyewitness reports of a major UFO sighting close to where they said his plane had come down?

Seems to me, you get some information like that, you should ask some serious questions. Maybe wonder about the truth of statements like "Dr Andres Garcia crashed his Cessna in the jungle of southern Mexico and suffered fatal injuries on impact".

Why am I the only one wondering about this? Seems totally normal to me. But the more I go on, the more Mum thinks I'm losing it.

What is it with UFOs, anyway? Why are you automtically a headcase just because you say you've seen a UFO? So many people nowadays have – it's not hundreds of people; it's hundreds of thousands. From all backgrounds, all ages, all types of braininess. UFO sightings are rampant; you can't ignore something that so many people see.

I took those three facts about my dad's plane crash and I put them together like this: what if that body belongs to someone else?

What if Dad wasn't in the crash at all? What if he was abducted by the UFOs? What if he isn't dead, just missing?

Mum's first reaction, I have to say, was very reasonable. She said, "OK. Let's assume that there really was a UFO. What about the body in the plane? What about the luggage? No one else was reported missing, just your father." Then she gave me a big hug and said, "I understand, sweetheart; you don't want this to be true. Neither do I. It's unthinkable, unbearable." Then she slowly began to cry, and it was me who had to comfort her.

Which I can do, because now I'm not so sure that he's dead.

Comment (1) from TopShopPrincess

Hey Josh. Notice you say on your profile that you're from Oxford. Me too. Us UFO-philes should stick together. I saw a UFO once, you know. It was at night; my dad was driving me home after a party and there it was, for just a few seconds, hovering in a field. Dad said all he saw were the lights of an airplane. But he didn't get a proper look cos he was driving. It hovered all right, then swung into the air and shot off. Planes don't do that – at least, no plane I ever saw did. If you say you think your dad was abducted, then I believe you.

Reply

Thanks, TopShopPrincess. (I'm guessing you're an Arctic Monkeys fan, right?) It's good to know there's one person out there who believes me. The guys at school think it's a laugh. I only mentioned it once and I never will again.

Too right! Arctic Monkeys rule!

BLOG ENTRY: AEROMEXICO PILOT FILMS UFOS IN CAMPECHE!

ᐁᐊᒾᐅᐊᐞᐊᑕᐊᐃᐁᐊ

I've been spending a lot of my time looking through UFO sightings reports. It's amazing what you can find on the Web. People I might once have called "nutters", logging up hours online to post information, rumours, opinion. I can't get enough of it. If I keep looking, I might find the one report that will lead me to Dad. It's not unheard of. People often get abducted in groups. Years later, they find each other again. No connection in their normal lives, but they know each other, somehow. I'm not talking about déjà vu. This is real. Total strangers who know stuff about each other that they couldn't know if they hadn't met.

If Dad was taken along with anyone else, there might be hope.

We heard about the plane crash a few days back. I've been tracking rumours in the UFO boards. Now they've hit the mainstream news.

So I'm *not* just going on the words of some random UFO fans. A commercial airline pilot with Aeromexico is one of my key witnesses!

Aeromexico Pilot Films "UFOs"
"In the late evening of June 15, a commercial airline pilot flying Aeromexico

Flight 231 filmed six unidentified flying objects in the skies over southern Campeche state, a Defense Department spokesman confirmed.

In a sighting that bears an uncanny resemblance to the widely reported event of March 2004 – in which pilots of the Mexican airforce filmed eleven UFOs – a videotape made widely available to the news media shows the bright objects, some sharp points of light and others like large headlights, moving rapidly in what appears to be a late-evening sky."

Comment (1) from TopShopPrincess

I looked up the news stories you blogged. Awesome! I can't believe you've actually got airline pilots backing you up on this one.

Reply

For all the good it does! Remember, I'm working against total scepticism here. Mum's argument, basically, goes like this:

1. The plane was found on the nineteenth of June. The corpse was at least three days old, but could have been older. So we don't know for definite that the crash was on the fifteenth, the day the UFOs were sighted.

2. People are always spotting UFOs in Mexico. The stories amount to nothing.

3. If the body wasn't Dad's, then whose was it? No one else was reported missing.

4. Dad could have planned another trip, not just to central Guatemala, but to somewhere in Campeche, Mexico. There are lots of Mayan ruins in Campeche.

Comment (2) from TopShopPrincess

Hmmm. Well . . . not being funny or anything, but your mum does have a point.

Reply

Maybe so, TopShopPrincess, but she's wrong about UFOs. They haven't only been around since the 1940s. They go way back. There are ancient Sanskrit manuscripts from India that talk about flying-saucer-type objects. Ancient Sumerian clay tablets 4000 years old with carvings of flying machines. UFOs – they're ancient history.

While I'm reading TopShopPrincess's response to my blog post, I notice my mother standing in the doorway. She's wearing her dressing gown – again. She's scarcely been out of the house since we heard about Dad. I wonder if she'll ever get back to teaching history to those rich kids at the college.

"Mum, you have to look at this," I say, waving her over. "A pilot for Aeromexico spotted those UFOs too. Fifteenth of June. Almost the the same day they think Dad's plane crashed. What if they got it wrong; what if his plane went down on the fifteenth?"

Despite herself, Mum can't resist looking. She stands, reading over my shoulder as I hold my breath. Is this it? Finally, the point at which she takes me seriously?

After a few minutes, she says in a tired voice, "Read the bottom line of the report, Josh. 'Mexico has a long history of fanciful UFO sightings, most of which are dismissed by scientists as space debris, missiles, weather balloons, natural weather phenomena or hoaxes'."

"God, that is SO patronizing!" I shout.

She just stares blankly at me. "I'm getting tired of this, Josh. When's this going to stop?"

"Why won't you even talk about it?"

Mum explodes. "Because it's preposterous! People don't get abducted by aliens! UFO sightings . . . they're just some trendy zeitgeist thing. It's a mythology, a modern mythology!"

Then she sighs, sinks down on to the bed, runs one hand through her hair, exhausted and desperate.

"Please, *please* listen to me, Josh. We both know what happened to your father, and as ghastly, as unforgettably horrible as that was, we have to learn to live with it!"

"What about the fact that his plane was in northern Campeche . . . in Mexico? Dad was supposed to be in central Guatemala, the place where they found the murdered Mayan king. That's hundreds of miles away!"

"Josh, he makes these trips all the time," she says wearily. "He doesn't give me every single detail. That's why he always goes out to Tuxtla first and rents his cousin's Cessna. Otherwise it takes ages, driving all over the place, or else it costs a fortune on commercial flights. That's how it is with Mayan archaeology. All the new discoveries are in the middle of nowhere."

And she goes on to say more stuff, but I've stopped

listening. Instead, I think about what she said just a few seconds earlier.

"You said 'makes these trips'. 'Rents his cousin's Cessna'. You're talking like he's still alive. Is that what you really think too, Mum?"

Mum shakes her head very sadly. "No. But I can wish it, can't I?"

There's a knock at the door. We're not expecting anyone. I can sense it – something's wrong. Mum feels it too. Nervously, I open the door.

It's a copper. He introduces himself as Detective Inspector Barratt of Thames Valley Police.

"It's about Professor Garcia," he says, standing at our doorstep. "The Mexican police have been in touch. And I'm sorry to say it's rather bad news."

The head wasn't burnt to a crisp like the rest of him. It had been sliced off before the fire, which started in the crashed plane.

Barratt tells us, "The Mexican investigators reckon that wild animals must have made off with the head. They found it miles away, features ravaged, decomposed beyond any recognition. According to the coroner, the dental X-rays are conclusive; a match with Professor Garcia."

He goes on; there were something called *hyaloid fractures* – the hyaloid is a little bone deep in the throat that often breaks during strangulation. And *petechial haemorrhages* – tiny broken blood vessels in the eye, another classic sign of strangulation. Taken together, they point to one thing: murder.

Listening to DI Barratt, I feel like a lizard is slowly crawling along my spine. It's the most horrible and yet the most thrilling thing I've ever heard. Now our pain isn't just a twist of fate but something malign, something intended. There's a prickling of the hairs on my skin. Even the air around us seems to be charged. I look across at Mum, and I can't read her expressionless face. But her knuckles are white to the bone.

Barratt lets that news sink in for a few minutes, then carries on. As things turned out, Dad hadn't been seen at Cancuen for four days before his death. On 12 June, he'd flown out of Cancuen, told the other archaeologists he'd be flying back to Mexico. They'd assumed he meant Tuxtla, where he'd hired the plane. But the police had talked to the plane-hire guys. Dad hadn't been there either. At first, no one knew where he'd gone for those missing four days.

The Mexican detectives were certain that Dad was dead before the plane crashed, probably even before it took off – strangled to death, maybe by whoever flew the plane. The theory is that a second man was in the plane with Dad – he probably doused Dad's dead body with lighter fluid, then parachuted out. Since no witnesses have come forward saying anything about the crash or any parachutist, it's likely that the incident took place at night. They're putting the date of death at 16 June, based on the examination of the crash remains. It's a theory that works with the facts.

Then last week someone came forward. An anonymous tip-off. There'd been talk of a secret night-landing in a small beachside town.

"A place called Chetumal," Barratt says. "Do you know it?"

Mum shakes her head. "No. I mean, yes – I've heard of it. Never been."

"Well," Barratt begins solemnly. "There was a late-night meeting. So we've heard. The kind of small-town gossip police hear all the time. But this time it ties everything together."

"Do the police out there have any suspects?" Mum asks. Her voice seems artificially flat.

Barratt coughs. "They do, Mrs Garcia. I'm afraid so. They've already made an arrest. It's going to be another shock for you. I'm very sorry."

We wait. The air is thick with our anxiety.

"There was a woman out there. In this Chetumal place. The professor had been seen visiting with her, you see. This past year. Many times. Plenty of witnesses. Incidents of affection, you understand. In a small town like that, there's always gossip. But where there's smoke. . . Rumours spread, the wrong people get to hear."

Mum's face drains. Her voice cracks. "I see. Was she . . . a married woman?"

"I'm afraid so. Her husband, you see. . ."

And in a tiny voice, Mum says, "I understand."

"I'm sorry, Mrs Garcia."

I blurt, "Well, I *don't* understand. Can someone explain?"

Barratt turns sympathetic, watery eyes on me.

"The woman's husband. The jealous type. And a qualified pilot. No alibi. Motive. Opportunity. Far as they're concerned in Mexico, they've got their man."

"So we're supposed to just believe this – village gossip?"

"I'm sorry, lad. These things happen."

And I shout, "Not to my dad!"

Mum pulls me close. Her cheeks are already wet with hot, silent tears. I bite my lip. It's not easy to stay calm.

BLOG ENTRY: FOUR MISSING DAYS AND A MURDER

⚑⌐⚠⧓⧫⌐⬧⧫⊐⋛

So, it's official. My dad is dead. Not only dead, but murdered.

I thought it was bad before. But after today I'm just sort of tired. There's a weird kind of numbness. Like I've reached a limit.

Comment (1) from TopShopPrincess

Josh ... omigod, I can hardly believe you aren't making this up.

Reply

TopShopPrincess – I couldn't. I'm living it and I can hardly believe it's happening.

3

It's a bad night, one of the worst. I can hear Mum crying next door. She'll get up every so often to be sick. She's melting away, losing herself in tiny pieces.

I phone the doctor, but they only put me through to the health information service.

"Call your GP in the morning. If there's no difference tomorrow, she can prescribe something to calm your mother down. This will have been a terrible shock."

Mum doesn't get up until late afternoon. We sit together at the kitchen table. I trace patterns in a pool of spilled cranberry juice. I've lost all sense of the future. What do people do after a thing like this? I have no idea where to start.

Mum begins to shake. She asks for a small glass of brandy. A little later she stops shaking and begins, very softly, to cry. I don't feel like crying any more – just the opposite. I have an urge to run – anywhere. To get far away from this house of bad news.

She gulps down one of the tablets I picked up for her, wipes her face with a tissue and blows her nose. I've never seen her look so bad. Not even the very first day.

Finally I speak up. "Why do you believe it?"

"Because it's my worst fear."

"That Dad dies?"

"That he'd find another woman. Your dad is – was – a very attractive man, Josh. I've always known it. And these excavations, they go on for ever."

I'm quiet for ages. I had no idea. And I can't think what to say. "You never said."

"Of course not."

"Did he know?"

"Of course not, he hated jealousy."

I think about how my parents were together. OK, no one likes to see their parents kiss and stuff. Obviously, it's gross. But I sort of liked that Dad was always really affectionate with Mum. She is shy, reserved. Very British and all that. Not him, though. Always pleased to see her, big hugs and kisses when he came home. My whole life, they'd held hands, watched TV in each other's arms. All that, had it been a lie?

"But how?"

She sighs. "Men . . . are that way, I suppose. DI Barratt said the woman is in her late twenties. Late twenties! You probably think that sounds old. But to a man your father's age. . ."

She leaves that one unfinished, goes back to her brooding. I can sense waves of anger building inside her.

I chip in, "Not Dad, though."

Mum snaps, "Why not? He's just another man, isn't he? I should have been more suspicious. What a fool I've been! *La casa grande y la casa chica!* Not as though I haven't seen plenty of Mexican men behave this way. It's finally happened to me."

"'*La casa grande.* . .'?"

"The big house and the little house. A nice little euphemism for a married man's family and his mistress's. Haven't you wondered where some of your uncles disappear to when they're in their forties? To their younger women, that's where. But the first wife, if she's in the know, then she's supposed to be quiet, dignified. She's supposed to cover for him! 'Where's your husband?' 'Oh, away on business!'"

I stare at Mum. I can't believe how easily she believes it. She's judging my dad without evidence, as if he were just any macho latin husband. If she thinks that about him, is she going to start treating me like just another one of "them"?

"No. It's not fair to accept this without hearing Dad's side. I don't believe he'd do it."

She's quiet for a long time. "I wish . . . I'd like to believe that."

"Well, why not?"

She looks at me with a faint glimmer of hope.

21

"Do you think we could? Just, not believe it?"

I take a deep breath. "*I* don't believe it."

But she can't meet my gaze. She looks down, begins to tremble. "I must be a terrible person," she says, her voice quavering. "Because I think it must be true . . . why else would they arrest someone?"

Why else?

I wonder about that all afternoon.

BLOG ENTRY: THIS IS A LOW

930Λ6Δᵁ̈Λ◍ᴎ

Mum spent today in bed again. It's been over a week. Well, I feel like I'm grinding through it, going to school every day, which takes my mind off stuff for a few hours. But each day I come home to find that Mum hasn't moved. When I came home today, I found her listening to "Waters of March". She and Dad didn't have one tune, but I'd guess that one was probably in their top five. She'd put it on a continuous loop and was lying flat on their bed, staring up at the ceiling.

Since Dad's death, jazz has been banned from our house. Miles Davis, Oscar Peterson, Stan Getz, Tom Jobim and all those guys – that's my dad's music. Me, I'm not a fan, but you get used to it. Mum and me – we have this unwritten rule now. Hearing jazz is just too miserable – for us both.

And yet there she was, wallowing in it.

Well, I said nothing. Just closed the door quietly so that I didn't have to listen.

I'm trying to keep things going here. I even cook sick-person food for Mum. Tomato soup with soft white bread. Chicken broth and buttered crackers.

But still she won't eat. Finding out what really happened to my dad seems to have finished her off.

What the heck am I supposed to do?

Comment (1) from TopShopPrincess

Jeez . . . Josh. You need to get some help, man. I'm out of my depth here. Call the doctor!

Reply

So . . . I did it. Called the GP. Told her that Mum was hardly responding. Just staring. And that was it.

They sent some paramedics round. Said Mum needed some time with specialists. I don't know if Mum even understood what happened. I prepared a bag for her; make-up, toiletries, spare clothes. As she walked through the front door, she got this look in her eye.

It made me crumble. I feel like a traitor.

Comment (2) from TopShopPrincess

Josh – you've done the right thing. You're only thirteen. How can you look after your mum when she's like this? She'll be all right in a bit. You wait and see.

Reply

I know you're just being nice. But I'm the one who feels guilty here. I have to come up with something quickly, something that will get Mum's hopes up again. If only I can get some bit of proof that this affair is a lie. Or come up with another reason why someone might have killed Dad.

Comment (3) from TopShopPrincess

Well – yeah. You could try. But how?

How am I going to prove that Dad wasn't having an affair with that woman? It's pretty tough to prove a negative.

I think about those four missing days. The way I see things, the police have accounted for just two of them: Dad's plane landing late at night in the town of Chetumal, Mexico on 12 June. And the plane crash on 16 June – the night of the murder.

What about all the days in between? Did the mystery woman hide Dad away somewhere? Where had his plane been? But the police aren't asking those questions. They don't believe a word the woman says. They reckon she'll say anything to keep her husband out of jail. Meanwhile the husband pleads his innocence. "But he would say that," insist the police. They have their man, and that's that.

I figure that something like this doesn't come from nowhere. People meet, they communicate. Emails, phone calls. Maybe even old-fashioned letters.

Until I make some headway, school is off the agenda. At my school they don't chase truants right away. I figure I have at least one day to get something done.

I've been eating supper next door at Jackie's while Mum's in the hospital. Afterwards, I go through Dad's emails on the home computer. There are no suspicious emails from any Mexican-sounding ladies. So either he's innocent or else he's smart enough to set up a secret email account.

I check the history of his Web browser. No record of any other email accounts. So either he's innocent or else he's smart enough to delete his history files.

I go back to the emails and read through the last few he's sent or received. That's when I find something interesting about Dad's plans for those missing days in June.

And it has nothing to do with an affair.

The day before he left Oxford, Dad emailed a Dr Marius Martineau of the Peabody Museum of Archaeology and Ethnology in the US. It was the last email he sent.

Dear Dr Martineau,

A manuscript that has come into my possession leads me to believe that there may be some truth in rumours of the existence of a fifth codex of the Maya. The manuscript appears to be a part of a letter from a Mayan citizen of Cancuen to the Ruler of Calakmul. This "Calakmul letter" is dated 653 AD. It speaks quite clearly of

a book named the Ix Codex, a book it describes as a kind
of Mayan Book of Revelations – about the end of the world
in 2012.

I gather you have a rather formidable collection of rare
inscriptions taken from stelae in the Rio Bec region. Have
you come across any inscriptions from the city of Calakmul
that might shed light on such a story?

Perhaps we could meet between 12–20 June? I plan to
be in Mexico for several days following a trip to the ruins at
Cancuen.

Regards,
Andres Garcia

The reply from Martineau came in the same day.

Dear Professor Garcia,

A "fifth" codex, prophecies about the "end of the
world" on 22 December 2012. . .? If I listened to every
crackpot idea I heard in this field, I'd be too busy joining a
cult to get any work done.

You say the document is dated 653 AD? That sounds
suspicious. All surviving codices date from the fifteenth
century.

I think you've got a fake on your hands. They can be

quite convincing – I've seen the Prague Codex and it might well have fooled me.

I'm pretty busy at the minute. I'm sorry, but I don't really have the time for something that looks this controversial. Maybe someone else can help out with authenticating it?

Sincerely,
Marius Martineau

My pulse races as I read the dates in Dad's email: 12–20 June. So he left Cancuen exactly as planned. Did he fly somewhere to meet with Martineau after all? Martineau's email seems pretty indifferent – which suggests that they didn't meet. I move on and read the second-to-last email Dad sent – two days before he left Oxford.

Dear Dr Montoyo,

I wonder if you remember meeting me at Palenque Round Table last year? I have recently come across a fragment of a Mayan manuscript. It appears to be part of a letter written to the ruler of Calakmul. This "Calakmul letter" speaks of a Mayan book named the Ix Codex. The letter also mentions two Mayan cities – Chechan Naab and Ek Naab. I've never heard of these cities, nor been able to find any references to them in the literature. That in itself is pretty strange, don't you agree?

I remember that you told me you'd recently been leading a project to translate new inscriptions from Calakmul. Have you come across cities named Chechan Naab or Ek Naab? Or ever heard of the Ix Codex? If you can offer any help, I'd be more than happy to work together on this project. I'll be in Mexico later this month, 12–20 June. Perhaps we can meet?

Regards,
Andres Garcia

When I look through the reply, my heart begins to pound. This is it. There *is* more to this Ix Codex than meets the eye.

Dr Garcia,

Indeed, I do remember our meeting. I feel I must warn you that you are headed on a dangerous path. The existence of the I* Code* is a rumour that has persisted in some disreputable circles for many years. I speak of various dubious practioners of the occult. I never thought to hear about the codex from a renowned archaeologist such as you. Those who have sought it have so far disappeared without a trace.

Please take note that I do not even include the name in this email. If you value your safety, you will not search for that term on the Web or include it in an email again. Web searches and emails are routinely monitored by organizations whose interest in the I* Code* might surprise you.

I cannot say more except in person. I will find you during your visit to Mexico. It is best if we don't make a firm appointment.

Regards,
Carlos Montoyo

Without even thinking, I hit the reply button and type a quick message to Montoyo:

Dear Dr Montoyo,

I am the son of Andres Garcia. Maybe you heard the news that my father died in an airplane crash in June. I read your email to him. Did you and my father actually meet? I have some questions about his research. It would be great if you could help.

Yours,
Josh Garcia

My eyes flick back to the top of Montoyo's email; when had it been sent? The reply came through the very morning Dad left. And it *had* been read. Dad went on his trip knowing that this wasn't just an exciting hunt for a valuable piece of Mayan history. He'd stumbled across something else, something that could attract the wrong kind of attention.

But was it the kind of attention that could get you killed? And would the killers take the trouble to frame someone else for the murder?

All I am sure of is this: I've found another possible motive for Dad's murder. Not a jealous husband but a search for a historical treasure. A search that led my father on a one-way trip – deep into the Mayan heart of darkness.

BLOG ENTRY: RAIDERS OF THE LOST CODEX!

ᗝᘓᗢᗣᗞᗠᗣᗢᗩᗡᗣ

I am NOT even joking. Seriously, my dad was involved in some major stuff. I just found evidence (not going to give details) that he found some Mayan inscription that might lead to one of the rarest finds in Mayan archaeology. A long-lost book, or codex, with a Mayan prophecy about the end of the world – in 2012!

Looks like I might have to learn how to decipher Mayan writing.

31

Comment (1) from TopShopPrincess

OK, now you've got me thinking you're making this up. Are you a big fat liar, Josh?

Reply

What's it going to take to convince you? Want to come down the library with me to do some research?

Comment (2) from TopShopPrincess

Very funny, LOL. I'm sixteen. A bit old for you, Josh, if that's what you're thinking.

Reply

Huhhh? Who said anything about that?

I get right on to it the very next day. There are clues in Dad's emails. I'm no expert on Mayan history, but Dad's study in our house is chock-full of books. So I swot up on the ancient Mayan civilization.

When I was a little kid, we'd spend long summers in Mexico, usually around the site of one of Dad's excavations. The names have all faded into a blur now. Truth is, I didn't pay much attention to where we were. It was all pretty much the same; ruined temples, jungles, tents and trying to find enough flat land for a game of football with the local village kids.

I didn't pay attention to the archaeology. Which now, I kind of regret.

I've never heard of any of the Mayan cities mentioned in Dad's emails – Cancuen, Calakmul, Ek Naab, Chechan Naab. So, I look them up in Dad's books. Cancuen is in Guatemala – a Central American country next to Mexico. Calakmul is in southern Mexico – Campeche state.

Close to where Dad's plane crashed.

Cancuen and Calakmul were important cities of the Mayan kingdom. Calakmul had this powerful ruler once, a guy called Yuknoom Ch'een. He was on the throne for ages.

But I find nothing about Ek Naab, nor Chechan Naab.

I find an online Mayan dictionary. It's cool – even has a little button you can press to hear the Mayan words spoken. Ek Naab translates as *dark water*. Chechan Naab translates as *knotted snake water*.

I'm playing around on that website when the doorbell goes. It's been quiet lately – for obvious reasons I haven't felt very sociable. Outside the door is Tyler Marks, a guy I recognize from capoeira – my Brazilian martial arts class.

"We thought you was dead," he says with a big grin.

"Not me," I say, deadpan. "My dad."

That rips away his smile. "God, Josh, I'm really sorry. I didn't know. You didn't show up. We wondered if you'd lost interest."

"Sort of, yeah. I've got other stuff to do."

"Like what?"

"Just . . . stuff."

"You and me both," Tyler says. "But you should still practise."

"Hmmm."

We share an uncomfortable silence.

"What did your dad die of?"

"Of murder."

"You're kidding!"

"No."

"Wow."

"Yeah."

We stare at each other, saying nothing. But he doesn't leave.

"Thing is, Josh, there's a talent scout coming in from London. Picking guys for a British team to go to Brazil. Mestre Ricardo says they're looking to pick one person from Oxford."

"Fine," I reply. "It can be you."

Tyler looks disappointed. "They have to see me in action. Against someone of similar standard."

I get it – he wants me to make him look good. "What do you want?"

Tyler's brown face cracks into a gleaming white smile. "Just come to class a couple of times over the next few weeks. Then when this scout comes in September, I can put on a show."

I scratch my head. "I'm out of shape."

"Come on. Do you good."

"You'll owe me."

"Hey, mate, name your price."

I sigh. "OK, you win." I grab my skateboard. "But sooner or later, it's payback time."

So, down at the gym, we spar. Capoeira has all these pretty special rituals, so I wear the white *abada* clothes, I join in with the songs, but inside I'm strangely detached. We sing in Portuguese, the old songs of slaves striving to keep body and soul together. We flex our muscles against each other, aiming for graceful mock combat.

Thousands of miles away, a deteriorating corpse awaits a burial. Nearby, an innocent man languishes in prison for a murder he didn't commit. These thoughts don't leave me for a minute, even as I retaliate against Tyler's cartwheel attacks. I'm drawn to those steamy jungle towns with their mysterious-sounding names. Chechan Naab and Ek Naab.

Why are there no references to them in any books? Or on the Web?

Are they lost cities, like the ones in the movies where Indiana Jones found the Ark of the Covenant and the Holy Grail? Was my dad looking for some incredible, ancient relic with the power to change the world?

Well, now even I begin to think I'm cooking up some daft fantasy. But I can't help it. Dad was involved in something heavy. I'm sure enough of that.

After the capoeira, we hang out together at Tyler's playing XBox. Tyler talks non-stop about girls he reckons fancy him. I don't say much, just listen. I don't have those kinds of stories to tell; worse luck.

It's still warm and sunny as I'm walking home. I'm through the gate when I notice something odd.

The curtains are drawn – every last one.

I know I didn't draw them. I guess that it must have been Jackie. I'm about to go over and ask why she's been in our house, when I hear the sound of an upstairs door closing.

The noise comes from inside my house.

I take my key and open the front door. I'm still only slightly puzzled. I step inside and call out, "Hey, Jackie, I'm back."

There's no answer. I stand absolutely still, listening.

And that's the first time it strikes me that something is really wrong.

There's someone upstairs and it isn't Jackie.

I'm looking around for a weapon when a guy in a balaclava comes hurtling down the stairs like a hurricane. He vaults over the banister and lands right next to me, swings out with a punch. My reflexes are better than I'd guessed because without even thinking, I duck. He narrowly misses my head. With all that momentum, he overbalances and stumbles. I'm in a *ginga* stance right away and aim a *pontiera* – a high front kick at his chest. It lands squarely – he's knocked back. I follow it up with a *chapa baixa*, landing a hard kick to his knee. He staggers into the back room. He tries to slam the door closed but I jam my foot in the door. Big mistake. He crushes the door hard against my trapped foot until I scream and pull the foot free. Again he slams the door – this time it snaps shut. I try to shoulder-barge it but it's no use – he's got something up against the handle.

He's only got one way out now – the French windows.

I can feel the adrenaline pumping through me as I rush out of the front door. I'm round the back just in time to see him dashing across the back lawn, loaded with a black rucksack. I throw myself at him in a flying rugby tackle and get him to the ground.

It's the wrong move. I should have stuck to the capoeira. This time he's prepared for me. On the ground, I'm useless. He lands two punches to my face; I taste blood in my mouth and see stars. While I'm still reeling in a daze, he pushes me off him, starts to get to his feet. I lunge out, grab hold of his balaclava and yank. It pulls off just as he's moving away. In that second I catch a glimpse of him. He's tall, eyes clear green and almond-shaped, high cheekbones, square jaw. There's a faintly astringent smell – aftershave or hair gel.

I could swear, before he heads off, he actually grins at me.

I'm still dabbing at my bloody nose and cheek with Kleenex when Jackie and the police turn up.

They all look at me with an expression that's kind of embarrassed for me. One bad thing happening to you, that's bad luck. More than once and it's almost like it's your own fault.

Inside the house, everywhere I look, objects are strewn;

every drawer, every shelf, cupboard has been emptied and the contents tossed around. Jackie takes one look at me. She goes straight to the freezer, takes out a bag of frozen peas and makes me press them to my face.

"Horrible bruising you'll get from that, see if you don't," she says.

One policeman asks me to go to my room, see what is missing. I trudge upstairs in a daze. My room is every bit as bad as the rest of the house. The guy's taken my laptop computer. I'm trying to process what's happened as I slope back downstairs and tell the police.

Mum's laptop is gone too, and the box for Dad's computer, and a fancy digital camera. "They go for stuff they can get rid of quickly at the pub," the policeman tells me. "It'll be kids looking for money to buy drugs."

"It wasn't 'kids'," I say, annoyed. "I gave you his description. He was in his late twenties at least. He knew what he was doing."

The copper gives me a disapproving look. "You shouldn't tackle burglars, son. Not ever. I don't care if you're a black belt. You should consider pressing charges when we catch the perpetrator."

If they catch him, is what goes through my mind.

Then he leans in close, says, "Your neighbour seems to think this will be too upsetting for your mother to hear about. In her current condition."

He leaves out "in the psychiatric hospital".

I ask, "You think there's a connection?"

"With what?"

"Between my dad's murder and this burglary?"

He looks at me blankly. "I don't see how . . . but if you're worried, I'll ask DI Barratt to take a look at the case."

I nod. "Please."

"It's not a good idea for you to sleep here alone," says the copper. "Not after this. Sometimes they come back for what they might have missed. Or for what they think you'll replace. Best stay away. Just for a bit."

He makes it sound sensible, but there's no hiding the fact that within one month I seem to have lost my dad, my mum and my home. I feel pretty rubbish. When it came down to it, I wasn't up to defending what was mine.

"It's just temporary, Josh," says Jackie, laying a friendly hand on my shoulder. I just nod wordlessly. My eyes sting from tears I badly need to hold back.

I don't believe for a second that it's "kids". I think back to Montoyo's warning to Dad about the Ix Codex. *Those who have sought it have so far disappeared without a trace.*

Yet my dad was murdered, with evidence and everything. Whoever these people are, they're getting sloppy. They're beginning to make mistakes.

Probably because I'm dazed from the punches and my ice-cold bruise, it isn't until much later, as I'm about to leave for Jackie's, that I think to check Dad's study. Is there anything missing other than the computers? I notice a couple of books on the floor, swept off the shelves. By accident? I kneel down to take a look.

The books are some standard textbooks of Mayan archaeology. I pick them up, replace them on the shelf. There's a gap. I scan the titles of the remaining books.

One is missing.

Even before I really think about it, I know which one it will be. Because only one book really matters.

One of the John Lloyd Stephens books – Volume II of the two-book set: *Incidents of Travel in Central America, Chiapas and Yucatan.*

There's a whole story behind those books, one I've never heard all the way through. But the story is magical to us – the books that brought Mum and Dad together, the books that Dad read as a young boy fascinated with travel, discovery and adventure. The books that first gave him the archaeology bug; the dream of discovering a lost city of the Maya, just like his hero the American traveller John Lloyd Stephens, the first "white man" to see some of the Mayan ruins as they lay undisturbed for centuries, gobbled up by the jungle.

Well, Volume II *is* gone. I take a thorough look just in case, but I know, with a sinking feeling in my guts, that the burglar has nicked it. Why? It feels like spite, but I know it can't really be that. Maybe Dad left a note in there? I slump down into his chair, trying to think.

I can't face telling Mum that her book is gone – not on top of everything else. It isn't just a valuable first edition of *Incidents of Travel in Central America, Chiapas and Yucatan* – it was her first present from my dad, inscribed with the very first romantic note he'd ever written her.

All I can think of is how I can find some way to replace it. Somehow it has to be possible.

Jackie isn't all that surprised when the first thing I do round at hers is to get straight on to the Internet. I get on to some second-hand book websites and hunt around for any bookshop that has a copy of that book. There are four or five in Oxfordshire, as it turns out. And one even has a first edition.

I almost laugh when I see the address. It's right here in Oxford – a shop in Jericho.

The next day, after school, I take the bus straight there. Tyler calls me on my mobile phone as I'm riding over Magdalen Bridge.

"I got your text about last night. Mate . . . what are you like?"

"Didn't arrange the burglary myself, you know,"

Why does everyone act like it's somehow my fault?

"Yeah, mate, I'm only messing. It's just . . . what's going on with your life, hey?"

"Well . . . there's some stuff I haven't told you about," I tell him.

"Like?"

"Stuff about why my dad was murdered. Stuff to do with his work."

"He's a university lecturer, innit? Who'd kill a teacher?"

"He's an archaeologist," I say, sighing. "And it's . . . oh . . . complicated."

"What you doing now?"

"I'm going to Jericho, actually. Looking for a book. Not far from where you live."

"Can I come with?"

I meet up with Tyler outside the Phoenix Cinema. The bookshop is close by. I go straight to the owner, tell him I'm the one who sent the message through his website. He's put the book aside and fetches it from behind the counter.

It's in good condition, but not mint – not as good as

Mum's copy. There's a chance that Mum wouldn't notice if the book was just spine-out on the shelf. I take it to the corner of the shop and inspect it. Tyler peers over my shoulder.

"Any good?"

I tuck a finger into the flyleaf, check the inside. That's when I see this inscription:

My dearest Arcadio,

Meeting you has been an inspiration. I trust you'll recognize yourself in this book. Many thanks for fascinating times at Chechan Naab and Tikal. JLS, 1843.

JLS?

It couldn't be . . . John Lloyd Stephens himself? And mentioning Chechan Naab – a place that I can't find any mention of in books about Mayan cities? The date sounds right to be Stephens, but I can't tell anything apart from that.

I show the bookshop owner. Did he know about the inscription?

Smugly he replies, "Yes, it's a hoax, obviously."

"Why?"

"Well, John Lloyd Stephens didn't know about Tikal. In fact, he describes its location without realizing what he's written. He describes it in this book as a legendary city of the Maya where the Maya are still living – 'a living city'."

"A place where the Maya were still living? In the nineteenth century?" I ask, puzzled.

"So rumour had it. Course, Tikal was discovered a few years later. Abandoned, like every other Mayan city. Stephens was propagating a local myth, nothing more."

"So. . .?"

"Well," the owner says, a bit condescendingly, "he'd hardly write an inscription about Tikal, a city he didn't even know existed, now would he?"

"And what about Chechan Naab?"

"Now that's the other problem," he says. "There's no such place."

The bookshop owner is convinced. Turns out that he's looked into the whole thing. My guess is that he'd secretly hoped it was signed by Stephens. It would have made the book worth a big chunk of money. But he's happy to sell it for "only" £200.

"Two hundred pounds?" I say, shocked. "You didn't put that on the website!"

"I'll take your best offer in the vicinity," he says.

My "vicinity" isn't even close. I give Tyler a nod and we step outside on to the pavement.

"I can't get two hundred pounds," I tell him in a low voice. "Not unless . . . unless I nick my mum's cashcard."

"Do you know the PIN?"

"I sort of . . . do."

Tyler shrugs. "It's for your mum, isn't it?" he says. "Hardly Grand Theft Auto."

As we're standing there, a studenty guy in a hoody pushes past us on his way into the shop. I'm about to say something but Tyler distracts me. He's right – it's only a loan. Mum would want the book.

I'm looking over Tyler's shoulder when I notice the hoody guy getting all chatty with the owner. Soon enough they're standing at the cash desk, then a book and money are changing hands.

The owner keeps looking over at me. With a funny look in his eyes, sort of embarrassed.

The hoody guy didn't have much time to find a book. A horrible thought strikes me. I take a harder look at the student, realize that there's something familiar about him. I didn't see his eyes, only his mouth and jaw.

It's when he comes out of the shop, walks towards us, that I catch a proper look. He's trying to avoid my gaze. I look at the paper bag in his hand.

And that's when I remember where I've seen him before. Those green eyes – unmistakable.

"Get him!" I shout to Tyler, as the guy breaks into a sprint behind us.

"Wha. . .?"

I'm already turning and pelting after the bloke. "He's the burglar," I yell. "And he's just bought the book!"

I get a flying start but Tyler catches up with me in a few seconds.

The burglar is fast. He's up the street and past the cinema by the time we're even really moving. Before the corner shop he turns left. We're there two seconds later and make the same turn, heading through a gateway and under a brick archway into St Sepulchre's Cemetery. The burglar dashes past the yew trees, vaults a couple of broken gravestones and we do the same.

The whole cemetery is surrounded by a massive building site. There are plasterboard facings all the way around. He runs the whole length, trying to find a way through.

We're almost on him when he finds a gap and dives through.

Tyler squeezes through first, then me. On the other side, we're just in time to see the burglar scooting up the road into the backstreets of Jericho.

We chase him, chests all puffed out, follow him into a little square where there's a bridge over the canal. He's on the bridge, giving us one final look at he crosses.

We're on the bridge less than two seconds later. But he's already nowhere to be seen.

On the opposite bank is another stream of the canal. It's parked with houseboats, bumper to bumper. There are a couple of guys fishing. They ignore us.

I stop, bend down, trying to grab my breath. Between gasps, I manage to ask, "Did you see a bloke in a hoody? Carrying a paper bag?"

The fishermen look at me in silence. One of them shakes his head.

"Nah."

"You must have!"

"Din't see nuthin'."

Tyler and I exchange a grimace. Our stares fall on the long row of brightly painted houseboats. The guy who robbed my house and swiped that first edition of John Lloyd Stephens, he's in one of them. I know it. But which?

I grab a handful of long grass in my fist, tear it off and scatter the shreds in frustration. Tyler watches in sympathy. The one thing I tried to do to help, and I couldn't even pull that off.

How can there be any doubt now? That burglar was looking for clues about the Ix Codex.

Whoever these codex hunters are, they have long arms. I might be thousands of miles away from Mexico, but suddenly I don't feel safe.

BLOG ENTRY: LEAF STORM

Well, the police are no help. I told them all about the burglar being in one of the Jericho houseboats. They just told me they'll "add it to their list of potential locations". I don't get it. OK, burglary isn't a

48

big deal when they've taken nothing massively valuable – but burglary after a murder? But no. No connection, that's what they believe.

Jackie's a nice lady. She takes good care of me. But she hasn't got broadband Internet access. It was one thing to find a second-hand book, but for the full-on Mayan investigation, I really need that. So I've ended up at the library after all. Ha ha, TopShopPrincess. You can come by if you fancy. Or not. Whatever.

Mum asked me to come and spend the night in her hospital room, which has a little extra bed. I was a bit nervous but it seems pretty cool. The doctors don't wear white coats. You can't tell who's sick and who isn't.

I didn't tell her about the burglary, of course. I didn't tell her that I tried – and failed – to replace one of the few possessions she might really care about.

There was a full moon. Its light filled the room with a soft glow. I woke up to find Mum awake, standing by the window.

I said, "Please, Mum, please get better. What am I supposed to do if you fall apart?"

She only shook her head. "You don't know how this feels, Josh. I hope you never do. It's all gone for me – vanished, like mist."

"They're wrong about Dad," I told her. I wanted to tell her about the emails I've found, but I couldn't – not until there's a bit more to go on. "I'm going to prove it. You wait and see."

I didn't know what else to say, so I turned on to my stomach and slept. I've noticed that my dreams are more vivid when I sleep on my

49

front. But last night's dream was really weird – one of those where you could actually believe you're there.

In the dream, I'm dizzy, floundering, caught in the middle of a leaf storm. The leaves surround and enclose me. I close my eyes. In the heart of that storm, I'm suddenly calm. When I open my eyes again, the leaves are gone. I'm standing in a small room with a thatched roof. There are candles everywhere, and the smell of autumn smoke mixed with something acrid, like linseed oil. My eyes sting a little and I blink hard. The room is filled with smoke. There's a man lying on the straw-covered floor. I don't recognize him – in fact, I have no clue who he could be. He's oldish – late forties, maybe, grey hair. And he's coughing, choking, shaking. His eyes almost pop out of his head. He turns purple. This guy is in bad shape, no doubt about it. I don't move, though; I don't help. I just look on and I feel nothing, not a shred of pity. It feels like the incense is making me dizzy. Looks like the guy on the floor is breathing his last. In fact – I'm sure of it. I don't take a closer look, but I light a candle I'm holding. I hear myself mumble a string of strange words. I could swear he's done for. But then, without warning, his eyes snap open. And he looks me dead in the eye and says something that sounds like "Summon the Bakabix".

The rest of the dream was just flashes; a small statue of a Buddha-like figure, water lapping around a decrepit old boat, a pier with two matching straw huts, a mist hanging low over water.

Ideas, anyone?

50

Comment (1) from TopShopPrincess

Well, I could try out some of my A-level psychology.

Maybe the dying man symbolizes a father figure. He's choking – didn't you say your dad was strangled? Could you be imagining your dad's death? What about the "Eastern" references – incense, a Buddha-like statue, the straw huts on water?

Reply

I hadn't thought that those symbols could be "Eastern". I've never been to the Far East, though. As for the rest of it, I don't know. Guess you could be right.

Comment (2) from TopShopPrincess

If a person who's actually died appears in one of your dreams, it can be a way of telling you to move on with your life. I think your mum really needs you now, Josh. Concentrate on supporting her. Time to stop thinking about your dad. Hasn't he already hurt you both enough?

7

When I see TopShopPrincess's comment the next day, I'm so mad that I type a quick, angry reply. I call her all the names under the sun. Who is she to judge my dad? If I don't know what to believe, then how dare she assume?

But in the end, what's the point? She's just some stranger. What do I know about her, really? She's taking a psychology A level, she lives in Oxford and as far as UFOs go, she's a believer. She could be a wacko, for all I know. Far as I'm concerned, you give friends a second chance, but someone who'd write a thoughtless comment like that?

It's up to me how I deal with the death of my dad, and the problems with my mum. I don't like TopShopPrincess's tone. Typical, patronizing older girl. What's she doing reading my blog anyway?

But there's another, much scarier idea that's occurred to me – a reason why I need to close down that blog.

Since the burglary, I've been worried about the fact that whoever took the computers may have read the emails between my dad and Montoyo and that other guy, whose name I can't remember, from the Peabody Museum.

Of course, that's not all they could have read. If they tracked back in my browser history, they might see the Web address of my blog. And then they'll know . . . way too much!

So I move the blog to another server, put a password on it. Now it will be for My Eyes Only. And I delete the old blog.

Adios, TopShopPrincess. You can keep your comments to yourself.

But at least she was someone to talk to about this. I don't want to carry it all alone, and no way am I telling anyone at school.

So I decide to tell Mum about the emails.

It won't be easy to get through to Mum while she's all vague from those tablets, but I have to try. I take the bus to the hospital. As I pass the trees on Headington Hill, I'm jolted by the ferocious lime-green quality of their colour – practically fluorescent.

Come on, Mum, get better fast. You're missing the best part of summer.

In Mum's room, I take her hand in mine.

"I found something out," I begin.

Mum groans, rubs her forehead. "It's always something with you. Can't you just comfort me? God knows I tried it with you."

"Dad wasn't killed by a jealous husband," I tell her. I watch for her reaction. There's definitely interest. "He was looking for a valuable Mayan codex. Something to do with the Mayan prophecy about the end of the world in 2012. This Carlos Montoyo guy sent him a warning by email. He told Dad not to even mention the name of the codex in an email! But Dad did email at least one other guy. And we don't know who else he talked to. I think he's been killed for that codex. I reckon that 'jealous husband' has been framed."

I'm not sure how much Mum hears after my first sentence. She's quiet for a few seconds, mulling it over.

"I'm sorry, Josh. What are you saying?"

"I'm saying that he was in some kind of danger."

Mum looks confused. "What's this got to do with . . . anything?"

"Well, maybe he wasn't killed by that woman's husband."

"Not killed by the husband?" she echoes.

I sigh. I'm not really getting through.

"Look, Mum – don't you think it's all a bit convenient that this has been wrapped up so quickly?"

"Another one of your conspiracy theories?" she says with a thin smile.

"Dad's been murdered," I continue, "so now they need a

54

suspect. And quick, or else . . . I dunno, maybe the British police are going to come over and look into things as well. So they listen to some rumours, some local gossip, and throw together a case against a local guy. Slam him into jail, charge him. Open and shut, everybody's happy."

"Not happy."

"Well, no."

"Perhaps you're right, Josh," is all she says. It isn't clear that she understands what I'm getting at.

"Thing is, Mum, there's something we can do. We can find out. Who this woman is. We can go and meet her."

"You're talking about going to Mexico?" she says in a dull voice. "I'm not well enough."

I squeeze her hand. "Maybe not now. But you could be. In a week or two? The summer holiday begins next week. We'll talk to this woman in Chetumal. Then we'll see. How about it, Mum?"

Mum hesitates. "Will we ask the doctor?"

I allow myself a little grin. This is progress.

"Yeah, why not? Something to look forward to. We'll see what's going on with this woman. And if we have to, we'll give her what for."

"I suppose . . . I suppose we could. And the funeral," she says hopefully. "We could have a funeral for your father."

So, we begin to plan it. It's just a matter of time before I'll be showing the Mexican police why they have arrested the wrong guy.

I feel a massive surge of excitement. This is it – I've cracked it. We'll get to Mexico, meet this woman, find out that she's just some friend of Dad's, or someone who's helping him with some Mayan archaeology thing. I'll show DI Barratt the printouts of Dad's emails and he'll convince the Mexican police that they've arrested the wrong guy.

It's amazing what you can do with a bit of snooping around on a computer. When all this is over, Mum will get back to slowly getting over Dad's death.

And she'll do it, too. I'll help her. We'll get through this.

But at the back of my mind, I can't stop thinking about the burglary. They've got our computers. They know everything I know, up until now.

Who are "they"? If they killed Dad for whatever he found, why are they still snooping around here?

BLOG ENTRY: A FIFTH CODEX OF THE MAYA

ꓶꓶꙄ⩕Ꙅ⩕Ɔ⩕Ꙅ

So – the first entry of my Really Secret Blog to track my detective work around finding who really killed my dad and why.

I'm blogging from a computer in the Summertown Library. When

I'm finished, I'll delete the blog address from the browser history. And anyway, you need a password to access the blog now.

Why would a lost ancient Mayan book cause such a rumpus? I couldn't really imagine why until I realized how rare they are.

Rare archaeological artefacts are Big Money. According to the stories I found on the Internet, all sorts of dodgy characters are involved in the trade. Rich South American drug lords can't get enough of the stuff. And their favourite flavour in antiquities is Mayan.

But an as-yet-undiscovered Mayan codex? It doesn't get any better.

The Maya made their books – codices – out of folded bark paper, painted hieroglyphics with bright colours. They should have been an incredible record of an ancient civilization.

Problem was, only four books survived.

Once there were hundreds of Mayan books. Most of them were about astronomy and mathematics. In 1652, after the Spanish had conquered Mexico, a Spanish bishop named Diego de Landa had all Mayan books rounded up and burned in a Mexican town called Mani. De Landa was apparently shocked by their "blasphemous" content. The Mayans who watched it happen were devastated.

Well, the Church called de Landa back to Spain and punished him for what he did. But it was too late for the Mayans.

And yet . . . four codices did survive. They'd been nicked from Mayan cities by Spanish soldiers, the conquistadors. Three codices turned up hundreds of years later, in the houses of these soldiers' descendents. A fourth was found hidden in a cave somewhere in Mexico.

There are only four, all owned by museums. No private collector owns one. A fifth codex would be *the* major archaeological find in the Mayan field – and the prestigous treasure for one of these collectors.

Could my dad have had some rich, powerful South American gangster after him for the codex? Did they kill Dad only to find that the secret of its location died along with him?

I stop writing my new blog and start to think.

In movies, these drug lords always have the local police forces pretty much under their thumb. These are the kind of guys who can kill a man and frame some local guy; probably someone who'd got on the wrong side of them once too often.

But then again, Carlos Montoyo wrote to Dad, *Web searches and emails are routinely monitored by organizations whose interest in the I* Code* might surprise you.*

He didn't even dare write out the phrase "Ix Codex", for fear it would be picked up by snooping programs on the Internet.

Dad couldn't have been too surprised to hear that drug lords were interested in a Mayan relic. It was part of his ordinary life – he'd often told me that he'd been offered bribes to pass Mayan artefacts on to these people.

Also – how the heck are cocaine barons going to have the

kind of technology to snoop on emails? That kind of thing has to be done by the government, and the military, surely?

Is that the kind of organization that Carlos Montoyo means?

I rack my brain trying to remember the exact contents of those emails of Dad's. Apart from the Ix Codex, the main thing I remember is that Dad mentioned a Mayan manuscript he had, which he called the "Calakmul letter".

He never mentioned it to us, so far as I know. It must have been a big, big deal to him. He usually talks about this sort of thing to Mum, sometimes even to me.

I'd never heard so much as a whisper about it in our house. Why not?

That night, I can't sleep. I'm still vexed about the burglary. OK, so by now I have to assume they've read my old blog, and all the emails. They searched the house. Unless they were much luckier than I was, they'll be out of ideas round about now. Where would they go next?

I have to find that Mayan manuscript – if it's still in Oxford. And there's only one place left to search.

I drop by Dad's Oxford college. The porters there know me. They let me by with a respectful little nod, just enough for me to know they're still in mourning for Dad. I've been dragged along to enough college events to know that Dad was a popular guy here. As I make my way around the immaculate edges of the central lawn in the main

60

quadrangle, I almost bump into one of Dad's colleagues, Dr Naomi Turnbull – she's always sweet to me. I tell her that I've come to start clearing out Dad's office.

"Oh," she says, with a sympathetic frown. "So your mum doesn't have to? You're a good lad, Josh."

Like everyone else, Naomi wants the latest update. Dad's death is making me feel like a news reporter.

"Yeah, he's definitely dead . . . turns out he was murdered . . . nope, they don't know yet who did it, they're working on some leads. . ."

I hate myself for censoring the rest. But not everyone is going to have my faith in Dad. For Mum, this is the worst thing of all. She's gone from the sympathetic widow to the wronged wife. Not an ideal move.

Naomi seems to be in a hurry anyway. "I have to be going, Josh," she says, "We had some trouble here this morning and I need to talk to the police."

"What kind of trouble?"

"Oh, just some stupid break-in. Or attempted break-in, actually, in the staircase where your father had his office. They tripped the alarm and ran off. Pretty daft place to try and burgle, though, don't you think?"

I freeze, and try to look casual. "Yeah. Weird."

Naomi gives me a sympathetic squeeze before she leaves. I hurry to Dad's office. Inside, a wave of sadness hits me. It's so strong that I have to sit down for a few minutes. Tears form at the corner of my eyes. I can hardly look around the room without sensing Dad's presence. His books, his papers on his desk. My photo, taken when I was eight years old, grinning, all gap-toothed. Eventually I get a grip, start hunting for a hiding place. Where would he stash a secret Mayan manuscript?

I gaze around the room, taking in all the objects. And suddenly it's obvious. My eyes land on a framed illustration of a Mayan ruin by Frederick Catherwood.

My dad loved Catherwood's illustrations. He used to say that Catherwood's drawings of some of the Mayan inscriptions were the best work anyone ever did. As good as photographs.

I lift the frame off its hook. There's nothing behind it on the wall. I run my fingers over the back of the picture. There's the slightest bulge in the middle.

I use my fingernails to scratch the brown paper that seals the back of the picture. A layer comes away in my hand. And underneath, something's hidden.

It's wrapped in several layers of tissue paper, folded, about the size of a piece of letter paper. I unwrap it carefully. A piece of very old-looking bark paper. I've seen this kind of paper before – in museums. It's the kind the Mayans used in their books. Three edges of the bark paper are smooth but the right-hand edge looks rough, as though it has been torn across the middle, vertically. The paper is coated in a white chalky substance and covered with fading Mayan hieroglyphs.

Whatever it is, it's incomplete. The section of writing to the right of the tear is missing.

Is this the Calakmul letter? As I wrap it back into the tissue paper, I notice that the final layer is covered with some writing. In ballpoint pen, just these words.

Josh, Eleanor, if I don't make it back from Mexico, BURN THIS. I'm serious. Don't make a copy. Destroy it. Love you both, Andres.

It's the lamest farewell note I can imagine. What about saying his goodbyes, telling us how much he loved us and all that? If it's so dangerous, why didn't Dad destroy the letter himself? Or was his note just an insurance policy – against a danger he never really believed he would face?

Is that all we were to him – just someone to burn evidence for him and leave it at that?

I decide not to tell Mum about the Calakmul letter – if it really is that. Dad's note doesn't paint the most encouraging picture of a devoted husband. Even I have to admit that.

And there's another reason. Mum might try to talk me into following Dad's instructions, burning the manuscript. But there's no way. There's just too much at stake.

I peel off the rest of the false back of the Catherwood picture. That's when I see that something else is hidden there.

It's so shocking that I simply stare at it for a long time. A small, square black-and-white photograph, printed on Kodak paper with the processing date – August 1964. The image? I recognize him immediately – it's the man from my dream. The man who with his dying breath whispers: "Summon the Bakabix."

I start boxing up papers, making good on my promise to start clearing Dad's college office. I can't resist taking one of the photos, too; there's a great one of Dad on top of Mont Blanc. I grab the *Dictionary of Mayan Hieroglyphs* and books on how to read the glyphs. I drop by my house with the two boxes of papers, journals and books that I've cleared out. The back windows are boarded up now, until someone comes to replace the glass. I take a few of the books, go back to Summertown Library and start deciphering the inscription on the Mayan manuscript.

I begin by cross-referencing the place-names mentioned in Dad's emails with any glyph I can easily make out on the Mayan inscription. Some place-names I've heard of, probably even been to at some point. The way it works is this: if they know the original Mayan name for a ruin, they use it. Like Uxmal, Chichen Itza, Calakmul. But sometimes the Mayan name has been forgotten. Like with Palenque – a ruin named for the Spanish-built town nearby.

With a list of known place-names in one hand, I recognize glyphs for Calakmul and Cancuen in the inscription. The symbols for *che* (knot), *chan* (snake) and *naab* (water) are easy to find too, clumped together to make one glyph. I've already researched the cities on the Web, but I haven't found anything about Chechan Naab. That is pretty unusual in itself. Most Mayan cities have been written about somewhere.

Could Chechan Naab be a lost city of the Maya? As for the other city mentioned in Dad's emails – Ek Naab – there's no sign of those glyphs on the inscription.

That's the easy part of the decipherment. As I stare at those columns of glyphs, it strikes me that I don't have the faintest clue how to read them. Left to right? Top to bottom? I don't even know where to begin. So I put the Calakmul letter safely out of view, tucked away in a paperback copy of *The Subtle Knife*. And I settle down to read a book called *How to Read Mayan Hieroglyphs*.

As I work, I can't help noticing out of the corner of my eye that a girl sitting diagonally opposite keeps glancing in my direction. For a while I'm not sure if she intends to look at me at all – there's probably some cute college student directly behind me. I lift my book to shield my face, then sneak a long look at the girl over the pages.

She's gorgeous.

She's wearing a blue and white cotton dress. Butter-blonde hair ripples across her shoulders. I swing around, survey the room behind me. There are plenty of students around, but they're all trolls. Certainly no one worthy of the Total Goddess sitting opposite. When I turn back around, she's staring openly at me, with this sort of bemused grin.

I redden, but manage to mouth, "Who, me?" in what I hope is a comic fashion. She nods. I push my chair back, walk over as slowly as possible, trying desperately to think of something cool to say.

In the end I go with, "Hey, stranger."

The girl grins. "Hey yourself . . . Josh."

I blanch.

"The boy with the blog," she continues. "You know who I am?"

It seems too incredible. But could it really be. . .?

"TopShopPrincess. . .?"

"Olivia," she says. "Olivia Dotrice. You can call me Ollie – everyone does."

"But you are TopShopPrincess?"

"Of course. How else would I know where to find you?"

"Um. About that . . . I thought we were both having a laugh."

"Well, yeah, until you went and deleted your blog. . . So, you can guess why I'm here?"

I stick my hands deep into my pockets. "Err . . . nope. I

really can't."

She frowns. "I wanted to apologize, Josh. When I saw that you'd deleted your blog, I guessed that my comment upset you. I'm really sorry. I didn't mean for that to happen."

I shrug. "It's OK."

"Were you upset?"

"I was annoyed, yeah. You didn't even know my dad."

"I know. It was stupid, thoughtless. I guess I felt for your mum. I just thought that's where your priorities should be. But it was a hasty judgement. Also. . ." She stops, glances around, lowers her voice. "I was getting worried about how much you were giving away on that blog. Didn't you think that the people who burgled your house might know about your blog? You even wrote about where you were. You should be more careful!"

"Actually, yeah. That's why I deleted it. Not cos you upset me or anything."

"Well, that's a relief," she says, smiling.

We're getting major shushing from the librarian, so we step outside into the garden and find a bench near one of the many sculptures dotted around. It's a fabulous summery day, sizzling hot. The garden is practically empty.

"I've been thinking about your mystery," begins Ollie. "Hope you don't mind. I don't mean to be nosy, but you've got me intrigued now, with the whole UFO thing and all. You really think it's a coincidence that your dad was

68

murdered round the same time that a massive UFO sighting happens?"

I haven't dared to go on about it, what with Mum in the state she's in. Ollie's right, though – I never thought it was a coincidence. I just haven't any idea how UFOs tie in with drug barons in search of a lost relic.

Ollie continues. "Seeing that UFO really changed me. Something like that, it makes you question everything you ever read, ever heard."

"Like what?"

"Well, like the links between the Maya and UFOs, for one thing."

If I'm honest, growing up, the part of archaeology that did excite me was the whole connection between UFOs and ancient history. That stuff is amazing. But of course, the subject was practically banned in our house. Dad worked hard to keep me from being interested in the more bizarro theories about the Maya that you find on the Internet.

"What, the whole ancient-Mayans-came-from-the-lost-city-of-Atlantis thing? Ancient astronauts and all that? My dad always laughed at that."

"I'll bet he wasn't laughing when he was abducted."

"*If* he was abducted."

"You don't think there's a connection?"

I sigh.

Ollie presses her point. "Wouldn't you like to be the one

to find proof that UFOs have something to do with the Mayan civilization? It's like – one of the major secrets of history!"

"Well . . . my dad was pretty down on all that new-age stuff. Plus, things have moved on a bit since you last read my blog. I know now why my dad was killed."

"I think I do too."

We stare at each other for a few seconds.

"What did you say?"

"Think about it," she whispers, tugging at my arm. "What if your dad found some link between the ancient Maya and UFOs? I mean, real evidence? What if the codex actually proves that the Mayans had contact with extraterrestrials? Wouldn't that be worth something?"

I'm confused. "Who to?"

"Well, lots of people. Art collectors. Those new-age religion gurus, they'd love that."

"Yeah . . . but they're hardly going to kill anyone. . ."

"The CIA."

"What now?"

"The CIA," she repeats, "NASA, 'Majestic', or whatever their latest name is. The government agency that does all the UFO cover-ups. The Area 51 people. You know what, Josh, I think you haven't been thinking big enough. This could be really, really huge!"

I thought I was getting paranoid, thinking about

government conspiracies. But it's beginning to make sense. There's a long history of UFO sightings in Mexico. Mum, of course, goes along with the old chestnut, "Mexican people are a fanciful bunch." And hadn't Montoyo written to Dad, *Web searches and emails are routinely monitored by organizations whose interest in the I* Code* might surprise you*?

The CIA!

"*They* could track emails," I say, almost to myself.

"They could."

"Maybe they read my email to Montoyo?"

"Who's Montoyo?"

I look at Ollie for a few seconds, wondering. She's looking at me, her expression eager. Should I tell her? I can feel it all bubbling up inside me. It feels so good to actually talk to someone about this. Now that I've started, I don't want to stop.

So, I fill Ollie in on the emails I've found between my dad, Carlos Montoyo and that Peabody Museum guy, Martineau. I tell her all about the hunt for the Ix Codex and finish off with my discovery of the Calakmul letter in Dad's college room. I carry it with me at all times now, still wrapped in its tissue paper. When she sees the manuscript fragment, her eyes widen; she's impressed.

"That is so wicked."

"I know."

"But it's torn." Suddenly she looks disappointed.

"Yeah. The right-hand side of the message is missing. But Mayan writing goes up and down, in columns. So I'll be able to decipher the first part of the letter at least."

"Where do you think the rest is?"

I frown. "I don't know . . . I sort of assumed that this is all that Dad found."

"Hmm," she says thoughtfully. "Do you think it is part of the Ix Codex?"

Dad's emails to Montoyo and Martineau don't suggest that. But then, I wouldn't know what a real Mayan codex looked like.

"Not sure," I tell her. "Maybe it's about the codex. Where to find it, perhaps."

She asks, "What's Montoyo's story?"

"He seemed to know all about this Ix Codex," I say. "Told Dad that people had disappeared looking for it. Funny really, because I've read lots of stuff about Mayan archaeology since this thing started. And I've never heard a single mention of the Ix Codex."

"That is weird. So how did Montoyo hear about it?"

I pause, thinking. "No idea. And he asked to meet my dad. I emailed Montoyo to ask if he ever actually did."

"What did he say?"

"Never replied."

"Did it ever occur to you that he might be the one who

really killed your father?"

"Of course," I lie. OK, maybe I'd had a background-level suspicion. Ollie's questioning is crystallizing all sorts of ideas I'd put out to dry.

She warms to her theory. "He knew your dad was on to the codex. So he pretends to help him. Then he meets up with your dad, gets rid of him."

"And this guy they've framed for murdering my dad?"

"That is a bit more tricky," she agrees eventually. "The CIA could frame a person for murder. And they could have your house burgled."

"So you really think it's the CIA, then?"

"I don't know, Josh. I'm just trying out some theories here. Isn't that what detectives do?"

I haven't thought of it that way. The main thing, for me, is to prove to Mum that Dad wasn't murdered for messing around with another woman. And to prove it to myself.

The codex thing has me intrigued, definitely. My father was looking for it. Now I seem to be picking up on the trail. There's a connection with his disappearance – I just know it. And something else, something weird I can't quite put my finger on. It feels pretty thrilling to be following in my father's footsteps. Thrilling – and a little dangerous.

"You know what you have to do?" says Ollie. "Decipher that inscription. Maybe even find the codex. I could help you.

You up for that? We'll be like Mulder and Scully."

I grin. "If you're Scully and I'm Mulder, then shouldn't *you* be the sceptical one?"

"What's the difference? In the end they were both believers."

Ollie's theories spark one of my own. Maybe the woman in Chetumal has something to do with Dad's search for the codex? It would explain why Dad had spent so much time with her. She might know something about the codex. Maybe framing her husband was their way of keeping her quiet?

No two ways about it; we have to talk to Chetumal Lady.

I ask, "Are you a university student?"

Ollie laughs. "Not yet! I'm in the lower sixth at St Margaret's."

I know the school. Some of those girls have modelling contracts. It isn't, after all, so surprising that Ollie seems so glamorous. I'm used to a more everyday type of girl.

"So you really think we should try to find this codex, hey? Assuming it's still out there."

Ollie's smile is a thing to behold. "It'd be amazing."

"Seriously, though. It sounds dangerous."

"Aren't you even a bit curious?"

"Me? Sure, but I've been warned off."

"Don't you want to get back at the people who killed your dad?"

"By finding the codex?"

"Yes," she says. "By beating them at their own game."

Ollie's blue eyes shine with excitement.

I don't know how much of what Ollie has said I actually believe, but her offer is tempting. All I know is that if this codex is still out there, other people will want it. And the codex will buy all sorts of things. Including the answer to the question, *Who killed my dad?*

If I had the codex, they'd have to negotiate with me.

"Well, to be honest," I say, "I could use the help."

That's how we team up. All because of Ollie's powers of deduction.

I've never met anyone like her. She. Is. Amazing.

BLOG ENTRY: DECIPHERMENT!

There are a couple of reasons for today's blog entry. It's a secret record that I daren't leave on paper, or on the hard drive of any computer I'm known to access.

But no one knows about the blog. I haven't even told TopShopPrincess/Ollie that I've started the blog again. I'm kind of embarrassed about what I might write about her.

Jeeeez. Ollie! What a turnaround. I stopped being angry with her about ten seconds after she apologized. Thing is, I'd always kind of thought of her as a slightly weird, kooky type of girl. She's anything

but that. She looks like a goddess, with the brain of an uber-geek.

Ollie and I couldn't work together at Summertown Library – we were getting too many beady looks and warnings to be quiet. Tyler, an old mate from capoeira, owed me a favour. I turned up on his doorstep with Ollie and told him, "Debt collection time. I need you to let me use your computer for the rest of the night."

I needn't have said anything. With Ollie in tow, he'd have given his living room over to us, even if there was a big match on TV. When he offered to help out with the decipherment, we accepted. I figured there was safety in numbers: the more of us who knew, the harder it would be for Them to silence us.

Them. Now I'm really talking like a conspiracy buff.

We cracked open the drinks and the Pringles, put *Batman Begins* on the DVD as a decoy for Tyler's parents. Then we started on the inscription.

I quickly showed the other two what I knew about reading Mayan hieroglyphs. Mayan inscriptions were written in a grid format. According to the how-to book, the first glyphs give the date of the document. Then the writing proceeded in a two-column grid that could be labelled in reading order: A2, B2, A3, B3, A4, B4, etc. until the end of the page. Then it continued in the next two columns: C2, D2, C3, D3, etc.

We started with the easiest bit – the date. Mayan documents always start with the date. My dad taught me to read Mayan dates years ago, to stop me from whining with boredom. I still remember how, but I can't do it without a dictionary.

In Mayan, the date was 9.11.0.4.8 16 Pax 9 Lamat.

In English, that translates to 8 Jan 653 AD.

This letter was written in the seventh century!

Then we got started on the main part of the letter. We each took one glyph apart at a time. First we'd look up the whole glyph in case we got lucky. Sometimes a whole glyph can mean something – like the name of a place.

When we'd solved as many of those as possible, our eyes were getting blurry from looking at all the different glyphs. We took a little break.

By then we knew the inscription included the words Cancuen, Yuknoom Ch'een, Calakmul, Bakab, Itzamna, servant, sacred, book, Ix, and "it will occur".

Then came the really tough part. We crunched through the rest of the glyphs syllable by syllable. When we thought we had a possible solution, we'd search for the word on the Web, find out all we could about it. That's how we made sense of the translation.

Six hours later we were still at it. We ordered pizza, kept going. It it was like each one of us was daring the others to be the ones to wimp out. I kept asking, "Shall we stop now, go to bed?" but they'd go, "No way, we're almost there!"

And as the dawn light filtered through the blinds, we had the whole thing deciphered.

K'inich K'ane Ajk of Cancuen writes to Lord Yuknoom Ch'een of
   Calakmul
I am your servant

From Chechan Naab he emerged, from the Great Temple of the Cross
The Bakab was defeated
This sacred Book of Ix speaks of the end of days
13.0.0.0.0 it is written in the Sacred Books of Itzamna
It will occur

I stare at the inscription for a few seconds and let out a slow, "Wow."

Tyler says, "What does it mean – 'end of days'? Is that like. . .?"

". . . the end of the world?" I say. "Yeah. My dad told me about all that years ago. The Mayan calendar ends on the date 13.0.0.0.0 – Thirteen Baktun."

Tyler stares, expectant. "Um . . . when's that, then? In our calendar, I mean."

I try to sound calm. "Well . . . it's pretty soon, actually."

"When?"

"The twenty-second of December, 2012."

Tyler's mouth opens, as if he's trying to think of something funny to say. But nothing comes out.

"People have been trying to work out what that date – Thirteen Baktun – means for *ages*. No one knows."

Tyler stabs a finger at our translation. "This 'Book of Ix'

seems to know!"

"Book of Ix – that must mean the Ix Codex," Ollie says thoughtfully.

"I can't see any mention of Ek Naab here. . ." I mutter.

"Can we talk about this end of the world thing a bit more?" Tyler says, voice rising.

"It's not *literal*," I say. "Not *literally* the end of the world. More like the end of an era. That's what my dad told me."

"Good thing you're so sure about that!" Tyler says. "I've never heard of it until now, but it seems pretty worrying to me! I mean – I've got plans, you know!"

I say, "This is about a rare Mayan book – some book that maybe finally explains just what the Mayans meant by ending their calendar in 2012."

"Yeah," Tyler says, emphatically. "And what if it really is about the end of the world?"

Could it really be? The idea is so far from what I've been brought up to believe about the Maya that I can hardly take it in.

I can't answer Tyler's question, so I look again at the Calakmul letter.

The manuscript consists of two sets of two columns. The final sentence is incomplete.

Not only are we missing part of the letter, we can't make sense of the final sentence. The final glyph is a verb, the beginning of a sentence: *utom* – "it will occur".

Everything to the right of that is ripped away. Without the second half, we can't even make sense of the first. Without it, we've no hope of picking up the trail of the codex. And without that second half, my dad wouldn't either. So if he thought he'd found the codex – he must have hidden the second half of the Calakmul letter somewhere else. But where?

"There's that word again," Ollie says. "Bakab. Wasn't that in your dream? The one you blogged?"

"I dreamt *Bakabix*."

"That's right," says Tyler. "*Bakab, Ix*. They're both in this inscription."

The possibility that my dream might have some connection with the inscription hits me like a kick to the stomach. It's all too weird. For a second, I imagine myself back in the leaf storm of my dream. There's a flash of memory; a curtain of fragrant smoke behind which a stranger chokes to death.

I suddenly need to be alone, to think. I manage to say, "I really need to get back now."

I drag myself back to Jackie's just as the paper-round kids are hitting the street. The dream is still with me. It isn't so much what I actually witnessed in the dream but the feeling of utter foreignness. Nothing about it felt familiar.

The dream of the misty lakeside straw hut with its cold,

unmoving death scene – like nothing I've ever seen. It feels otherworldly. Disturbing.

That date turning up in the Calakmul letter – 22 December, 2012 – and the mention of the "end of days". Written about in the Book of Ix – the Ix Codex.

And those words together. Bakab. Ix.

Summon the Bakab Ix.

What – or who – is the Bakab Ix?

Could it really be the guy in my dad's photo? I'm feeling more and more like I've stepped out of reality.

Later that morning I'm at school for an ICT class. Well, they say "ICT", but this close to the end of term, it's pretty freestyle. Most of us just surf the Web. I Google "Bakab". The Bakab is a figure from Mayan mythology – one of four sons of the Mayan deity Itzamna. Itzamna is one of the top gods as far as Mayan deities go – the bringer of writing and agriculture to the Mayan people. Only the Creator Gods are above Itzamna. In Mayan mythology, Itzamna married a goddess named Ixchel. They had four sons, who were named Ix, Cauac, Muluc and Kan. The Bakab Ix must be one of these guys.

Why would someone want to summon a Mayan god? Is it some weird occulty thing?

After school I take the bus up to the hospital. I'm hoping to hear that Mum's coming home this weekend. The attendant tells me how much better she is; they've changed her medication; it's very light now and she's "more herself again". He lets me into her room, but she's asleep. Fine – I'm pretty zoned myself. I lie down for a little nap in the second bed. And I'm out in seconds.

Sometime later I'm vaguely aware of someone fumbling through my schoolbag. I'm still half asleep and in that state, all I'm thinking is that it's fine; Mum's always searching for neglected letters from school. Then there's a long silence. Mum remains quite still.

I wake up to find her staring at a photograph in her hand.

It's *that* photo – the one I found in Dad's office.

Mum's tone is bewildered. "Where did you find this?"

"Dad gave it to me."

Sharply she replies, "No, he didn't."

I pause, surprised. "He did." It's a small lie, I decide; a detail.

"He kept that photo on him. He was never without it."

"Why?"

"If he really gave it to you, he'd have told you what it meant to him."

I stay quiet. No doubt about it – she's sounding much better.

"So you lied to me." It isn't a question.

"I found it in his college room. I went there to get some books."

"Why?"

83

"Just . . . cos I wanted to learn about Mayan hieroglyphs."

"Why?"

I groan, fall back on to the bed.

"Jeez, Mum. Wow, you really are sounding like your old self! Look, it's to do with the Mayan codex Dad was after. OK?"

Mum looks puzzled.

"You do remember me telling you about the codex he was searching for?"

She says yes. But I'm not convinced.

I snap, "Come on, Mum, we've been through this." Then I remember where we are. And I'm filled with regret.

Mum stares at me with a searching expression. "You tell me why you're so interested in that photo and I'll tell you what it meant to your dad."

"OK. Only. . ." I hesitate. "You're not going to like it."

"Why, are you going to lie to me again?"

"No, it's just that . . . well, you're going to think it sounds stupid."

"Try me."

So I tell Mum about the dream. I tell her everything, with every detail I can remember. Relating it, I feel my spine prickle. And when I come to the end of the dream, I say, "Then he looks at me and he says. . ."

"'Summon the Bakab Ix'," says Mum.

"How?" I whisper. "How could you know?"

84

"Because I've heard this before," Mum says simply. "Your father had the exact same dream. All his life. Since he was a little boy. And he never, never understood it. It obsessed him. Andres researched the myth of the Bakabs. Wrote lots of papers about them. He wasn't any closer to understanding the dream. Then, about a year ago, his mother wrote to him. The man who raised him, whom he called 'Papa', wasn't his real father. That kind of family secret – it's not unusual, especially in a Catholic country like Mexico. Young women who got pregnant out of wedlock didn't broadcast it then, and they still don't. She married a close family friend and that was that – they forgot about the real father. You certainly didn't go telling your children that they were illegitimate.

"But she's getting old, so she decided to come clean with Andres, to admit the truth. She told him that his real father was a museum curator, a man she met when she was nineteen. At least he said he was a museum curator. He was the man in this photo. He was looking to buy old manuscripts from local collectors, take them back to his museum. One thing led to another between the two of them. Then one day he just upped and disappeared. Your grandmother – Abuelita – called the museum he said he worked for, but they'd never heard of him. No one had. He arrived as if from nowhere and went back the same way. This photo of him was the only evidence Abuelita ever really had that he'd ever existed. That and your father, of course."

I have no idea what to say.

Mum continues, "Your dad was raised by the man who was kind enough to marry Abuelita. He never knew or suspected. Then when he was about ten or eleven he began to dream about the man in the hut. And 'Summon the Bakab Ix'. It haunted him. When he discovered that the man in his dream was his father . . . well. . ."

She pauses, seems wistful at the memory. "He didn't know whether to laugh or cry. It was as though a missing part of him had been found. But it still didn't make sense of the dream."

Then she turns, stares intently at me for a second, and asks, "Josh, did Dad ever tell you about that dream?"

I shake my head. Seems like Dad had been pretty close-mouthed about the whole matter.

"Then," Mum says quietly, "how can this be happening to you too?"

BLOG ENTRY: CAPOEIRA O LE LE

ℕℙℤℍ○○Ʒℍℂ♈

I was desperate for a bit of normality, so I let Tyler persuade me to join the capoeira players in a demonstration for the Summertown Arts Festival. We pitched up outside the bank on a sunny Saturday morning

amidst the curious Summertown residents. A light breeze wafted the last of the loose cherry blossoms from a nearby tree and they drifted over us like snow. Mestre Ricardo took the *berimbau*, the main musical instrument we use in capoeira; I took the *pandeiro* drum. The whole group stood in a circle as we drummed up a crowd with a song. Pretty soon supermarket shoppers were crossing the road to watch us launch ourselves in combat. In capoeira, the trick is to just skirt the edges – no contact. It's a flirtation with violence, a ballet. The beauty of the game lies in the controlled, acrobatic restraint of the players.

After a few turns I was up against Tyler. We'd rehearsed the cue. As the *roda* struck up with the song "Capoeira O Le Le", we began. *Ginga*, handstand, *au malandrau, cocorinha, armada, queixada*. I executed my moves perfectly, just as we practised. Then Tyler left the script and pulled out some style moves – a headspin, a handstand whirl. I could see him grinning at me, delighted to have caught me on the hop. From then on we improvised; we dropped into the music's groove.

That Tyler – he's a show-off. But he knows how to please an audience. The crowd loved it.

Then Ollie turned up. And the subject turned to the codex. . .

11

I glance around the faces, hoping to see Ollie – and then there she is. Luckily, Tyler's also thrown off balance at the sight of her. With her eyes on us our pace picks up a notch. I can feel my skin warming where her gaze lands.

"That was coolness," she says afterwards, grinning. Tyler has another bout to prepare for, and he strips off to the vest underneath.

"He's in good shape," she remarks to me as Tyler takes up position against Mestre Ricardo.

I sigh. "Yeah. I know. Probably be selected for the British team."

"I should hope so," she says. "He's terrific!"

It's definitely time to change the subject. "So guess what," I say. "I've found out something about the man in my dream."

Ollie swivels around, eyes wide. "Go on."

"He's my *grandfather*," I tell her. "My secret grandfather. Turns out that Dad was illegitimate. His mother only confessed to Dad about a year ago. She sent him a photo of his father. And that's how I know. Dad's father – he's the guy from my dream."

Well, that does it. I have Ollie's undivided, even fascinated, attention.

I glance at Tyler, who completes a series of intricate moves, a breathtaking sequence of handstand whirls, headspins and a clock movement. He's not improvising against Mestre Ricardo, I notice. Each time the players attack, they plant precisely aimed blows within millimetres of each other's bodies. The crowd surrounds us even more densely. They murmur their appreciation.

Ollie stands next to me, lost in thought. "So in your dream," she says, speaking very slowly, "you're seeing the death of your own grandfather?"

I nod. That's it exactly – like a premonition. Only, it's already happened.

"And *he* is asking for the Bakab Ix?"

"Right on."

"Wow." Her voice drops to a breathless whisper. "So this Mayan thing – it's been going on in your family for, like, years?"

Again I nod. "My grandfather found the Calakmul letter – the one we deciphered. That's how Dad started on his search for the Ix Codex."

"But if your grandfather had the Calakmul letter, then maybe he was searching for the Ix Codex too."

89

"That's the whole point. Grandpa was hunting for the codex. Then Dad. Now me."

Ollie punches me lightly on the shoulder. "Way to keep your family legacy going!"

"Some legacy," I say. "They're both dead. And still no codex."

"Still," she replies, "I wonder why your grandpa was looking for it."

It seems pretty obvious to me. He was a museum curator, a seeker of rare Mayan objects.

"What does his museum say?" Ollie asks.

That was the odd thing. They'd denied all knowledge of him, right from the start.

"Abuelita – my grandma – she tried. Years back. She doesn't even know where he really came from."

Ollie's eyes glisten. "Fabulous! And you know what else is interesting – the missing half of the Calakmul letter? Your dad must have had it once."

"That's what I think," I say. "Or else how could he think he'd found the trail of the Ix Codex?"

Ollie goes quiet for a while, her eyes drifting off as she watches the capoeira players.

"So," I tell her, "I've decided. I've got to find a way to go . . . to find Dad's woman in Chetumal."

"'Dad's woman'? I thought you were in denial about that. . ." she says with a sly smile.

"We'll see. Maybe she's a contact, something to do with the codex hunt."

"From where? How many people do you think know about this?"

There's Carlos Montoyo, we know that. He still hasn't replied to my email, which has me more than a little spooked. Then there's Ollie's own theory – the CIA – or some US agency looking to cover up UFO incidents and evidence of alien-Mayan contact.

"Let me get this straight. You think that your dad went to Mexico, met with Montoyo and then disappeared?"

"Went looking for the codex. *Then* disappeared. The missing days – remember?"

I watch her as her mind computes away.

"Maybe Chetumal Lady knows where your dad went. Maybe she even saw Montoyo."

I smile with satisfaction. "Bingo. Man, you're brilliant."

Then she asks me about Mum. I relate my discussion with the psychiatrist. He was just about OK with the idea of me going to Mexico – I told him I'd be staying with an aunty in Cancun who'd pick us up at the airport. For a minute I was worried that he'd ask for a phone number, but he seemed OK about it. I told him about my plan to confront the woman in Chetumal. (I didn't mention the codex or any of the complicated stuff.) He saw how it would "resolve some key issues". But as for Mum coming along – there was no way.

91

Ollie says, "Your poor mum. She's had such a rough time. I bet she'd enjoy a trip to Mexico. But she could probably do without the stress of meeting your dad's ladyfriend."

Mum's not being able to go just makes me more determined to sort everything out. "You bring me back his ashes," Mum insisted at my last visit, gripping my arm as I turned to leave. "Have them blessed in a church by a priest, then bring him back to me."

When I tell Ollie this part, she frowns. "Creepy," she says. "You'll be, like, carrying your dad around."

"Don't remind me."

And then Ollie hits me with her own bombshell.

"I'm coming with you," she announces, with not a hint of a request. "Sounds to me like you could use the moral support."

"What a mate you are." I'm caught on the hop, but I'm thrilled and I don't try to hide it. "You're serious? I mean – you hardly know me."

"It's true. It doesn't feel like that, though, does it?"

I'm relieved to hear her say that. It's exactly what I think – but I didn't dare believe that Ollie thought so too.

"You'll need to ask your parents, though, won't you?"

Ollie waves a hand. "That's nothing. They're always on at me to travel. They travelled all the time when they were young. We can get them to buy the tickets for us over the Web, in fact."

I'm secretly relieved that I won't have to use my mum's credit card.

"Really? They sound really cool!"

"Yeah, they're OK," Ollie says, and she looks away, almost uninterested. Her eyes come to rest on Tyler. "Mind you, it could be dangerous."

"No way to know what's gonna go down," I agree. "What about bringing Tyler along too? Capoeira moves can be wicked deadly, you know."

Ollie raises an eyebrow. "'Wicked deadly'? Maybe we *should* invite Tyler along."

"Let's do it."

And with Ollie's almost matter-of-fact comments, the summer horizon opens up. The three of us are off to Mexico, to crack open the mystery of my father's murder, the identity of his Chetumal Lady and maybe even to find the Ix Codex. With my two mates with me, I feel like anything is possible now.

BLOG ENTRY: THE DOLPHIN HOTEL

♠⟆⩚⪦⩞⩟ⴳⵝ⪦⟆

Well, I should have dragged Mum along. It's too great here, definitely beats summer in England. Sunny, bright blue skies and HOT! I almost

feel like relaxing, just hitting the pool. But . . . there's work to be done.

Hotel Delfin (Dolphin Hotel) in Chetumal is a tidy white hotel in a small seaside town. The beach here is made from dredged-up sand. It's nothing to write home about, but works fine as a cooling-off point: a drop-in for anyone wants to explore beyond the mega-famous Mayan ruins at Chichen Itza.

We flew into Chetumal after a connecting flight from Mexico City. It's only the second time in my life I've flown without my parents. The first time I was ten, and had to be accompanied by a stewardess the whole time, along with the other little kids. This time, because Ollie is sixteen, they let us travel with her.

I'm still the expert of the team, though. For one thing, I'm the only one of us who speaks Spanish. I quite enjoyed showing Ollie and Tyler around Mexico City Airport, where I've been almost every year since I can remember. I made sure to pick up Cinnabons before we boarded the domestic flight to Chetumal.

Ollie and Tyler admit that the warm, juicy, cream-cheese-frosted Cinnabons are the best cakes they've eaten, ever.

The hotel is on a main road, roughly a hundred metres from the beach. The lobby is small, marble-floored and only just has room for the reception counter and a small set of upholstered rattan furniture where people can wait. A ceiling fan moves the warm air around uselessly.

When we arrived, the place was deserted – we had to ring the bell for attention. A cramped little room off the lobby serves as the

"Internet Café" – it's where I am right now. In an alcove next to the reception area there's an ice machine and a drinks machine selling Fresca and Delaware Punch. Grape soda – yum!

When I checked in, the receptionist (name badge said "Paco") lingered over my passport. "Are you related to Professor Andres Garcia, also from Oxford?"

It's not a big town, few enough places to choose from. Turns out that I'd chosen the same hotel as my father. Paco was tickled pink by the coincidence, but it didn't strike me as so unusual.

You don't find many Mexicans at the Hotel Delfin. It's mostly ecotourists who want to hug trees in the rainforest, or tourists on the "Maya Route". There's something of an effort to provide a slightly "groovy" atmosphere. Hence piped jazz music in the central courtyard around the pool, and scattered gardenia petals floating on its clear blue water.

I can see why my dad chose it.

The grooviness of Hotel Delfin isn't lost on Ollie. She smiles, amused, as we stand in the courtyard, taking a good look around.

"Stan Getz," she says approvingly. "Nice."

Back in our room, Tyler and I change into our boardies. I sit down to phone Detective Rojas, the Mexican policeman in charge of the murder investigation. Before we left Oxford, I managed to get through to the police station in Chetumal, trying to get hold of a name and address for Chetumal Lady. They weren't willing to give out that information over the phone. "But phone Detective Rojas the minute you arrive in Chetumal. He will come to your hotel and take you to meet her. This is safest for you, for her."

I've got my UK mobile phone, but the local Mexican call will cost me a small fortune if I use it. So I head for the lobby, to call from a payphone, when Tyler stops me.

He scowls. "Leave it out, just for a bit, hey? We need to

cool off. Let's have a laugh first."

I hesitate. He has a point. It's late; Rojas has probably gone home. The call can wait until tomorrow.

So we head for the pool, to enjoy the late-afternoon sun. Ollie emerges minutes later from her room. She's changed into a pink sarong with matching bikini. She stands close to Tyler, dropping chunks of ice into tall glasses of fizzy grapefruit Fresca.

I leap into the pool and Tyler follows, landing on top of me. We begin to wrestle, glad to release some of the tension of the past couple of days. Ollie lowers herself gracefully into the water, where she watches us with a lazy gaze.

"Why don't you two practise your capoeira?"

We stop grappling for a minute. Tyler eyes me expectantly. "How about it? I'm up for it if you are."

"Or. . ." I say, "or we could order cheeseburgers with fries, and chocolate fudge sundaes, and eat them by the pool."

Tyler groans with delight. "Mate, you're so right. What are you waiting for? Call a waiter!"

"Cheeseburger, yuck," Ollie says, wrinkling her nose. Then she perks up. "I'll just have a piña colada."

Everyone's happy when I take their orders to the bar. Tyler's standing with his back to me when I stroll back, and I can't resist shoving him into the pool. He topples and lands with a spectacular splash. Ollie's soaked but she's laughing too much to care. For a second I wish we were just here to hang out by the beach and take in the sights. Why didn't I ever think of bringing friends to Mexico before? It would have made things so much more fun.

We're interrupted by a hassled-looking hotel porter who leans out of the lobby. He shouts in Spanish, "Someone's looking for an English boy named Josh Garcia."

I pull myself out of the water. I'm thinking that somehow, it has to be Detective Rojas. But when a young woman strolls into the courtyard, I just sense it: this is Chetumal Lady.

She's dressed in tight white, low-rise Gap jeans with a jewelled belt and a strappy lime-green top that shows off a slender, deeply tanned, toned body. She walks effortlessly on high-heeled gold sandals. Her deep chestnut hair is long and sleek. She reminds me of a movie star.

She stops in front of me, pushes back her wide, tinted sunglasses.

"Joshua Garcia, right?" she says in Spanish. "Man, but I can read you like a book! The same hotel as Andres? C'mon up here and give me a kiss, willya?"

For a minute I just stand motionless, dripping, exchanging incredulous looks with Tyler and Ollie.

I reply in Spanish with the line I've been thinking about for weeks.

"So you're the woman who ruined my parents' lives."

The reaction isn't what I expected.

"Don't tell me you're buying the same garbage the police are putting about," she snorts. "Thought a guy like you would have more sense. Don't you know Dad?"

"Dad. . .?"

"That's right, hotshot. He's my father, too. So what if he hadn't got around to telling you and your mother about it? He was only a teenager. It doesn't make him the world's worst villain."

"He's your dad too?" I echo. "You're my sister?"

She grins. "Now you're getting it. That's right, baby brother. So how about that kiss?"

She takes another step towards me and plants a kiss on my cheek. "Oops," she says. "You got some lipstick there." I'm frozen, too surprised to react as she carefully wipes my cheek with her thumb.

Then she looks at me, and for a few seconds we just stare into each other's faces. That's when I know she's telling the truth. No doubt about it – my dad's eyes are gazing out at me.

I have a sister.

Nothing has prepared me for this. It is something I hadn't suspected, even in the tiniest corner of my mind. I just stare at her in dumb shock.

"You feel it too?" she asks with a rueful smile. "It's like some weird kind of mirror, isn't it? A mirror of feeling, of sensation. That sense of being split in two. The very same thing happened to me when I first met Andres."

I'm on the edge of understanding what she means. In her face, I see tiny aspects of myself, of my father. When she touches me I catch a scent of something familiar.

"Look at you," she murmurs. "What a cutie!" She stretches her hand across her face, just touching the tip of her nose. "From here down to your chin, you're Andres."

"You've got his eyes," I admit.

"Yep, I did OK there," she says with a grin.

"Mum knew he was pretty handsome," I tell her. "It's why she was so sure the stories about Dad having a girlfriend here were true."

She wrinkles her nose. "She did? Unbelievable. You can see why the people round here went for it – they love a bit of juicy scandal. And since I'd never told anyone who Dad was, of course they gobbled it up. Kind of thought you'd know better."

Of course I had. But her words feel like an accusation. I don't like to hear my mum slated.

"What did you expect? If you go around keeping a secret, having mysterious meetings with an older, married guy. . .?"

"Hey, the secrecy was all his idea," she says, with just a flash of anger. "He kept insisting he'd tell you both when the time was right."

I scowl. She notices and touches my arm.

"Come on now. Our father, he was all about the

100

archaeology. Well, that, and you and Eleanor."

"Really?"

"Sure. He talked a blue streak about the two of you. And the plans he made! How he was going to tell you about me, how I'd go to Oxford to meet you all, how you and I would become best buddies. How you'd always wanted a big sister."

I tell her, "I used to want a big brother."

"Well, bad luck, kiddo. Better learn to make do with me."

By now Ollie and Tyler are out of the pool. They look faintly dazed. My sister suddenly seems to become aware of their presence.

"You gonna introduce me to your buddies?" she says, switching into a heavily accented, Americanized English.

"Maybe you should introduce yourself to us first," says Ollie. "After all – Josh doesn't exactly know who you are, does he?"

"They don't speak Spanish," I tell my sister. "I'll tell them later what you just said."

"My name is Camila Pastor," she says to Ollie, "and I'm the daughter of Andres Garcia."

"Which makes her my half-sister," I tell the others.

"And that's your story, is it?" continues Ollie. Now there's no mistaking her hostility. Camila gives a tiny shrug, turns her full attention on Ollie, looking her up and down. Ollie's taller, prettier, but Camila's attitude is out of Ollie's league.

"That's right, sweetie."

Ollie says, "And you believe her, do you, Josh?"

I'm stuck for words. It hasn't even occurred to me to doubt it. I can't explain that kind of chemistry – the sisterly-cousinly-motherly thing you feel when you touch a female family member. Camila reeks of it. I can't believe it isn't obvious.

Camila beams Ollie a kind smile. "Sweetie, it's nice to see you're so keen on protecting my baby brother. I know he believes me. We recognize each other, see? I don't expect you to understand. As it happens, though, I have proof."

Tyler asks, "What proof?"

"The Mayan manuscript – the Calakmul letter. You've got half of it. I'm right, aren't I? You've got the first half. I've got the second."

Ollie stares at Camila, and a smile suddenly appears on her lips. She looks surprised and delighted. Slowly, Ollie says, "You've got the other half of the Calakmul letter?"

Tyler interrupts, "That doesn't prove she's his sister. She could have stolen it from his dad."

"Sure, buddy. But I got the other letter too, the one that says, 'Destroy this manuscript'. Addressed to me."

"You've got the second half of the Calakmul letter?" I echo. "And we've got the first half! That means we can decode the entire inscription. That means we can find the Ix Codex."

Maybe I sound a little bemused. But that would be a

major understatement.

I'm absolutely, entirely floored. We've been in Chetumal for less than two hours, and we've already solved two of our three mysteries. I feel a rush of triumph. This trip is turning into a huge success. With Camila's help, we might only be a few steps from finding the Ix Codex – or solving the mystery of who really killed my dad.

BLOG ENTRY: SISTER ACT

ᴙᴄᵾɔ◊ΛΛᴙɔӜ

Here's what happened when I met Chetumal Lady.

She turned out to be my long-lost half-sister. No messing. Ever since Dad found out that his real father wasn't the guy he'd grown up calling "Papa", his guilty conscience prickled at him. Because in his case the sins of the father had been passed on – and Dad had his own dark secret from a misspent youth.

The girl's name was Araceli; she was the maid's daughter in the house where Dad grew up. They'd known each other since they were kids, and early teenage fumbles in the laundry room eventually led to much more. When they were fifteen, Araceli fell pregnant and the weight of Mexican middle-class society descended on her and my dad. He was sent away to a Franciscan seminary. She was sent away too, back to her village. There was no discussion and no argument. Any feelings they might have were less than irrelevant. And naturally,

103

abortion was out of the question. So Araceli's family raised baby Camila. But when it came to schooling, Dad's family relented. They couldn't take the scandal of their perfect little family having an illegitimate child in its midst – especially given the fact that it seemed that history was repeating itself. Then again, they couldn't condemn one of their own to a life of poverty and no education. So, they sent money. Every month, bang on the dot: school fees and enough to cover clothes and piano lessons.

The money paid for her to go to a posh girls' convent school. Tough for Camila, though, being the only one from a poor family. It wasn't the best of situations, but she didn't let it get her down too much. She beat all the rich girls to a college scholarship in the US, studied tourism and returned to Cancun, where she ended up selling real estate until she met Saul – the guy who is now locked up in Chetumal jail on suspicion of murdering our dad.

Camila insists that we drive out with her to her house. "No way can I be seen with you," she tells us as we drive along the beach road. "Detective Rojas won't want you to speak to me until he's had his chance to set up his twisted little piece of theatre."

It all feels a bit paranoid, even to me. Yet Camila is adamant, practically drags us out of the hotel. "It's not just that I'm known in this town," she explained earlier. "But you've chosen the same hotel your dad always stayed in. I had to wait until the reception was empty to walk in – you can't trust the police not to leak information. Anyone who really wants to find you, Josh, will know just where to look. So we need to get out of here, like now."

It's a pretty nice place, her *hacienda*, very tastefully furnished. Her husband, Saul, must be a pretty cool guy. From discreetly placed stereo equipment, I hear the faint strains of "East of the Sun". Over iced tea and grilled cheese-

and-tomato sandwiches, Camila tells us the whole story of her childhood. We sit in her lush garden under shady banana palms, amongst the hibiscus and allamanda flowers, overlooking the sea.

"I didn't know Dad stayed at Hotel Delfin," I say. "I just thought it looked OK from the website."

"The owner has a jazz bar in Cancun," Camila says. "The Dolphin Bar. Andres was crazy for it. You didn't know that?"

I listen, say nothing. It's not every day you meet a long-lost relative. I don't really know how to react. As the afternoon wears on and Camila tells us the whole story about her and my dad, I begin to feel something new: jealousy.

Because the way it looks to me, Dad liked Camila a whole lot more than he ever liked me.

The sun sets in the hills behind us while Camila gives us her version of Dad's disappearance and the murder investigation. Ollie, Tyler and I screw up our faces, trying to work out what was really going on. Did Saul know that Camila was Andres's daughter? That would certainly throw out Saul's motive for killing Dad – why would he kill his father-in-law? If the police didn't believe it, why didn't she prove it to them? Why would they want to hold Saul for something he didn't do? Why wouldn't they want to find the real killer?

Camila sighs. She sounds a little irritated. I guess she's been over this. "It's not so complicated. You have to understand that many of the police here are corrupt. If some local *narco* wants a favour, then they deliver. But I have a friend who works at the police station. And she feeds me information."

Her theory is that Saul is being framed as revenge for not joining in with the drug cartel. The local drug guys reckoned that Saul's avocado farm had a few too many fields of avocados, and not enough of marijuana. Saul turned down what he called their "interesting business proposition". He expected trouble, and he was right.

As for telling Saul that she was Andres's daughter, of course Saul knew. So did the police. Camila and Saul protested as much when they arrested Saul as a jealous husband.

"But as Ollie so cleverly pointed out," Camila says, "I couldn't prove it. Andres only wrote me that one letter."

She passes it to me.

My dearest daughter,

This letter, should you ever read it, will doubtless come as too little, too late. How can I hope to make up for the years I've missed? Since I tracked you down, I've experienced a rush of tenderness that's entirely new to me. The lifelong love of a father for his daughter has seemed to be compressed into such a short period of time. Then there are regrets over lost time, guilt over continuing to keep you secret from Eleanor and Josh. I'll admit that it's been almost more than I can bear.

If words could ever say it, I would tell you how much I've been with you your whole life. Even if you never knew me, I never forgot you. In my heart I was with you every day.

But enough of that. I'm starting on something, you might call it old family business. A search for a lost Mayan codex – the sacred Book of Ix. It is possible that it could be dangerous. As I write this, truthfully I don't believe it is, but then, some strange things have happened recently. And there have been warnings. So I'm taking heed.

Which is why I'm entrusting you with something that is at once dangerous and priceless. My real father – a man whose death I've seen in my dreams since I was a boy – left my mother something else as well as me. The Mayan inscription I call the "Calakmul letter" has brought me to the point at which I'm ready to throw caution to the wind and venture into the depths of Mayan history in search of something I barely dare to believe can exist.

If I don't return, the search must end here. This is why I tell you nothing of my journey, of my research. This search has already destroyed more than one life. If I fail, I daren't risk anyone else in my family.

So I'm asking you, my darling Camila, to destroy the Calakmul letter. Don't be tempted to decipher it – you can't. I've left the other half with someone else, someone I trust, also with the same instruction.

Destroy it. Burn it. Tell NO ONE about it. Take the secret to your grave.

Do this for the father who loves you and wishes with all his heart that he'd known you as a baby.

Your adoring father,
Andres

Camila, she gets pages and pages. Us? We just got a few words.

My dearest daughter. Your adoring father.

I've crossed an ocean in search of the truth. But now I'm not so sure I want to hear it.

Camila stares at me, her eyes wild with excitement. "You didn't destroy your half, did you?"

"Nope," I say, trying to keep it together. It's tough not to sound bitter. "So much for Dad's trust. Why didn't he just destroy the bloody Calakmul letter himself?"

Camila says. "I think he planned on coming back with a huge, important discovery. This would have been a pretty important piece of evidence. An ancient document – it's not the kind of thing you destroy just in case things go wrong."

"Yeah, but what about all the danger?"

"Guess that's why he said to destroy it. To save us from any danger." She turns to me with a grin. "He didn't know his own children, though. Both just as curious as their father."

"Well, yeah."

"You see now why I couldn't show this letter to the police?" Camila says. "At least until I've had a chance to find out what Dad was searching for. And that's what they want. That's what this is all about."

"Whoever killed Dad did it to get their hands on his secret."

"I hate secrets," Camila says. "Don't you?"

Ollie leans over the wrought-iron garden table, pours herself and Tyler more iced tea.

"Have you deciphered your half of the manuscript?" she asks.

"Sure," replies Camila. In Spanish she says, "You trust your buddies, do you?"

"Course! They helped me to crack my half of the inscription."

Camila looks thoughtful for a second, then gives a little shrug and disappears into the house. She returns a moment later holding a small lacquered box. She opens it, removes a piece of bark paper.

There's a tear along the left-hand side of the manuscript. I reach into my back pocket and take out my half. I spread it out on the table next to Camila's half. No question about it – they match.

Camila gives me a look that's somewhere between sisterly love and pride. "Here it is," she says. "The Calakmul letter. My father talked about how he was studying this letter written to a king of Calakmul. But in my half there's no reference to Calakmul at all."

"It's to Yuknoom Ch'een, the ruler of Calakmul," Ollie tells her.

"From his servant," adds Tyler.

I want to fume quietly at this extra evidence of how much Dad preferred Camila – he'd even discussed his work with her. But even more than that – I want to look smart.

"A letter," I say, "telling how the Bakab was defeated.

How the Bakab came from a place called Chechan Naab. And it mentions the Book of Ix."

Camila nods. "That's it. The sacred book of Ix. That makes sense. Well, look, let's read it."

So we do. First we read out our translation, then Camila reads out hers.

**K'inich K'ane Ajk of Cancuen writes to Lord Yuknoom Ch'een of
   Calakmul**

I am your servant

From Chechan Naab he emerged, from the Great Temple of the Cross

The Bakab was defeated

This sacred Book of Ix speaks of the end of days

13.0.0.0.0 it is written in the Sacred Books of Itzamna

The Black Road will open the Heart of Sky

It will be destroyed

Healer of Worlds will be born

In the Moon it walks

In their Holy City of Ek Naab they wait

They are still. They wait

In wonder I stare at the inscription. There it is – the final clue from Dad's emails to Montoyo and the Peabody Museum guy.

And the other city name, the city that no one seems to have heard of, the one that doesn't exist.

Ek Naab.

"The 'holy city of Ek Naab'," I say, pointing to a glyph. "Dad emailed some Mayan scholars, asked about that place. No one's heard of it."

"*Utom*," murmurs Ollie. "So that sentence at the join says *The Black Road will open the Heart of Sky*."

Camila's section of the Calakmul letter is more baffling than ours.

"It's all Mayan mythology," she tells us. "And although it sounds pretty strange, I know, I think maybe it has a real meaning for us too. I've spent days studying what it means. You wanna know?"

We nod.

"The Black Road – *Xibalba be* – is kind of the Mayan concept of the Road to Hell. But," explains Camila, "there's another interpretation."

She watches us closely, to make sure she has our full attention. "From astronomy. The Maya were really crazy for astronomy," she continues, almost conspiratorially, "and no one really understands why they paid so much attention, or knew so much about what goes on in the sky. The Maya believed that you could see *Xibalba be* in the sky. Astronomers know it as the 'Great Dark Rift' in our galaxy: the Milky Way."

I'm impressed. This is much deeper than we've gone.

"How about 'Heart of Sky'?"

"Well," muses Camila, "the Mayan creation myth says that the world was created by the Heart of Sky and the Plumed Serpent. But there are scholars who say that it's also an astronomical thing, that 'Heart of Sky' could mean Polaris – the Pole Star."

Two astronomical terms together.

"Could that be some kind of astronomical event?" Ollie suggests. "The Great Dark Rift meeting Polaris?"

"In the Calakmul letter," says Camila, "it says *it will be destroyed*. Doesn't that sound kind of like a prediction of some cataclysmic event?"

I feel a ripple of energy pass through me. The hairs on my arms prickle. What if a 2012 doomsday scenario is real?

"Thirteen Baktun," she continues gravely, "the twenty-second of December 2012 – the end of the Mayan Long Count Calendar. Even nowadays it's thought that our galaxy will be aligned in a special way on that date. Maybe the Ix Codex describes what will happen then. And what if it's not some harmless shift in the collective consciousness, or whatever these New-Age types would like to believe. But a *real end*, some terrible event. *It will be destroyed*. What? The whole world?"

"Maybe not," I point out, "The Calakmul letter mentions this 'healer of worlds'?"

"Sure, that's also interesting," Camila muses.

"What does it mean?"

"Well . . . what if it's a reference to something that could reverse the cataclysm, or protect people, something like that?"

"What, like a spell or something?"

Tyler makes a tutting sound of disapproval. "What's wrong with you? That's madness, man!"

Camila shoots him a withering look.

I compromise: "Or something."

"'In the Moon it walks'," she quotes.

"Now *what* does that mean?" mutters Ollie.

She's got a point.

"OK," admits Camila, "I don't have all the answers. Who knows – maybe I've interpreted everything completely wrong! But I do know this: Andres believed that the Ix Codex is a true document, that it contains a Mayan prophecy about the end of the world. The Calakmul letter – it's giving only a hint of what's in the Ix Codex."

"I knew it," Tyler says, half-angry, half-smug. "This Mayan prophecy – it's for real, man!"

"Someone believes it," says Camila. "Someone believes that codex is worth killing for. Someone with the power to murder Andres and frame my husband."

"Carlos Montoyo," I breathe.

Camila seems thrown. It's clear that to her, Montoyo isn't a suspect. "Who, the archaeology teacher from Yucatan University?"

"Dad was supposed to be meeting him. He knew all about the Ix Codex. He warned Dad off."

"Andres did meet him – in Guatemala," says Camila, shrugging. "He didn't seem suspicious of Montoyo. In fact, Montoyo gave him some useful information. About a small ruin not far from here, where Dad found some new emblem glyphs."

"Emblem glyphs?" I say. "He found some new city names?"

"You'd better believe it! He was really excited."

"And that's all that happened with Montoyo?"

"Yeah. That was it."

"So if not Montoyo," I ponder, "then what about the CIA?"

Camila gives me a strange look. "Why do you say that?"
I reply, "It's Ollie's theory."

"Someone who could trace emails and Web searches," Ollie says loftily. "Someone who could organize a burglary. Someone interested in extraterrestial encounters with the Maya. And the alien secrets they might have shared."

Camila stands up, clearly troubled. "There's been something really weird about my father's death, right from the beginning."

"The UFO incident?" I ask.

Camila gives a wry smile. "Yeah. To be honest, we all wondered. But then my girlfriend, the one who works in the police station, she brought me a photo she took. In the plane wreckage, they found something attached to the flight controls – a small machine. My friend never saw anything like it before. Then, she told me, some *gringos* came. They had badges; CIA, FBI, something like that, but she didn't see which kind. And they took it away, the little machine. None of the police ever mentioned it again. It was deleted from a list of exhibits recovered from the crash."

"A machine attached to the flight controls. . ." I murmur. "Something that could have made Dad's plane crash?"

Camila completes my thought: "By remote control. No need for a pilot to jump out of the plane mid-flight. Just put the dead body in the plane and send it up. Then crash it – and you've got a perfect accidental death. If everything goes to plan, you don't even need to frame someone for murder. So, that only happens as an afterthought. When they inconveniently find the missing head of a strangled pilot. And that's when they start looking around for a victim to pin with their dumb story.

"These US agents," she says, "They killed Andres. It's as clear as a bell. And the reason is in this Mayan inscription."

Camila leans back in her chair, takes a sip of tea. She picks up and stares at my half of the Calakmul letter for a few moments, concentrating. Then quite suddenly she stands up straight.

"Oh my God! I can't believe I didn't see this right away!"

We stare at her, expectant. When Camila looks at me again, her expression has gone from one of wonder to anxiety.

"There's one thing these people – whoever they are – they cannot know. Something Andres only told to me. Something that tells us *exactly where Andres went before he disappeared.*"

BLOG ENTRY: CHECHAN NAAB

꒱Oⴷ◊O꒳Ɜ꒳ⴷ꒰

When we met Camila Pastor – my sister – I wanted to know everything: when Dad had first made contact with her, how he found her, what they'd done, where they'd been together, how many times she'd seen him, why he'd ignored her for so long, why he didn't tell us. That last one more than anything.

But once I'd seen the letter Dad left for her, and her half of the Mayan manuscript, the whole codex mystery dominated our minds again.

117

How weird was it that we'd both become obsessed with finding out what really happened to Dad and why?

Well, according to Camila, not at all. When I brought the subject up, she seemed nonchalant. "Of course. Every day I sent you mental messages, willing you to decipher the inscription, to get interested, to come over."

"You didn't even know I had the other half of the manuscript!"

"I knew *someone* had it. I sent my telepathic message to him," she countered, grinning. "And it worked!"

It sounds odd when I write it down. But in Mexico, people really talk that way.

Camila reckoned our half was the important bit. "Andres didn't realize it, but he told me where he was going. That last day. He was all excited, because he said he'd worked out something really important. He'd worked out the real Mayan name of the ruins at Becan."

Becan, a ruin not far from Chetumal, was named by archaeologists, just like lots of Mayan cities where the original name has been lost. Nowadays no one knows its Mayan name. But Dad reckoned he'd made that discovery. It was a name we'd seen before, another city named in the Calakmul letter.

"Andres found the Becan's emblem glyph on a marker in the forest nearby. He told me that the name translated as 'City of the Watery Snake Knot'."

"Knotted Water Snake – that's what Chechan Naab means," I said.

I remembered that bizarre inscription to "Arcadio" in that book

118

that the burglar was so keen to get his hands on, the one by John Lloyd Stephens.

"When was Becan discovered?" I asked.

Camila wasn't sure. "The 1930s, I think."

"So not discovered by John Lloyd Stephens?"

"Hey, that guy didn't do everything, you know."

I breathed out slowly. That inscription in the book must be a fake – not scrawled by Stephens after all. It mentions Tikal, discovered a few years after Stephens wrote the book. I could just about believe that he'd been on a secret trip to Tikal. But Becan, or "Chechan Naab" . . . if it wasn't even known about until the twentieth century? Still . . . it was all pretty odd. Whoever really wrote that inscription – they'd heard of a Mayan city I'd seen mentioned nowhere else.

Ollie broke in then, quoting from the Calakmul letter: "*From Chechan Naab he emerged, from the Great Temple of the Cross.*"

"There ya go," Camila said. "I knew you would see it too. That's what I realized when I looked properly at your half of the manuscript. The morning he left, he was so excited you can't believe it. Like he was really on the brink of something. That was June 12. I saw him leave in his plane. He flew west. Towards Becan. It has to be! To *Chechan Naab* – to where 'he' emerged, according to the Calakmul letter. Can't be a coincidence."

"But who is 'he'?"

"It's not clear. Maybe it's K'inich K'ane Ajk of Cancuen. Or maybe it's the Bakab, the one who the letter tells us was *defeated*."

"You're sure Dad went to Becan?"

"Look," she demanded, "Becan is the only Mayan city surrounded by a moat. It goes all the way around. What's a moat but a knot of water? The archaeologists who found it – they almost got it right – 'Be'kan' means *way of the serpent*. And one of the stone motifs you find in Becan is the open-mouthed serpent."

"The snake," Tyler said.

"Exactly. The snake that swallows its tail. The circle – a moat. And there's more. Your half of the inscription has this line – *By the Great Temple of the Cross*. Well, another motif you find in Becan is a cross made with recessed bricks. Nope, it seems pretty clear to me – the ruined city we all know as Becan was once called Chechan Naab. Which means that Becan is at the heart of this whole mystery of the Ix Codex. That's what Dad discovered, that last day before he disappeared. That's what made him so excited. I'm sure of it."

I have to admit that my sister's done it again. She's some kind of genius. Even more than Ollie. I feel proud to be related to her.

Maybe it's like father, like son and *like daughter too*.

A silence falls over us as we struggle to absorb all these new ideas.

"We're gonna find this codex," Camila says. "And hold it to ransom. Get whoever's really in charge to order my husband's release, or I destroy the codex."

"What makes you so sure it's still out there?" Ollie asks. "What if they already have it?"

"Maybe they do," concedes Camila. "But I don't think so. They are still looking. My phone is bugged, I know it. Every so often I sense I'm being followed."

"My house was burgled," I say. "And they tried to rob Dad's college room too."

"They're looking for the Calakmul letter," Camila says. "They know we have it. Which means that the codex is still out there," she adds. "Somewhere. And I'm gonna get it."

"All this to free Saul?" says Ollie.

"Sure. It's that or betray my father. These people killed

him for what he knew. You think I'm gonna let them win?"

"Let's say you do find it. If you destroy the codex," says Ollie, "how have you won?"

"At least," Camila says fiercely, "I'll know that those jerks will never get their hands on it. And my father will have taken his secrets to the grave."

With a perplexed smile, Ollie tilts her head to one side, asks, "And if this codex does turn out to contain some secret to save the world?"

"Oh, I'm counting on it," answers Camila.

Then she turns to me, looks me dead in the eye.

"So, baby brother, can I count on *you*?"

"I'm in," I tell her. "All the way."

Camila convinces us that it isn't safe to stay at Hotel Delfin. There, it will just be a matter of a day or two before Detective Rojas gives up waiting for me to phone him the way we agreed. And then he'll come looking for us. "And maybe not just him," warns Camila, driving us back to pick up our stuff. "Maybe the guys he's taking orders from will finally show up."

It's still not clear to me who she thinks these guys actually are. Like Ollie, she's mentioned the CIA/NASA/Majestic – whatever their name is – the UFO-Encounter Cover-Up Guys. But then she's also going on about the *narcos* – the local drug barons. When I ask her, she seems annoyed.

"The *gringos* – the agency – tell the police here the result they want. They want Dad's murder pinned on someone local. Fine. They don't care *on whom*. So Rojas looks for a candidate. And that's where the *narcos* come in. They want Saul punished. As an example to the businessmen around here. Play nice with the *narcos* or you could end up in jail too. Everything is sewn up: the police, the military, the secret services. And all of them – when the *gringos* jump, they ask, 'How high?' Is the same in your country, no?"

"No," I say firmly, "it is not."

Camila gives up on me. "Well hey, man, believe whatever you want."

It's past seven when we arrive at the Hotel Delfin. As Tyler, Ollie and I are getting out of the car, Camila tugs gently on my T-shirt, pulls me back.

"Listen," she whispers, "is there gonna be a chance for us to talk privately? There are some things, you know, that I didn't wanna say in front of your buddies."

My pulse quickens. This is exactly what I need – time alone to really get into the whole long-lost-sister thing. So I call out to Tyler, ask him to pack up my stuff too and bring it to the car, telling him that I'll pay the bill in the meantime. Tyler nods his agreement. Ollie gives me a final, curious look as we separate.

"Don't be too long," she says. There's almost a note of longing in her voice, but I couldn't swear to it.

It's a temporary goodbye. Nothing in it to indicate that by

the next time I see them both, my entire life will have irrevocably changed.

Even though the sweltering heat of the day has begun to wear down, the air still feels like soup. Before I go back to Camila, I dip into the alcove to pick up some more cans of Fresca. I'm feeding coins into the slot when American voices in the lobby stop me in my tracks. They're talking quietly; understated, calm. They sound nothing like tourists.

In Spanish they ask the receptionist, "Do you have a group of British students staying here?"

The receptionist asks to see their identification. "I can't give out guest information just like that," he tells them politely.

There's a pause while the Americans show their identification. I hear him ask, "NRO?"

"National Reconnaissance Office," replies one of the men. He doesn't sound all that keen to explain any further.

"You're US military?" asks the receptionist.

"That's right, sir," replies the second man.

The receptionist shrugs. It's obvious he has no idea what the NRO might be.

"OK."

I start searching for an escape route. There's no other way but to walk out behind them. When I poke my head around the alcove, I catch sight of the two men. Both are in their thirties, heads bent over the guest list. They're both wearing

Hawaiian shirts and board shorts but their regulation hair cuts give them away – these guys are no beach bums.

In the broadest Mexican accent I can manage, I call out to the receptionist in Spanish, "There ya go, pal – I fixed it. One of the Delaware Punches had gotten jammed. Call me if there are any problems, all right?"

The receptionist glances up – and when he sees me, for just a second, he hesitates. I make an imploring gesture. In his eyes, I see his agreement. One of the agents eyes me curiously. I'm careful to return him only the most uninterested glance.

"Thanks, Tony," he replies in Spanish. "See you next time."

I'm walking across the lobby when I hear one of the agents say, "Here they are. Josh Garcia, Tyler Marks, Olivia Dotrice. Rooms Twelve and Thirteen."

It takes all my willpower not to break into a run until I'm safely out of sight. Then I sprint to the car park, where Camila's touching up her make-up in her mirror.

I leap into the car, hissing, "Drive!"

I don't have to ask twice. Camila steers her car effortlessly out of the car park and hightails it out of there without the tiniest shriek of tyre-rubber.

"The people after us," I tell Camila, "are with the NRO."

Camila's shades hide her eyes, but I see her lips press together tightly. "National Reconnaissance Office. That's joint CIA, US military and Department of Defense." She gives a low whistle. "Yep, this is it, kiddo. The big test. And don't even think I'm unprepared. I've been waiting for this."

As we hit the coastal road, she steps on the accelerator.

"What about Tyler and Ollie?"

Camila shrugs. "How good are they at keeping their mouths shut?"

"I dunno. . ." I say. "What will those guys do to them?"

"Probably won't hurt them. After all, they're just kids. They don't need to hurt us; they just want the Calakmul letter. And what it leads to – the Ix Codex."

My hand goes automatically to my money belt; I finger around the edges, feeling for the manuscript. It's still there.

"Your buddies know where we're headed. It was a big mistake to talk so much in front of them."

I'm on the defensive. "Hey, they're in this with me. Ollie's been helping me right from the beginning."

"Yeah . . . interesting, that."

"What do you mean?"

"Just seems odd to me that some British kids should get so interested in Mayan archaeology."

"It didn't start out that way. It was about why my father was murdered."

"Are they good friends of yours?"

"They are now."

"But not before all this?"

"Well, no, but. . ."

126

Camila shrugs. "All I'm saying is – how much can you expect them to be in trouble for you? How long d'ya think they'll hold out before they give us away?"

There's no way to know. There's a lot of information. If they tell it slowly, reluctantly, piece by piece and from the beginning, it might be an hour before they get to the bit about Becan.

Camila concentrates on the road. "I'm betting their first stop will be my place. They'll go back there. So we need to call the maid, get her to hide the box with the manuscript." She hands me her mobile phone. "Press 2 and hold it down. Ask for Fernanda."

Then, her voice tinged with regret, she says, "We should get to Becan in, like, an hour. Well, with the way I drive, anyhow. Too bad for you and me, bro. I was hoping we'd have time for a heart-to-heart. It isn't every day I get a new brother."

I smile at her. "Yeah. I guess we can't really do that while we're on the run."

Camila stretches out an elegantly-manicured hand, seeking my own. When our fingers meet, she squeezes my hand. I can't say anything, but I squeeze back, waiting for Fernanda to pick up. I pass on the instructions and hang up.

Ten minutes later we slow down, turn off the road and through the gates of a smart-looking hotel. "I'm a member of the health club here," Camila explains. "And for a few weeks now, I've had an emergency bag packed, ready to go. In case of exactly this eventuality."

I follow her as she jumps out and marches up to the door of the Mil Suenos Health and Spa.

"A few weeks?"

"Yep," she replies. "Father murdered, husband locked up in jail for something I know he didn't do, no one believing my story, strange sounds on my telephone, engineers in front of the house at odd times of day, a guy in a blue Nissan who follows me. . . What, you think I'm a moron? How could I *not* be suspicious?"

"Well, when you put it like that. . ."

"Right," she says, taking a key from a chain around her neck. She uses this to open her locker, where she has a tan-coloured Louis Vuitton backpack. She removes this, as well as a pair of black-and-tan Skechers trainers. Then she changes into the trainers, takes off her rings, bracelets and earrings, stashes them in the locker and turns to leave. The whole operation takes less than five minutes, and as we leave Camila pulls a Fendi baseball cap low over her face.

When we reach the car park, instead of heading for her yellow Beetle, she turns towards a red Dodge Stratus.

"The Stratus?"

Camila nods. "Right again. Everyone in Chetumal knows my Beetle. So I bought this car two weeks ago. Been keeping it here ever since. Like I say, just in case."

"Wow," I murmur with admiration. "You're really good."

"Had a lot of time to think, bro. Lot of time on my own."

"It's a good plan."

"Not really," she says. "It depended on one thing – you. Only I didn't know it. I didn't expect that you'd be the one to put me on the road to Becan. And now you're here . . . well, I didn't bring anything for you."

"Oh," I say, not knowing what to add.

"S'OK," grins Camila. "We're brother and sister; we're supposed to share. There's enough food, money and water for both of us."

We pull out of the hotel's driveway. I stare into the dusky road ahead. The sea's already turned a flat mauve colour. A warm breeze drifts across the bay, rustling through the fronds of coconut palms. In the distance are faint sounds of tropical music playing on someone's car stereo. I lean an elbow out of my window and enjoy the sensation of rushing air as we turn west, head for the interior, towards the jungle ruins of Becan. I know I should be scared, worried about my friends.

But I'm not. As my sister and I drive into the shadows, I feel alive, energized, free.

Highway 186 stretches out ahead of us, plunging deep into the depths of the jungle. Any minute now we'll pass the state line of Quintana Roo and enter the state of Campeche. I feel the jungle closing in behind us, thick shadows encroaching on either side of the road. Every few minutes the trees give way to a small lagoon or a mangrove swamp, black holes of water that shimmer reflections of a purple, moonless sky.

I rummage through the contents of Camila's backpack. There is a sealed water bottle, a dozen high-energy snack bars, a waterproof torch, a Swiss Army knife, spare batteries, matches and cotton wool (sealed in a plastic bag), water purification tablets and ten thousand pesos in cash – around £500. And a pink iPod. "In case I got bored," Camila admits, smiling. "I didn't know I'd have you along for company."

Where was she planning on going?

Camila was prepared for anything. Me, on the other hand, I wasn't prepared at all. I had no idea what I was getting into. I have all the preparedness of a kid out on a jaunt with his big sister.

"Don't you wish we'd known about each other before?"

"Uh huh," I reply.

"No, but seriously. It's sad to be an only child. I'd love to have grown up with a little brother."

I can't imagine growing up with an older sister. That world of teenage girls, lip gloss and hair straighteners, pink trainers, pin-ups of Orlando Bloom and Brad Pitt. I've had glimpses when visiting my mates with sisters.

"It's so cool that you actually chose to stay at the same hotel as Andres."

"Not cos of the jazz," I point out.

"No, but still, you chose it. And so much of you is like Andres. The way you roll your eyes when you don't believe what you're hearing. The way you eat with your hand in front of your mouth. How you scratch your sideburn when you're happy."

"I don't do that."

"Sure you do," she says with a wry grin. "You're doing it now."

"What makes you think I'm happy?"

"You don't have to play it cool with me. I'm not Ollie, after all." She arches an eyebrow as she says this. I pretend not to notice. "You like her, don't you?"

"Yeah."

"Too bad," Camila says, shaking her head.

"You don't like her?"

"It's not even that. It's just that – there's something strange about a girl like her being so interested in a kid like you."

"Cool, isn't it?" I grin. "I think maybe the mystery about my dad made me interesting."

Camila frowns. "I'll bet. How old is she? Like, twenty?"

"She's only sixteen," I say, laughing. "She just knows how to look *fine*."

"Hmmm."

"No offence, but – why are you bothered?"

Camila turns to me with a sly grin. "Just looking out for my *hermanito*."

For a few minutes, there is silence. Then Camila says, "Plug in my iPod. Might as well have some music."

I dock the mp3 player. The car fills with yet more jazz.

I groan. "Not you too?"

"That's right." She's grinning from ear to ear. "I grew up apart from our father my whole life, and yet what do you think is my favourite jazz album of all time?"

"I dunno. *Kind of Blue* by Miles Davis?"

"Way to go, kiddo," she says, giving me a little shove. "Not such a space cadet after all."

"I lived with him, remember? He must have played that CD every week."

"Well, when we listened to it together for the first time he got tears in his eyes. Seriously. It was quite a moment."

Another silence.

She asks, "What do you most miss about our father?"

I take a few seconds to think it over. There are so many things, but the one that hurts most when I think about it, is knowing that when the phone rings it will never again be him. Calling from his college, saying he'll be home late. Calling from Mexico, in the middle of nowhere.

"Not hearing his voice on the phone," I reply.

She releases a long, slow breath. "Just the same as me. It's like in the song: *A telephone that rings, but who's to answer?*"

When she puts it like that, I get a little shiver. I'd never thought of it quite that way, but. . . "That's exactly it."

Camila grips the driving wheel a little tighter. "Well . . . I guess none of us know the time or place. That's why you have to live with death at your shoulder."

Maybe she senses that our cheerful mood is in danger of slipping, because she adds smartly, "But you know what? Next time you miss his voice on the phone, you call me. Deal?"

I gulp slightly, nod.

"Good. Got your cell phone?"

I dig my UK mobile phone out of my pocket. She dictates her number and I punch it in.

"Put me in as 'Camila, Call Me!' Or 'Call Me! Camila!' Either way it's with a C."

And eventually she asks, with delicacy, "How is your mother?"

"Not great."

"I'm sorry."

"She's on the mend," I say. "In fact, when we get five minutes I'll call her again. The news about you will be a big help."

"Should have called earlier. It's getting kind of late in England."

I look at my watch and realize she's right. It's eight thirty local time – the middle of the night in England. I feel a pang of guilt. I really should have phoned my mum, put her mind at rest about Camila. Somehow the whole afternoon has passed in a blur.

And it isn't over. The last traces of dim light remain in the sky, but the road ahead is gloomy.

Then, in a quite different tone, Camila asks me this: "Tell me, Joshua, did Andres ever tell you about his dream?"

"The one about his father? The one where he watches him die in some smoky straw hut? *Summon the Bakab Ix*?"

"That's the one," she says. "Did he tell you?"

"Nope."

"I thought not."

"But he told *you*."

"Once. He told me he dreamt the words 'Summon the Bakab Ix'. And that it was about our grandfather. The rest of it, well, I dreamt it myself."

I stare at her, stunned. But Camila doesn't take her eyes off the road. Very simply she says, "You've had it too, haven't you?"

It's a few seconds before I can reply. "How'd you know?"

"Since Dad disappeared, am I right?"

"Yes."

She nods thoughtfully, as though considering the matter from many angles. "Figures."

"You know what it means?"

"I think so. It's like a telepathic message. Someone saw our grandfather die, all those years ago. And they're sending out a message to the next of kin. Now, that's us."

I give a loud chuckle. "You're kidding, right?"

Her eyes grow huge. "No way. That stuff goes on here in Mexico. Lucid dreaming – entering people's dreams. There are Olmec Indians who can do those things. Really."

I'm still laughing as I say, "So you think our grandfather died in front of an Olmec Indian?"

"Could be."

"You tell Dad that?" I smirk.

"Well, hotshot, what's your theory?"

I shrug. "Simple. Dad told us about his dream. You remember him telling you, I don't, but I must have forgotten.

And our subconsciouses took all those elements, turned them into a crazy dream."

Camila doesn't smile. "Laugh it up, fella," she says. "But the way I see things, it all connects – the Bakab in the Calakmul letter. Then there's the dream of 'Summon the Bakab'. And finally – Dad's final trip to Becan."

"I really can't see how."

"Me neither," she admits. "But I sense it. And I have a great nose for these things."

As lights appear behind us, Camila checks her mirror a couple of times.

"That car's been behind us for a little while now," she notes.

"When did it join the road?"

"I didn't see," she says. "I think it just caught up. Now it won't overtake."

Camila keeps checking her mirror. She hasn't said anything for five minutes and I don't think it's because she's wrapped up in the Jamie Cullum track that's playing on her iPod.

"You think we're being followed," I venture.

Now that she's worried and deadly serious, Camila's eyes look like my dad's more than ever.

"I've slowed down quite a bit. And they just match my speed." She turns to me briefly. "Sorry, bro. I think they're on to us."

"What's the plan?"

"Well," she says, "We're gonna be in Becan pretty soon. There isn't much choice in hotels. If they want to follow us right to our door, they easily can."

"Why don't we go somewhere else? Lose them further away, then double back?"

"Not a bad idea, kiddo. OK. Let's keep going."

So we drive. Watching.

Then the car behind begins to gain on us. Until now, it's maintained a nice distance, far enough back to make it impossible to identify the car. As it gets closer, I hear Camila's voice fill with dread as she says, "Oh no."

Her knuckles are white as she grips the wheel. I look behind, get a good view of the car.

"It's the blue Nissan," she says. There's genuine fear in her voice now. "This guy's been hanging around me for weeks."

"You're sure it's the same guy?"

Camila explodes, yells at me, "Of course I'm sure, what, you think I'm making this up?"

"Who is he?"

"I don't know," she screams. "How should I know?"

I figure I should stop asking stupid questions. If the NRO guys have been in position since Dad died, then they've probably had a tail on her all along.

The blue Nissan finally starts to overtake. I twist around, try to catch a look at the driver. I see only shadows of his face lit by the dashboard. Then, with a sudden swerve, Blue Nissan rams our car. We veer horribly for a second as Camila leans hard on the pedal and pulls us out of the start of a spin.

Within seconds we're up to eighty miles an hour. Blue Nissan's speed increases too, and he's about to catch up. Camila takes us up to a hundred. Blue Nissan speeds up again. But Camila's car has the edge now. She goes even faster. I even see the beginnings of a triumphant grin on Camila's lips as we start to pull away from Blue Nissan.

And then we hear a shot. Camila almost jumps out of her skin, and for a second I think she's about to lose control of the car.

"Slow down!"

"Are you crazy? They're shooting at us!"

Another shot rings out. This one hits the car, somewhere in the trunk. We both yell, then duck. More shots follow. I'm flooded with electric panic. Camila's foot pounds even harder on the accelerator. But it can't be fast enough for me – the instinct to run, to get out of there, is overwhelming.

There's a part of me that knows that it's practically suicide to drive that fast in the dark. But as bullets start to hit the road around us, it's hard to take any notice.

"They're going for our tyres," Camila shouts.

And a second later, we're hit again.

There's a hideous explosion on the lower-right-hand side of the car as a tyre blows out. We spin violently to the right and within a second, we're off the road. Our car crashes through metre-high grass, then for a split second, we're flying. I'm screaming, watching the rush of looming black water.

My last thought before we hit the water is a desperate prayer that this is a small mangrove swamp, not a lagoon.

The car plunges down with terrifying speed. The airbags inflate on impact. I struggle to comprehend the fact that we aren't stopping. The car submerges completely, and water begins to churn in through my half-open window. The airbag pins me into my seat, and only when the car comes to a violent stop against the bottom of the lagoon am I able to move.

Adrenaline takes over and I fumble for my seatbelt. The water's already up to my thighs. I find the buckles and release my belt, then Camila's. But when I look up at her, I freeze. Her eyes are closed; she's not moving. There's a small wound on her head. As I wipe the blood away, I'm still trying to work out where she could have hit her head. And then I stop. I remember.

There'd been a second explosion, coming almost on top of the first. The rear windscreen has shattered. A bullet's come straight through the car. I've no idea if she's dead or alive – and there's no time to check. In less than a minute the car has filled with water. My head is about to go under. I take a huge lungful from the last remaining bubble of air, and I try to yank Camila out of her seat.

But it's no good. She's all tangled up in the airbag. Without her help, there's no way I can get her out. My chest is stinging to release some carbon dioxide and I blow a few bubbles out. I probably only have seconds left. I drag uselessly at Camila for a few more seconds. But in my own mind, I've already made the dreadful calculation.

And then, some cold, mechanistic part of my brain takes over. I'm like an appalled bystander, watching myself grab the backpack, wriggle out of the open window, and use the last ounce of air to swim as far away from the car as possible. My lungs are ready to explode when I surface. I'm already thinking about Blue Nissan, who's sure to be looking out for us. The water is warm, deep. I keep my head underwater as much as possible, surfacing only occasionally and with as little noise as I can manage. I've no idea where I'm going, and I'm amazed at how long this lagoon goes on. Finally I reach the edge. I stop, turn around, bury myself deep amongst the reeds, and gaze backwards.

One of the lights of our sunken car still beams out along the bottom of the lagoon. It casts an eerie, hollow light on a sickening scene. My breath comes in short, desperate gasps. I can just make out the dark shadow of a man shining a torch down into the depths. Then he flashes the torch upwards, in the water surrounding the submerged car. The torch moves further away, tracing a path along the edges of the lagoon. It's almost upon me when I take a deep breath and duck down. I stay down for almost two minutes, my eyes open, looking up through the water.

By the time I'm desperate for air, the torch beam has gone. The water finally seeps into enough of the car's systems to blow the headlamp fuse, and under the water the light blinks out. It's as though Camila's life-force has just been extinguished. For now, I can only register this as another bizarre fact: a guy in a Blue Nissan has shot us off the road; lungs need a few practice breaths to stretch before you can take a really long-lasting breath; my unconscious sister just drowned.

It doesn't hit me even then. I manage to remain calm for quite a bit longer, treading water. Slimy creatures that I badly don't want to see brush against my arms and legs. The shock hits me later when I climb, exhausted, out of the lagoon. I drop, soaked, muddy, bedraggled, on to the shore. Clutching Camila's backpack close to my chest, I begin to shake violently.

I try telling myself to relax. But shocked limbs don't want to move; it feels as though there's a whole apple stuck in my throat. I can't seem to make a sound. I retch and throw up. Briefly, I feel a little better.

Then I hear another car brake and stop on the highway nearby. Voices carry over to me. The torch flashes around again, still searching for survivors. I force myself to my feet. And heading for the darkness of the forest, I run.

I do pretty well for the first half hour – if "doing well" means managing to keep running forward through a dark forest. Staying on my feet, that's job number one. It isn't easy. Running in a straight line is impossible. The hardest job of all is trying not to remember that I've just seen my sister die.

I keep thinking about what I've seen on TV survival shows. You're supposed to sit down, stay calm, make plans. Well, that's great, but what about when you're on the run from secret agents?

I must give myself away. No sooner do I stop, double over to catch my breath, than the shooting starts again. So I run, deep into the woods. Planning and "don't panic" are not options.

When I finally stop, it's only because I can't take another step. I sink to the ground and beg God to make it be over quickly. I lie there for hours; fall asleep from exhaustion, waiting for them to find me and finish me off.

When I wake up, for a few seconds I can hardly breathe.

I've never known a burning darkness like this – it's as though I'm blind. The night sky of Oxford always has a slight glow. Even in the villages around the city, the sky never gets really velvety black. I'm stunned to realize that I can't see my hand in front of my face. Night has well and truly fallen. After a few minutes my eyes adjust, and I can make out some outlines. I stare into the sky, but the stars are invisible.

I'm still drenched from the swamp. The air is heavy, wet, thick. My clothes haven't dried out and I doubt they will. I hear the distant rumble of thunder.

The sound of the jungle is deafening. Birds, insects, reptiles and monkeys all chime in with clicks and chatters and whines. I think I can hear snakes sliding over rustling leaves, lizards crunching on beetles.

Lying there I remember everything my dad taught me about the Yucatan jungle. Jaguars. Pumas. The brown "recluse" spider, whose harmless-looking bite turns into rotting flesh within days. The "ten-step snake" whose bite can kill you before you take ten steps.

I fumble in my back jeans pocket for my mobile phone. I'm not surprised that it isn't working. I drop it back into my pocket – I've heard that you can dry out a soaked phone.

Thanks to Camila's foresight, I should have everything I need in her backpack – or so I'm hoping. Until I notice that I didn't fasten the top properly when I last opened it. The backpack looks empty. Furious with myself, I throw the bag to

143

the floor and start swearing, until some part of me remembers that someone might still be following me. I force myself to calm down by slowly counting to ten in English, then Spanish. Then I have another rummage through the backpack.

There are just two things left – the plastic envelope of money and the torch. The water or penknife would have been much more useful, but I'm grateful for what I have.

I'm about to switch on the torch when I think of all the creatures the light might attract. And never mind the creatures – the guys who are after me. I half-expect to hear the clatter of helicopter blades. Alone out here, I'll be an easy pick-up. I've seen TV shows where they chase bad guys in the dark using infrared goggles. The more I think about it, the weirder it seems that I haven't been found.

I test the torch under my T-shirt, just for a second. It works.

Without any way of telling where I'm going, it's too dangerous to keep walking. We came off Highway 186, heading east to west. From what I remember of maps, it is the only major road for hundreds of miles. Sure, there are dirt tracks. I might happen along one of them. But they won't be easy to find. They won't hum with the sound of faraway traffic the way a smooth highway does.

It's as though hours go by; hours in which I'm rigid, frozen. I can't make a decision without changing it two seconds later. *Stay put*. (But I might be wasting valuable time. Tomorrow I'm going to be pretty thirsty. It'll get hot. I'll pass out before I can get closer to safety.) *Keep moving*. (But I might walk into a snake's nest, or a jaguar. I might go in the wrong direction – even further from safety.) *Keep the torch on*. (It might attract creatures, or Blue Nissan and the other US agents.) *Stay in the dark*. (Spiders! Snakes!)

Slowly, surely, the nightmarish quality of my predicament dawns on me. It's like being suffocated. I feel the panic rising in me, swamping me. It takes hold of my legs and I literally can't move. If a helicopter appears, I decide, I'm flashing the torch at it. I'll take my chances with the NRO any day rather than face this jungle. What was I thinking, running? I must be crazy. Watching Camila's motionless body sink under the water, seeing those headlights flicker and die; it must have sent me over the edge. Fight or flight and I'd automatically gone for flight.

But the helicopter doesn't come. The sky bulges with sounds, though: distant airplanes on their way to Cancun, the grumbles of thunder, the whoosh and flutter of bats. And a low humming, which I'm guessing is a swarm of bees or insects. But bees at night? It's weird, but that's the closest match to the sound.

I can hardly even think about Camila. Every time my memory starts to revisit the horror of that crash, it seems like I'm quickly led away. Something inside my brain is taking me firmly by the hand, saying, *Pal, you really don't want to go there again*.

Come on, Garcia, I tell myself. Think of it as an adventure.

145

What would Ray Mears do? Now that I'm feeling a bit calmer, I run through every detail I can remember from his wilderness survival TV show. I decide that he'd make a fire. He always makes a fire; it cheers you up and keeps you warm while you make a plan.

Of course, he always carries a hefty knife and dry tinder. Camila packed that stuff, but it's gone. I could go looking for it, but then we're back in the whole *to-move-or-not-to-move-that-is-the-question*.

Survival is all about making decisions.

I can't remember if Ray Mears said it, but it sounds like something he'd say. I take a deep breath and make my first survival decision.

I turn back the way I came. I try not to think of the fact that I ran every which way I could, then fell over, then fell asleep. It's a guess, based on a feeling, the faintest memory.

I switch my torch on. The beam lights up a short corridor in front of me. Dark shadows twist around and behind it. I walk for about ten minutes but it's impossible to walk in a straight line. I can't see where I'm going or where I've been. There's nothing to get a fix on in the cloudy sky. Every so often a tree completely bars my path and I make a turn. Pretty soon I realize I've probably turned all the way round. This was a stupid decision. I've taken a step closer to death.

Then I hear an unmistakable sound – a twig crackling. A soft rustling; movement through leaves. I swing the torch around lighting up the trees in a circle around me. On an impulse, I switch the torch off. I realize that the hairs on my arms and neck are totally standing on end. I have to fight to stay still.

Something or someone is out there in the jungle. And they know I'm here.

There's another sound. It seems low, close to the ground. I move backwards and then I hear an unmistakable hiss. That's followed almost immediately by a bite. Just one – to the ankle. I fall to the ground screaming. I couldn't care less if there's a great big jaguar ten metres away. A snake's bitten me and I'm probably a goner.

The last thing I remember is like a hallucination. There's a loud crunch in the undergrowth. Something rushes towards me. There's another sharp pain as something new bites into my leg. The pain around the snakebite becomes intense, like someone's holding a blowtorch to my skin. I see a flash of movement above me.

Someone's here.

All I catch is the golden-yellow of their shirt. My vision becomes blurry and my breath starts to come in shallow gulps. A hand grabs my leg and I feel a sudden burst of ice against my skin. The pain of the snakebite eases at once.

There's a soft voice, a girl's voice.

"Take it easy, keep still."

I try to move around to see her, but I can't move . . . and then I fade out, fall into blackness.

I wake up to find myself next to a roaring fire. A girl, not much older than twelve, throws a handful of something on the fire. The air fills with a sweet, lemony smell that takes me back to evenings on verandas of holiday homes with my parents, listening to crickets and Stan Getz's saxophone; watching Dad smoke Cuban cigars while Mum drank gin and tonic.

I sit up, look at the girl. She's looking at me too.

"You were bitten by a snake," she tells me bluntly, speaking in Spanish.

"Yeah, I know," I reply. Obviously not the ten-step variety though – I seem pretty much alive.

This seems like enough conversation for the girl. From a shoulder bag made of woven sisal cactus fibres, she takes out a bottle of water and offers it to me. "*Muchas gracias*," I say, taking a long drink.

She doesn't answer – there's no "You're most welcome" or "It's nothing".

We stare at each other again. There's something odd about the way she looks me over. It actually makes me feel pretty uncomfortable.

So – I check her out too. She's taller and fairer-skinned than you'd expect for a local Mayan girl. Her eyes are rounder and her shoulder-length hair looks like it's been conditioned and styled. She's dressed in blue jeans, scuffed old Nikes and a soccer top – the golden-yellow shirt of the Mexico City Pumas.

The more I look at her, the more suspicious I become. She's no typical village girl.

Who is she?

"You saved me?"

Without looking up, she nods.

"You had antivenom?" I ask incredulously. For a second she flashes me with a contemptuous grin, as if to say, *Sure, bozo; what kind of idiot goes into the jungle without antivenom?*

"Who are you?" I ask.

"Ixchel."

"Ixchel," I repeat carefully, pronouncing it something like *Eeshell*. "Is that Mayan?"

She nods.

"I'm Josh."

Again she nods.

"You like the Pumas?" I ask.

"Uh huh," she replies, but she doesn't sound convinced.

"I prefer Chivas," I tell her. Her only reply is a shrug that seems to say *whatever*. "I even prefer their kit. Y'know, stripes. They're cool."

"My clothes are second-hand," says Ixchel, breaking across my attempts to make conversation.

I have sudden visions of charity collection bags and I'm embarrassed. I'm silent for a few minutes, trying to find another way in.

"Where are you from?" I say.

"From a place nearby."

"There's a village close by?"

"It's not too far."

"Wow." For a second I'm brought back down to earth. Looks like my terrified ravings about being miles from anywhere were way off.

"How did you find me?"

Ixchel doesn't answer this, but rummages in her bag. She takes a Snickers bar from it, passes it to me.

She watches me tear the wrapper, then says, "You were in a car accident?"

I give her a confused look. "How did you know?"

"I heard it."

"Well, yeah. A car ran us off the road. A guy driving a blue Nissan."

She mulls this over for about ten seconds. "You and who else?"

And I literally can't answer – the words stick in my throat, right under the chocolate. Ixchel just gives me a little nod, then goes back to looking all self-contained and impassive.

"How old are you?" I ask.

"Fourteen."

"*Fourteen?* Are you sure?" It's out of my mouth before I can stop myself. One look at her reaction tells me it was definitely the wrong thing to say.

"It's just that fourteen . . ." I mumble, "seems pretty young to be out here all alone."

Blandly, without a trace of irony or resentment, she comments, "I'm doing better at it than you."

I'm about to reply when she cuts in with, "How's your ankle? Can you walk yet?"

I stand up, test the foot. "I think I can, yeah."

I'm lying. My ankle is burning like crazy; walking on it will be torture.

"We should get going, then," she says. "It'll be light in two hours."

She gathers up all the litter into her bag, carefully stamps out the fire and picks up my torch.

I ask, "Where are we going?"

"Where do you want to go?"

"Your village?"

"Is that where you were going?"

"No."

"Then where *were* you trying to get to?"

I hesitate for a fraction of a second. Can she be trusted? The dressing on my snake-bitten leg seems to say yes.

"Becan," I reply. It's the only thing I can think of doing – to keep going, to find what my dad found, to discover whatever it is that Blue Nissan and his pals are so keen to stop me doing.

"OK," she says, apparently quite uninterested.

"You'll take me?"

"Mm-hm," she says vaguely. Her mind is already elsewhere.

"Is it close?"

"Maybe two hours."

"I hope it's not out of your way."

"No."

"You really don't mind?"

"No."

I follow Ixchel through a maze of trees. I'm mystified as to how she's keeping us walking straight until I notice that she keeps shining the torch on her wristwatch.

"You've got a compass there?"

There's silence, which I take to be another of her famous nods.

"You're pretty well set up for this wilderness stuff," I comment.

"Yep."

"What were you doing out here, all alone, at night?"

"Same as you," replies Ixchel.

"Hmm. I don't think so. I was running away. . ." *From a guy who killed my sister*, I'm about to say, but I remember just in time that despite the way she talks, she's still a kid, like me.

"Yeah, you said – from the blue Nissan guy. Well, me too. Not from the same guy, but running away."

"From where."

"From home."

"I get it," I say. "Hence the Dick Whittington set."

"What?"

"Sorry," I say. "Guess you don't know that story. Why are you running away?"

"It's long and complicated."

"I've got time."

"No . . . you wouldn't believe me anyway."

"Try me."

"It's really none of your business," she says, with such an air of finality that I shut up.

And it's like that all the way. Ixchel won't talk about herself or her village no matter what. She has this world-weariness about her that seems practically oblivious to my presence. I get the definite impression that to her I'm just a huge chore, something standing between her and fun.

I keep wanting to say, *Hey, what's your problem?*

We walk in silence for a long time. I think about Tyler and Ollie being interrogated by the NRO. Even though I try hard not to, I think about Camila, drowned in the lagoon.

I can't bear to think about what will happen to Camila. Reduced to being a body in a bag. At that moment I wish with all my heart that I were safely at home.

But that wasn't really much better. Watching my mum crack up, forever trying to make sense of my dad's pointless death in Mexico.

My breathing must give me away because Ixchel stops to look at me.

"You're crying," she says.

"I'm not."

"Why bother to lie? I can hear you. What's wrong?"

Blood rushes to my cheeks and I realize that I'm in danger of serious blubbing.

"I don't want to talk about it, all right?" I shout. "Just lead the way!"

For a moment I sense a crack in Ixchel's expressionless mask. Her eyes grow wide, soften. It's a disaster. The more sympathetically she looks at me, the worse I feel.

"Come on!" I insist. "Who asked you, anyway?"

Tears roll down my cheeks and I wipe them away quickly.

154

Ixchel stretches out a hand to touch my arm, stops when she notices me flinching.

I work hard on concentrating on the mission, to solve the mystery of Dad and the codex. I have to – it's all I have left.

As we walk, I feel for the Calakmul letter in my money belt. It's still there. Probably soaked and ruined, but by now I have the whole inscription memorized. Looks like I finally obeyed Dad's instruction to destroy the document.

After my outburst, Ixchel stays quiet but keeps glancing at me. She asks me just one more question as we walk.

"Why are you going to Becan?"

"I'm looking for something," I tell her. "A lost Mayan codex."

Her reaction is almost the last thing I expect. With a resigned sigh, she says, "Not you as well."

"You know other people who've been looking for a lost codex?" I ask, astonished.

Ixchel stops again. Her clear eyes stare straight into mine. "Some things are just *lost*, you know. People, things, causes. Sometimes all that counts is knowing when to give up."

"Maybe you're right," I admit slowly. "But that's the way I am about lost things. Even the word . . . *lost*. Doesn't that make you want to . . . find? When I lose something, I can't stop looking for it. It's as though there's a thread that connects me to everything I've ever cared about. Every now and then I'll feel this tug from an invisible source. I can't explain it any better. And I can't give up, not now."

"You're looking for something else, aren't you?" she says. "Not just this codex." Ixchel stares at me with an air of sadness. "Just look where it's got you."

I shrug, keep walking. I concentrate on the future. Me with the codex in my hands. Me handing it over to a museum, the police, the NRO, whoever it takes; so long as they let my friends and Camila's husband go free.

I'm curious about Pumas Girl and why she seems so out of place, like a city girl who's completely at home in the jungle. She isn't an obvious hottie or anything, but there's something about her. She's light and graceful on her feet. She bounces around roots and skips over fallen trees as easily as a deer. I find myself wondering how she'd be at capoeira, decide that she'd probably be superb. If I weren't so afraid of falling apart in front of her, I might feel more talkative. But I'm just not in the mood.

For some reason, though, walking along with Ixchel, I feel a tiny shift inside me. I can't put my finger on it, but there's something about her. It's like a kind of recognition – the way I felt with Camila, but different.

Different. But just as strong.

Two hours and twenty minutes into our walk, the sky begins to light up behind us. Ixchel turns off the torch. Our eyes adjust to the blueish-grey light. We cross a small opening in the trees, wade through a light mist and pass a huge iguana sleeping on the stump of a tree. We stumble into a ravine and then climb up the steep bank on the other side. Then we're lost again in a thick maze of trees. Frustrated, tired and thirsty, I call out, "How much further?"

Ixchel pulls up sharply, spins round and grins. It's the first time I've seen her smile and I'm momentarily disarmed.

"We're here."

"Becan? I don't think so. Where are the restaurants, souvenir stalls, visitor centre?"

"*That* part of Becan?" Ixchel shakes her head. "I thought you meant the ruins."

"The ruins? No. They won't be open yet. I need to get some food and drink, find a place to stay."

"You should have said," she mutters. "You said Becan, so here we are. As for the ruins being open or not . . . you don't need to worry."

And she pushes back a hefty branch. I'm so stunned that I almost trip over. We're smack-bang up against a huge stone pyramid that rises almost a hundred feet into the air. She's led me right in the middle of the ruins of Becan – Chechan Naab – the last place my dad went before he disappeared.

"Becan, OK?" says Ixchel. "I did what I promised. And now I really, really have to go."

"OK," I say, shrugging. "Thanks."

She gives a quick nod, turns to leave and then seems to think better of it. She gives me a strange look from out of the corners of her eyes, like she's hoping I won't notice or something.

"We probably won't meet again," she says, her voice suddenly very soft. "But whatever you hear. . ."

There's a long pause, into which I interject, "What?"

Ixchel breaks off her gaze. Now it's her turn to look embarrassed. I'm becoming more baffled by the second.

"Nothing," she says, staring uncomfortably at her hands. "If anyone asks, tell them not to worry. And that my decision . . . it's a matter of principle."

"Principle," I repeat, nodding. "Got it."

"It's not personal. OK?"

I'm still nodding vaguely as she backs away.

And then she really does leave. I call out after her, "But who's going to be asking?"

Her answer stuns me more than anything she's said so far. Because for the first time, *she answers me in perfect English*.

"The third layer on the western wall, Josh. And good luck!"

By the time I rush after her, she's disappeared into the ravine. I don't see her climbing up the other side. She simply vanishes into the undergrowth at the bottom. I now realize that the ravine is the dry moat that runs behind the towering pyramid and surrounds the ruins of Becan. I hear sounds of movement but it's too late to give chase.

Ixchel knows me. It's the only explanation. It even explains my strange feeling of recognition. Have we met before, maybe? Could she be one of the local kids I used to play with around the sites of my dad's archaeology excavations?

She was looking for me. She's delivered me to the exact place I wanted to be. The question is: who sent her? Who else wants me here?

It was as though she knew all about my mission. She saved my life in the jungle. *She came prepared*. That's why she didn't seem surprised when I told her I was looking for the codex. Her final shout had to be a clue to its location.

I gaze into the undergrowth where I last saw Ixchel. How do I know whether or not to trust her? She appeared from nowhere!

But what else am I going to do? Dad might have led me to Becan, but he hadn't been helpful enough to leave a map. Ixchel – whoever she is – obviously knows her way around these ruins.

Did she know my dad?

All sorts of theories run through my head. Maybe she's another long-lost sister? Maybe she was part of whatever led my dad here?

Maybe she saw my dad climb this very pyramid?

The dawn light is turning the sky salmon-red; the grey stones of the ruins glow with a pinkish hue. I push further through the undergrowth to find myself in a wide clearing. The massive pyramid is part of a city. It towers above a plaza, flanked by smaller buildings, including one with a wide staircase and two towers, each one almost as tall as the pyramid. The ruins stretch to the south and the east. Patches of morning mist hang low over the grass. Some of the ruins are fully excavated, but others are still partly covered with grass and trees. It's as though buildings are crawling out from under the hills.

I'm surrounded by ancient history that's being revived. This city is being rescued from the green of the jungle that choked it for the past few hundred years.

And it's all for me.

This moment I share only with the beetles, the lizards and birds. I can almost hear them now, hopping around in the fresh morning dew. A sweet smell of warm grass and loam rises from the ground. There's a stillness to the air that makes me catch my breath; a reverential, natural silence. I'm entranced.

And then I begin my climb.

The big pyramid that dominates the northern plaza is composed of five layered tiers, with a single front stairway that goes to the temple at the top. The dawn chorus begins – a huge racket starts up all from the trees behind the pyramid. When I reach the third tier, I step off the main staircase and follow the ledge towards the western face. In places the stones are loose. I have to watch myself or I'll slip. The third tier is almost at the top and the view is amazing. With the sun behind me I can see all over the site, right across to the highway.

When I reach the western wall I lean against the stone and groan. This side hasn't been restored properly. The ledge is narrow and looks treacherous. Worst of all – there's no sign of any opening in the wall. I guess I was hoping for a convenient little tunnel. Can't anything be easy?

Standing about halfway along, I notice that my clothes are still damp from the lagoon; swampy water mixed with sweat. It's pretty grim. No wonder Ixchel kept her distance. I lie flat against the side of the pyramid, pressing my cheek right up to the stones. I reach up with fingers outstretched, grab all the stones in my reach, tugging and pushing to see if they come loose. Nothing.

I begin to scrabble around desperately, moving along the pyramid. I grip hard with my fingers and scramble up the side of the third tier. Not very successfully. I don't have the footwear for sheer rock-face climbing – plus, I've never tried it in my life. Then, as I've just about given up hope, something unnerving happens.

My whole body falls against a rocky panel that suddenly lifts out of the side of the pyramid. Within seconds, it's horizontal, and then it pitches me towards an opening in the wall. I can't stop myself sliding. I fall straight down into a dark tunnel. The rock panel begins to slide back, upwards and out. The opening to the outside is being closed. I just lie there, mesmerized, watching it happen, watching myself being shut in. A moment later, the rock panel seals the opening.

For the second time in twenty-four hours, I really have to ask myself, am I making the right decisions here? The first decision resulted in Camila drowning, and now I seem to have buried myself alive.

Sometimes, instincts can mislead you.

I still have Camila's torch. Who knows how long it will last, though – in the jungle we had the light on for most of the past two hours.

The tunnel is about three feet high and wide. The ground is hard-packed dirt. The air is warm but dry. It smells only faintly of limestone dust – a smell that takes me back to those summers on excavations with my dad. Usually the interiors of Mayan ruins smell of dank, rotting guano. This place hasn't been recently infested with birds or lizards. I begin to crawl ahead on my hands and knees. Within a few metres, the tunnel slopes down, then straightens up. I switch on the torch. Straight ahead, the tunnel takes a right turn, towards the south.

The sound of my own ragged breathing echoes in the silence. I follow the tunnel a little further, until it comes to a dead end. There's an opening to the left. I flash my torch around. It looks like a small chamber – tall enough to stand in. I crawl inside. The room is empty. I'm holding my breath, scared stiff. It looks as though I'm trapped inside this pyramid. I've no idea how to get out. But the thought of Ixchel keeps me going. I just can't believe that she'd save me only to set me up for something worse.

I wait there for a few minutes. Nothing happens. I check all the walls and the floor, hoping to see some special stones or recesses. But no. I'm just about to give up when, without warning, the whole floor of the room begins to lower.

Down doesn't look like a way out. Now I feel myself losing my grip – this really could be grounds for panic. The room stretches longer and longer until the doorway I came through is only a small, dark opening near the distant ceiling. Pretty soon, my torchlight won't even reach that far.

I stare at the walls around me. The room is like some

huge long elevator whose shaft was cut into the dirt, packed with occasional limestone bricks and mortar. I hear a mechanism whirring under the floor. I'm being lowered back to ground level and beyond, deep into the earth under the pyramid.

Minutes later, it stops. The entrance to a tunnel comes into view against the side of the room. There's no other way to go. I could never climb up the shaft in a million years. I hear the mechanism moving again. The stone lift is about to head upwards again. The only thing I can do is to keep going.

This new tunnel is high enough to walk through. I walk ahead for about fifty metres, finally reach another opening. From the difference in the air quality, I can tell immediately that this is a large chamber. I flash my torch around. It's a pretty big cavern, around thirty metres across. Water drips from stalactites and stalagmites, which form columns from ground to ceiling.

My guess is that I've walked into something like the Loltun caves. The Loltun is a network of naturally occurring caves and tunnels that riddle the Yucatan peninsula. There are some archaeologists who specialize in finds from these caves, but for my family they were just a fun place to visit once in a while; a way of getting away from the jungle's heat. But with a guide! You didn't want to go down there clueless – unless you wanted to disappear without a trace.

Then, from behind one of the columns, I see someone step out from the shadows. I shine my torch directly at him. A tall figure stands about twenty metres away, watching me. I freeze. He approaches, and I can only stand there. There's nowhere to run, nowhere to hide.

Through the clammy air of that cavern, his voice resonates. "Good morning, Josh Garcia. I'm Carlos Montoyo. It's about time we met. Your father and I, we had unfinished business."

Maybe his words should mean something to me but right then, they don't. I'm so tired, so bewildered that for a moment I wonder if the walls of my reality melted when I leaned against the pyramid. And whether, at some point, I'd crossed over into a parallel world.

Carlos Montoyo? For the first second or two, the name means nothing to me. *I'm sorry*, I want to tell him. *What are you doing here?*

It's funny how context is everything. Carlos Montoyo; if I've imagined him at all it's as a benevolent academic, some crusty old college professor who took an interest in my dad.

Definitely not a Bond-villain type of guy you'd meet in an underground lair beneath a Mayan pyramid.

Montoyo steps towards me. He's solidly built, around fifty, wears black jeans with a silky shirt and a black leather jacket. His long hair is flecked with grey and pulled back in a ponytail. His brown eyes look sad, tired, deadly. His face is marked with deep crags. I can't quite decide which he looks more like – a trendy college lecturer or a hired assassin.

Or maybe one of those trying to pass as the other?

He stops when he's just two metres away, looks me over with a strange smile. He sticks out a hand. I answer him with a damp, limp gesture of a handshake.

"You seem confused," he comments in fluent English, with a hint of an accent that I can't place, but I don't think Spanish is his first language.

I nod. "Yeah," I manage. I want to say, *You? Here? But how?* But I don't think it will come out quite so coherent.

"OK. First of all, I owe you an apology."

"Uh huh," I say, wondering what he's going to apologize for. The burglary? Using some weird-but-helpful girl to lure me to a cave deep under a Mayan pyramid? Killing my dad?

"Why are you here?" I ask.

"Long story."

"Short version?"

He shrugs. "I live here. Nearby."

I watch him closely. He doesn't seem to be joking.

"Right, sure, in a cave? It's, um, nice."

He ignores that, instead saying, "I have to apologize for deceiving you. Or at least, for economizing with the truth."

I'm none the wiser. "Um . . . OK?"

"Some weeks ago I became aware that you'd taken up your father's quest to find the Ix Codex."

"How?"

He stares at me, seems slightly irritated.

"Believe me, you're gonna have more important questions. And you don't have all the time in the world. You've been reported missing already. Every minute you are away, people are looking for you. So we'll stick with the *necessary*, OK, Josh?"

I nod, trembling slightly from the sudden cool. Maybe it's fear. Or maybe it's excitement. I'm awash with adrenaline, tingling from head to toe with anticipation.

Montoyo gives a low whistle. "Hey, kid. You're really scared. Aren't you?"

I shiver, shaking my head. "No. I'm not."

"Yes." He nods once, slowly. "You are."

Something about his tone makes me suddenly suspicious. In a firmer voice, I tell him, "I don't think so."

"Your sister," he says softly, "I want you to know – I'm really sorry about her."

That does it. I launch myself at him, aiming a high capoeira kick straight at his throat, and I scream something at him.

He's definitely taken by surprise. I land a kick somewhere on his head as his tries to duck. He reels slightly. Before he can recover, I aim another kick to his ribs. But somehow he's able to swerve out of the way, spin around and get behind me. It's all done so fast that I don't see it coming. Next thing I know I'm pinned to the ground and he's on top of me, pressing my face against the cold rock floor of the cave.

"*Bravo, Josh. Que barbaro!* But now you're gonna listen to me. All right?"

I give a quick nod, tears of frustration springing to my eyes.

"I didn't kill your sister. You got that? I wasn't in the car chasing you. OK? The fact that I know what happened under no circumstances makes me guilty of her death. Can we agree on that?"

I nod again and close my eyes. I'm really losing it now.

"And, in case you need to hear this too, I didn't kill your father. OK?"

He releases me and sits back. I sit up, looking down all the time, ashamed of my tears.

"Grief is nothing to be ashamed of, son. You should cry for your father, you should cry for your sister. What happened to her – and almost happened to you – it's very sad."

I'm choked with emotion as I mumble, "I couldn't save her."

"Of course not," Montoyo says soothingly. "A situation like that, every second counts."

"I tried," I tell him, staring straight into his eyes. "I really tried."

He looks back, deep brown eyes studying mine. "I know."

I breathe deeply, trying to get myself under control again.

Watching me, Montoyo tells me, "I know what happened, because we were following you. Not from the road." He glances upwards. "From the sky."

"What. . .?"

Montoyo nods. "Yes. Later, I'll show you. But first, tell me, what did you think of Ixchel?"

"The Pumas-shirt girl?"

Montoyo breaks into a grin. It transforms him entirely. "Yes, the 'Pumas-shirt girl'."

"She's got a pretty big chip on her shoulder."

Montoyo chuckles. "That's true. But did you like her?"

"Why?"

"Hmm. Just wondered. Kind of hoped you'd get along."

"I wasn't really in the mood for getting along. Neither was she." I shake my head, annoyed. "Will you please just tell me . . . what the hell is going on?"

"OK. That's fair. But we need to get moving. Can we walk and talk?"

We both get to our feet.

"We're going somewhere?"

"Going somewhere? Oh yes. You could even call it the adventure of your life."

I hesitate. I don't feel afraid any more, even though maybe I should. I've already thrown out the idea that Montoyo is a psycho, hell-bent on killing me. He's had plenty of opportunity – he could have crushed my skull against the ground only a moment ago. Wherever he learnt to fight like that, he's been taught well. I didn't stand a chance.

Even so, I want to see if I'm still free to go.

"What if I say no? Can I go back?"

He seems genuinely taken aback. "Of course. It's your choice, Josh. You can go back to the top, back to your life. Forget this happened. Or you can come with me, and discover what's behind all of this. But you need to know one thing. If you come with me, you'll leave behind everything you thought you knew about the world."

I stammer slightly, saying, "But my mum . . . and my friends?"

"You'll see them again. I won't lie to you, it won't be the same. Nothing will be the same. In many ways, your childhood will be over. But then . . . I imagine after what you've been through today, that's already the case. Isn't it?"

Today? This is about so much more than today. I feel as though everything in the last few weeks has been leading up to this. Maybe longer. Like grandfather, like father, like son – is this where it's all been heading?

There's an unstoppable drive inside me that tells me that it is.

"OK. Let's do this. I'm in."

I follow him into a narrowish tunnel, about ten feet high and six feet wide. Hanging from some kind of rail in the ceiling are what I can only describe as something like ski chair lifts. Montoyo gestures towards one of the chairs. He waits for me to sit down properly, then sits in the second chair. He pulls down on two metal lapels sticking out of the top of the chair, above the shoulders. They extend to reveal two cushioned straps, which he crosses over his chest, then plugs into two slots in the sides of the chair. He turns expectantly to me, so I do the same. When Montoyo seems satisfied that I'm correctly strapped in, he presses another button in the side of his chair. A small console rises out of a central panel that separates our two chairs. It swings into place over his lap. For a couple of seconds he's preoccupied with a small visual display unit that lights up in the console.

I speak up. "Um . . . where are we going?"

He doesn't look up from his button punching, but grins.

"To Ek Naab, my friend. To the eternal city of Dark Water."

I remember the line from the Calakmul letter.

In their Holy City of Ek Naab they wait.

Ek Naab. It's not just some obscure name in an ancient inscription. It's real. Hidden, secret and lost – under Becan.

Abruptly, Montoyo stops pressing buttons. The console returns to its position in the central panel.

I ask what he's doing.

"Navigation," he replies curtly. "This isn't a route for the uninitiated. We don't take kindly to intruders."

"What happens?"

"Booby traps," he says with an unpleasant smile. "You don't want to know."

"You kill people?"

He doesn't answer my open-mouthed question. A large stud lights up on the central panel. Montoyo presses it. After that all I can hear is my own voice, yelling.

There's a sound like a small explosion of hydraulic pressure. Our chair is catapulted forward. We're yanked back into our seats. We hurtle towards what looks like a solid wall of rock. At the very last minute, the chair plummets, falling into the void. I feel my guts lift up inside me. We fall crazily, in a dizzying downwards spiral, plunged into the darkness, like a rocket totally out of control, like a Catherine wheel released from the pin. We pull out of the drop into a steep climb. After that I lose track. The wall of the tunnel speeds past. Every so often I spot openings, turnings. Some we take, some we miss. I understand then what Montoyo said. At this kind of speed only an expert could navigate safely through the tunnels.

Every so often we pass through a wide opening and I catch a glimpse of something. I see a cavern filled with the glow of phosphorescent stones, see our blurred reflection in a pool of mirror water, see a stalagmite as tall as a telegraph pole and thick as a redwood, see another chair skim by, the occupants a white fuzz in the distance. We tumble into a tight loop that crushes us into our seats, then shoot out into another hard curve, before beginning a series of steep climbs. Then a sudden deceleration.

As we slow down, I catch my breath. I stare ahead. I can see bright lights. It's like coming out of a tunnel in the London Underground. When we finally stop, that is exactly how it looks to me: like an underground station. Empty, clean, no turnstiles, but basically, somewhere to dock.

There's no one around. This is like nowhere I've ever been. The doorways are arches in the classic Mayan corbelled style. The building material seems to be local limestone, just like above the ground. But there is also metal, wood and ceramics. The walls are tiled with Spanish-style decorated ceramic tiles; except the designs are Mayan. The floors are lined with traditional terracotta Spanish floor tiles.

Montoyo helps me out of the chair and I step on to the platform. I stare in awe, speechless. Finally, Montoyo seems happy to stop, to let me take a moment.

"This is it, Josh; the place your father was *really* searching for. The centuries-old secret of the ancient Maya. Ek Naab is *alive*."

I gaze at Montoyo, see raw emotion cloud his eyes.

"You see, our civilization is not so finished after all. Some of us did escape the Spanish, the *conquista*."

I just gawp. "What . . . what are you saying? Mayans live down here? *Ancient* Mayans?"

Montoyo nods.

"A living city," I breathe. "Just like John Lloyd Stephens said. . ."

Montoyo breaks into a delighted grin. "You've read Stephens," he murmurs. "I'm so glad."

"OK . . . not actually . . . not myself. My mum and dad had his books. They told me about it. . ."

He looks a teensy bit disappointed. "You should read him, he's really excellent."

"I can't now," I comment. "Someone broke into our house, took the Stephens book along with all our computers."

"Why would someone steal that book?" Montoyo asks with a frown.

I shrug. "I've been asking myself that."

"Well, Josh, I can confirm that we are the descendents of one particular ancient Mayan community."

"But *you* . . . I mean . . . you're Mayan?" I can't bring myself to say it, but his face is obviously not pure Mayan. He's as Hispanic as most middle-class Mexicans.

As if guessing my thoughts, Montoyo smiles sadly. "I didn't say we were completely exclusive. We'd have become completely inbred long ago, if not for bringing in new blood. A few travellers found their way to us; explorers. My ancestors include men from Spain and Germany. Yours were from Spain. But we can claim *continuity*. The people who lived here were never conquered. We trace a direct line back over two millennia, to the very dawn of Mayan civilization."

My ancestors? I guess I should have seen that coming. But the surprises are arriving so thick and fast that I'm not getting time to process properly.

Montoyo helps me out. "Your great-great-great-grandfather was a Spaniard, Isidro Garcia de Vega. He married a woman here. And your grandfather, well, that's a whole other story."

Then, maddeningly, he begins to walk again.

"Come on, Josh. There's a lot to see. We have to get you back before a search begins in earnest. We've much to do."

I follow him, trotting to keep up.

"Why *am* I here? And if it wasn't you in the blue Nissan, then who?"

"The man chasing you, his name is Simon Madison. According to his passport, a US citizen, occupation listed as a systems engineer. . ."

"Never heard of him."

"Of course," Montoyo says. "It's probably not his real passport. Most likely he's undercover."

"With the NRO?"

"It's possible."

"And you've been watching him?"

"We were watching Camila Pastor. And he was watching her too."

"Why were you watching Camila?"

"Because she talks to the police – she knows what they know, or at least what they think they know. We have to investigate this from all possible angles, Josh. We must find out what happened to your father."

I haven't realized until this moment just how badly I've been hoping that Montoyo knows something – anything that might help. But he doesn't. It's a nasty shock, stops me in my tracks.

"You . . . don't know?"

He gives a deep sigh. "Your father came to Ek Naab – that much you've probably guessed. But shortly after he left we lost track of him. There was an air crash."

"Yeah . . . I know."

"No, you don't understand. He left here in one of our flying craft. Like the one we followed you in when you ran into the jungle."

"What. . .? You mean you weren't in a helicopter?"

"No, my boy. We have something rather better than helicopters. As you will see. Your father needed to go on a mission for us, to Veracruz. He used one of our aircraft – which we call 'Muwan'. Shortly after leaving here, we tracked five other craft in the vicinity. They chased your father. And then – he just disappeared from our radar."

"What?" I'm staggered. "Aircraft. . .?"

"That story about the Cessna crash is just as much of a mystery to us as to you."

"Maybe he was forced to land and got into his other plane?"

"No, Josh. Listen to what I'm saying. One aircraft, the Muwan – your father. Then five others appeared. *Six craft.*"

Slowly, unbelievably, it dawns on me.

"The UFOs. . .?"

Montoyo nods, starts walking again.

"What did you call them? 'Muwan'? The UFOs over Campeche?" I repeat, incredulous.

"Pay attention, Josh. I said your father was in one craft. The other five were a total surprise to us also."

"Extraterrestials?"

Montoyo snorts with disdain.

"Then, what?"

"Simple; someone has stolen our technology. We've suspected it for a long time. These same people probably murdered your father."

"This Simon Madison guy and the NRO?"

"Possibly."

"The NRO must have organized the burglary. . ." I mutter, almost to myself. "That's when they started following me . . . they must have tracked me to Hotel Delfin."

"Hmm."

"Why didn't you reply to my email?"

"I promised your father. Not to involve you. It was a solemn promise, Josh. If I'd answered that email, I would have had to lie."

"But I did get involved."

"True, but not because of me." Then gently he says, "Look, we'll talk about this later. I realize you have many questions. But I need you to listen first."

We walk again, making our way along the tunnel, then up stairs. I make a huge effort to shut my trap. Tough, when my worldview, not to say family history, is being turned on its head.

"The first thing you need to know is that the Mayan inscription your father found originally belonged to your real grandfather, Aureliano."

I nod. "Yeah, yeah, I know."

"And your grandfather, he was one of us. He was born in Ek Naab."

That's not as surprising to hear now as it would have been outside Ek Naab. It certainly solved my grandmother's big mystery over where Dad's father came from – and where he went.

"Where is he now?"

Montoyo catches his breath. "He's dead."

"I know," I agree. "But where?"

"That's the big question. Because we believe he had something with him when he died."

Suddenly it's obvious. My grandfather had owned the Calakmul letter before my dad. He was searching for the codex too. *And his search hadn't been in vain.*

Breathlessly, I say, "The Ix Codex?"

Montoyo nods, apparently impressed. "Good boy. It's the only explanation. He was in charge of the search. For hundreds of years, one from your family has sought the codex. Then, miraculously, finally we found its trail. Your grandfather, he set off to find it. Our information told us it was in England. . ."

"England?!"

"In a place called Saffron Walden. In the house of the renowned Mayan archaeologist J. Eric Thompson."

I stop walking. Each new bit of information seems more

incredible than the last. "Thompson?! Thompson had the Ix Codex?"

I've heard about J. Eric Thompson all my life. He was probably the most famous British guy ever to study the Maya. My father had all his books. Until he died in 1975, he was the Big Cheese of all Mayanists.

"Your grandfather believed so. He tracked the codex to Thompson. Not easy, because Thompson didn't know what he had. Or at least if he did, he kept it very, very quiet. For understandable reasons."

"What reasons?"

"Later, Josh. We'll come to that. Your grandfather went to see Thompson in Saffron Walden. We received word that he'd found the codex. You can't begin to imagine the importance to Ek Naab, to the destiny of the whole world. And then, somewhere over Mexico, we lost track of your grandfather. He simply vanished."

"He died near water," I murmur. "In a hut."

Montoyo stops suddenly. We're almost at the end of the stairs. My legs are cramping with fatigue.

"Why do you say that?"

"I dreamt it," I say, rubbing my thighs. "One of two huts, on water. The ocean or a lake. A misty, watery place. He died, choking. And someone saw it."

Montoyo looks at me with a mixture of respect and wonder.

"Amazing. That's just what your father said."

He turns to the opening of the tunnel, a few metres away. Beyond, I catch a glimpse of buildings and the glow of natural light.

"Beyond this tunnel lies the city of Ek Naab, a city of a thousand wells. The city of a hundred fables. A city that exists for most only as a rumour, a whisper, a hope. It's the city to which you belong, Josh, as much as you belong anywhere. Ek Naab holds the only hope of survival for civilizations throughout the world."

We emerge from the subway tunnel on to a high platform overlooking a deep underground pool. Montoyo says, "This is the *cenote*, the fathomless 'black water'; a black hole of sacrifice for which Ek Naab became notorious."

I stare into the depths. The surface of the water is about twenty feet below the opening of the sinkhole. A nasty drop and a pretty impossible climb to safety for the poor human sacrifice. A metal fence and guarded walkway rings the entire body of water, which is roughly the size of the penalty area of a football field. At intervals around the walkway, tall lamps with five globes of yellow light illuminate the nearby shore of the lake. The smooth surface of the pool gleams, mirror-like.

Beyond the water, I glimpse the wide expanse of the underground cavern. I can see buildings that appear to be as much as two football fields distant. All kinds of buildings – everything from what look like gleaming office blocks to sombre, stone-faced Mayan temples. There are plazas and alleyways and canals of water, all bundled together. Like a weird fusion of Mexico, ancient and modern, with Venice.

And all underground! I can't get my head around it at first – how come it's so light?

Then I look up. Over the central part of the city, instead of the rock ceiling, there's a mesh-like fabric. Sunlight pours through the tiny holes. It's unnerving, confusing. There's a sense of vast space . . . then you look up and see that ceiling.

I stare back into the city. Colourful murals display the Mayan heritage. The five-globed lamps are dotted around the city. There's one spacious plaza covered with tables and chairs; open-air cafés. They're empty, so I guess it's too early for them to be open.

There are even *trees*. Exactly the kind I've seen in the central town *zocalos* of small Mexican towns, canopies neatly clipped. Warm light leaks from windows in the buildings. A background hum carries the faint suggestion of voices and music.

And everywhere I look, flowers. Potted, in hanging baskets or trailing over walls, crawling their way through the narrow alleyways between brick, glass and stone; the entire city blooms with violent pinks, regal purples, jubilant reds.

Montoyo watches me with a hint of a smile. "What do you think?"

I spin around, trying to take it all in, my head in my hands. "Amazing! I mean . . . where did this all come from? And how?"

Montoyo's enjoying watching my reaction, I can tell.

"Centuries ago, Ek Naab was just a shrine, dedicated to Itzamna. He brought us agriculture, writing and time-keeping. The Maya worshipped Itzamna as a god, you know. They came to Ek Naab to placate him with regular sacrifices of the city's young people, thrown into the *cenote* to drown."

He gives me a loaded stare.

"But that's all in the past, right?"

Or am I about to hear that the Maya of Ek Naab were sticklers for tradition, and I'm about to become the latest sacrificial victim?

Montoyo chuckles. "Of course. We're over all that."

I'm silent for a long time. "I . . . really dunno what to say."

"Don't you want to know about us?"

"Well, yeah. . ."

But where to start? I'm not in the mood for a history lesson. The damp of my clothes has cooled in the underground chill. I begin to shiver. Or maybe it's the thrill of discovery? I have this sudden urge to call Ollie and Tyler. Then I remember that my mobile phone wouldn't work underground, even if it wasn't soaked.

The thought that my father was here gives me a warm feeling. I'm sharing in his final secret. I wonder if it ever crossed his mind that I would? I'd like to think he'd be proud of me. I guess now I'll never know.

Montoyo finally snaps me out of my trance-like state.

"You look exhausted," he notes. He's right; my legs are turning to jelly, and my eyelids keep drooping. "We're gonna get you to a bed," he says. "And we'll talk more in a few hours."

I nod and follow him around the path, past the *cenote*, through a narrow passageway into a small patio crammed with bright red, potted hibiscus flowers. We cross the patio and take one of four doors, climb stone stairs to a third floor.

We enter a small apartment, minimally furnished, like a room in the IKEA catalogue. Montoyo leads me to a bedroom. There's a hammock, a reading light suspended from the ceiling and a thick mat of woven sisal on the floor. An indigo-coloured curtain is drawn across a small window. It doesn't quite blot out the dimmed daylight that floods the city. The sun must be up outside, high above the jungle.

From behind a cupboard door, Montoyo removes a fleece blanket.

I hold it for a minute, just looking at the label.

"This comes from Sears," I say, noticing the mark of the department store.

Montoyo nods. "Most things we use come from outside the city."

"And nobody knows about you?"

"They don't know about Ek Naab. Part of the city is above-ground. Doesn't look like the rest of Ek Naab, that's for sure. And it's all private land."

"Can I see?"

"Tomorrow, my boy."

I can't stop myself yawning. "OK. But . . . can I ask one more thing? When you said you had unfinished business with my dad. What did you mean?"

Montoyo's eyes take on a flinty look. "He took something of ours – or rather, something that once belonged to Itzamna."

Hearing this jolts me awake. "*Itzamna really existed?*"

"Of course."

"Not just a myth?"

"Absolutely not."

"And the Bakabs?"

"His four sons. And *their* sons."

"The guys who hold up the four corners of the sky, you mean those Bakabs? Bakabs are real?"

Montoyo gives me a stern look. "You're as bad as your father, you know that?"

"How do you mean?"

"A lifetime of education told your father that everything he studied about the Mayan religion was mythology and superstition. Even with the evidence before him, he could hardly believe it."

"Maybe that's why he took this thing of Itzamna's. To test it."

Montoyo laughs. "I doubt it."

"Why?"

"The Bracelet of Itzamna is not exactly the sort of archaeological artefact your dad is used to handling."

"The Bracelet of Itzamna?"

"That's what he took."

"Where is it now?"

"A good question."

"And . . . *what is* the Bracelet of Itzamna?"

Montoyo smiles thinly. "Ah! Now that really *is* the question."

For a second, I'm hopeful. Then I notice Montoyo's lips pressed tightly together.

"Oh. . ." I say, rolling my eyes. "I get it. You're not going to tell me, are you?"

This time Montoyo gives a wry grin. He pats my shoulder. "Get some sleep, Josh."

I climb into the hammock, wrap the blanket around me and snuggle up, trying to find a comfortable position. My mind buzzes with everything I've seen and heard. I hear Montoyo moving around in the living room. Piano music plays faintly in the background – it sounds like Bach.

This is all too bizarre. I still haven't quite recovered from finding myself sliding into a pyramid. I'd been expecting a cubbyhole, something I could stick my hand into and find a hidden manuscript in.

The city of Ek Naab is about a billion light years from anything I'd ever imagined.

It takes me a while to fall asleep. I think about Ollie and Tyler, feel a dig of guilt when I think about the trouble I've led them into. It's only the memory of how mad-keen Ollie was to come on the trip that makes me feel anything but a total idiot.

Camila is another story. I haven't dared to really think about her yet. Every time I get close to the memory, I can't help crying, like when I was with Ixchel. Now, alone in this darkened room, I forget where I am. I could be anywhere in the world. When I close my eyes, all I see is an image of Camila in the car, blood trailing through the water from her head. I force it away, try to think of anything else.

I imagine meeting my father again. Telling him about Ek Naab. Having a nice little chat about it. And that, finally, puts me to sleep.

When I wake up, a narrow line of light around the curtain tells me that it's still daytime. The music playing next door has changed – now I hear something that sounds like grungy rock music.

I slide out of the hammock. Underneath, someone has laid clothes in a neat pile. There are shorts and a blue shirt, and some canvas slip-on shoes. I change quickly.

In the living room, sitting on a wood-framed sofa is a guy I don't recognize. He looks around seventeen, eighteen. When he sees me, he smiles broadly, leaps to his feet.

"Hey, Josh! It's great to finally meet you!"

Another person who speaks terrific English. He shakes my hand vigorously, pats me on the back. Meanwhile I struggle to take in yet another new face.

"Where's Carlos Montoyo?" I ask.

"He had something to take care of."

"But . . . he said he'd be here."

The guy gives a huge, so-what shrug.

"I'm Benicio," he explains. "I'm your cousin!"

"Um . . . that's pretty random."

"'Random'?"

"Wild. Out there. It's unexpected."

My "cousin" gives a puzzled smile, then gets back to shaking my hand. He's slim and lean, only a little taller than I am. He has longish, floppy hair with a ragged fringe that looks a little greasy. His face is covered in a couple of days' worth of stubble. He wears blue jeans, a plain, crumpled white T-shirt and green tennis shoes.

"I read your blog, man," he says with a grin. "You and that TopShop girl. Cool! Until you hid it. What a shame!"

"You read my blog," I repeat. "How come?"

"Montoyo, you know, Montoyo's been watching out for you ever since your daddy disappeared."

I think about that in silence. I study Benicio's features for a second: sallow skin, almond-shaped brown eyes. I'm definitely seeing another mixed Mexican/Hispanic – *mestizo* – face. It's a fair bet that Benicio's ancestors are part Hispanic too, but his eyes and mouth show signs of a Mayan heritage.

I'm beginning to wonder if anyone in this lost Mayan city is actually a hundred per cent Mayan. Looks to me as though the Spanish *well* got their feet under the table in Ek Naab.

Benicio notices me checking him out. He folds his arms, saying, "So, Josh, you notice any family resemblance?"

"I dunno," I tell him. "What relation are we, exactly?"

"Your father, Andres, he was my mother's first cousin."

"So our grandparents were brothers?"

"Brother and sister. She's alive, you know. Your great-aunt – my grandmother."

"That's amazing. How many more relatives have I got here?"

"A few."

"The girl who found me, Ixchel. Is she one?"

Benicio looks momentarily shocked, then laughs. Emphatically, he says, "No way."

"Benicio," I say, "I really need to call my mother and my friends. Is there a way to do that?"

"Yeah. They'll be pretty worried, I guess. Listen, I can't call to an outside network from the underground part of the city – only to another Ek Naab phone. But later we'll be on the surface. Then you can call, OK?"

"How long?" I ask. I don't want to keep them waiting any longer than I have to.

Benicio checks his watch. "Like one, two hours."

I sit, anxious. I don't really want to insist, but that feels like too long.

"Come on, it's OK," he says, trying to cheer me up. "We can get to know each other! I've been waiting to meet you!"

"How long have you known about me?"

"Just a few months. When your father made contact with Carlos Montoyo. No one knew that your grandfather, Aureliano, had a baby in the outside world. Imagine! Was a big surprise for everyone here."

"How come?"

"Aureliano," says Benicio, "he was spending most of his time outside the city. Searching for the Ix Codex. Your grandpa, I think he was kind of a crazy guy. You know? Living to his own rules. We have our rules here, and when he was here, he lived by them. But outside . . . outside he was playing another game."

"Another game? What do you mean?"

"I mean, here, he has his wife. By arranged marriage, of course. But no son. Maybe he's not so happy, so outside, he hooks up with this other woman. . ."

"Wait, wait," I say. "Slow down. Arranged marriage?"

Benicio's eyes widen. "You don't know about this?"

"Look, I just got here, OK? This isn't easy to take in, you know!"

Benicio pats my back. "Hey, man, cool it! That's why your cousin Benicio is here, OK? To answer all your questions. Sorry – I thought Montoyo told you all about the Bakabs."

There it was again. That term – the Bakab. It was mentioned in the Calakmul letter, written way back in 653 AD. I dreamt about someone saying, *Summon the Bakab Ix*.

What on earth are the Bakabs?

"Arranged marriage is normal for the Bakabs," Benicio explains. "Has always been this way. All the Bakabs must have a marriage arranged by the *atanzahab*, the matchmaker."

"So you still have Bakabs in Ek Naab?"

"Yes. Your grandfather was a Bakab. You didn't know this? He, your father, and you. All Bakabs."

"Until yesterday, I thought Bakabs were Mayan gods."

Benicio nods gently. "Not 'gods'. But descended from Itzamna, yes. Is why the bloodline must be protected. And so, marriages must be arranged. To guarantee it."

Piece by piece, things fall into place. I lean back on the sofa, overcome.

I'm a Bakab. Descended from Itzamna. Not a "god" – but a real person.

Benicio stands up. "I'm gonna make some breakfast. You look like you need it."

He disappears through an archway into a kitchen, from which, after some minutes, delicious smells waft in my direction. I can't resist and I join him at the stove. Benicio gives me a friendly smile as he scrambles eggs, heats refried beans and tomatoes, and griddles maize tortillas. He indicates a fridge, says, "You want some juice? There's papaya and pineapple too."

We take our food out on plates and sit on the sofa as we eat. I'm so famished that I stop talking, even though I'm thinking of questions as I wolf down the breakfast.

When the initial pangs of hunger wear off, I ask, "So, Benicio . . . are you a Bakab?"

"No. Our great-grandfather was a Bakab, but only his son's sons can be Bakabs. It's through the male line."

"Like priests?"

"*Not* like priests," Benicio says. "We have a woman priest. Maybe I'm not explaining this very well. The Bakab thing – it's inherited. On the Y chromosome. You know what is the Y chromosome?

"Course I do," I say, a bit annoyed. "I've done biology. So what's passed along on the Y chromosome? Is it, like, some special ability?"

"Yes – a special ability. The power to resist the curse of the codex."

I can't help it; I laugh. "You're kidding me."

But Benicio's face is entirely serious. "Look, the Bakabs, they are the guardians of the four codices – known as the Books of Itzamna. Everything we know about technology, it comes from these four codices. Ancient knowledge, which has been copied down every fifty years by the Bakabs, since we received them from Itzamna."

"And the Book of Ix – is one of these?"

"That's right. The Bakabs are Muluc, Cauac, Kan and Ix. Your family carries the blood of the Bakab Ix. The Bakabs in your family, they protected the Ix Codex."

"'Summon the Bakab Ix'," I say wonderingly.

"What?"

"It's something I once dreamt."

"Well, the Bakab Ix, that's *you* now. You're the only one."

"Why do you need a Bakab?"

"To find the Ix Codex," he says. "Is why you come here, no? Only a Bakab can do it. The Books of Itzamna are protected by an ancient curse. Anyone but a Bakab – if they touch one codex – they will die."

They want me to find the codex. Well, fine, me too. But I need that codex for myself. Without it, how will I to persuade the police and NRO to leave Camila's husband and my friends in peace?

Benicio seems so normal that it kind of freaks me out. I watch as he disappears into the kitchen to return with two cups of tea and a packet of biscuits. He seems like any Mexican college kid. When I mention this, he says, "Sure, I have to work in the outside, see? So I learn to speak like the Mexican kids, even spend some time living among them. Is possible to live like this, Josh. But it's only on the outside. On the inside, believe me –" and he taps his chest close to his heart – "right here, I understand my priorities."

And he looks at me closely. "Just like you should understand yours."

Well, I'm beginning to. Everything is beginning to make a strange kind of sense. From the minute I started out on this quest for the Ix Codex, I've felt the bond between my father and me grow stronger. Just as he discovered the mysterious bond between himself and his own, secret father. I'm becoming conscious of the link between all the men in my family, those who've gone before me. The idea that this all ends with me, that I have to finish what they all began, sends cold shivers down my spine.

Yet I'm not afraid.

"You know what you're here to do?" Benicio asks quietly.

And somehow, I *do* know. It's as though the thought has been buried inside me forever, and I've finally uncovered it.

"You want me to find the Ix Codex."

Benicio nods. "First, you need to be officially installed as the Bakab Ix."

"Thought you said it was an inherited thing."

"Yes, of course, you already are the Bakab, but you know, rituals and ceremonies and all those things. Your Prince William, he isn't just the king one day, is he? They still have to make the coronation."

"It's different. And he's only *second* in line to the throne. He's can't be the king just because he's a Wales."

"Well, you, you're the first in line to be the Bakab Ix. So you need to be installed with the ceremony."

"Or else, what? There's another potential Bakab Ix wandering around?"

Benicio's features cloud. And he doesn't answer.

"The Executive will install you," he says.

"Who are the 'Executive'?"

Benicio says, "Is, like, the government. The four Bakabs;

197

our mayor, Chief Sky Mountain; and the *atanzahab* – the matchmaker."

"The matchmaker? Why?"

"Is kind of an honorary title," he says with a grin. "She's more like our chief scientist. These marriage matches aren't made with potions and incantations and things like that, not any more. She uses state-of-the-art genetic matching."

"But you're missing the Bakab Ix?"

"Exactly. That's where Carlos Montoyo comes in. When your grandfather left, we chose a proxy – someone to stand in for the Bakab Ix. Montoyo is the third one we've had. Then your dad came back and . . . well, we had our hopes, but, you know. . ."

He flashes a rueful grin, I return one.

"So anyway, we're back with Carlos as the proxy. He works undercover in a university. He files patents in the world outside, based on technologies from the Books of Itzamna. That's how come the city is so rich. Worth billions of dollars a year. All secret; bank accounts in Switzerland, Monaco, the Caymans. And with all the money, Chief Sky Mountain runs building, engineering and genetics projects. Makes Ek Naab what you see today."

I can see out of the window and it's hard to believe I'm not in a swanky neighbourhood of Mexico City. Albeit a very cramped one. Most buildings are separated only by narrow alleyways and the occasional small patio. It's like a modern version of a medieval town. With a Mayan twist.

"So all this, right under the nose of the Mexican government?"

"Pretty much. Cool, huh?"

"It's *am-a-zing*. It's the most incredible thing I've ever seen or heard of. And then some. You Ek Naab Mayans, you really stuck it to the Mexican authorities, hey?"

Benicio's reply is unexpected, and a bit odd. "Of course you'd think like that, it's to be expected. For you, all success means progress. And progress is success."

I'm not sure what he means. Sure, progress is good. So what?

"Fiddling while Rome burns."

That's his answer. I'm none the wiser.

"That's how we were in Ek Naab," Benicio explains. "Learning from the Books of Itzamna. Progress for the sake of it. We didn't have the Ix Codex, so we didn't worry about what we didn't know. We avoided it. Because we had some idea that it answered a pretty tough question. The toughest of all – the one that could really kill us."

And finally I get what he means. The Book of Ix is about the "end of days".

"*What is going to happen on the twenty-second of December, 2012,*" I breathe.

"You got it, buddy. And it's getting awful close. Whatever the Ix Codex is going to teach us, we don't have too much time to learn. So you need to begin your mission, and fast."

"Mission?"

"Yeah." Benicio gets to his feet and snatches away the packet of biscuits I've been picking at. "So, time to go. Just a little time before the ceremony. Lots to see."

With that, he leads me out of the apartment and into the alleys and plazas of Ek Naab, now bustling with people, a hive of activity.

Everything seems clean, everybody looks busy. Benicio takes me walking. He explains a bit about how Ek Naab works. Food, clothes, bread and tortillas are all sold at the daily market. Clothes are pretty simple for most people. Few dress in "Western" clothes; instead they wear white or cream-coloured loose trousers and brightly coloured stripey or plain woven tunic shirts drawn in with a simple belt. Women wear the same, or white cotton dresses embroidered with large flowers and bird designs.

"What we don't grow or make ourselves, we buy from the cities," Benicio says.

We stroll around the plaza as the market is winding down. I watch a guy scoop out the last of his ice cream into little cups and hand it out for free before the ice block it rests on melts away. I take a cup; creamed corn flavour (not bad!).

"This could be anywhere in Mexico," I tell Benicio, with heavy irony.

"Except everything's clean, there are no kids working

here, no one's hustling you for money, everyone has a nice apartment to go home to, the water's not contaminated. . ." he replies with a laugh.

"Montoyo said part of the city was above-ground."

Benicio nods. "The land above-ground, it's all ours. For many miles around. Bought hundreds of years ago by a Spanish lord who joined us. He gave the land to the Executive. They ordered it to be farmed, so we grow bananas, mangoes, vanilla, coffee, cacao beans. Plus, naturally, all the food we need for ourselves also."

"It's incredible, amazing. Like paradise."

Benicio licks his ice-cream spoon, pondering. "Pretty much," he decides.

I ask, "And you have phones in this paradise? Do you have the Internet?"

He looks astonished. "Of course."

BLOG ENTRY: OUR LADY OF THE HIBISCUS

ᛗᛟᛖᐃᛉᛗᛉᛗᚢᛉ

ᛝᛉᐃᛉᚲ ᛘ ᚲᛝᛟᐃᛦ ꝫ ᛝᛉᛘᐃᛗ ᛗᛟᛗᛘᛦ ᛜᐃᛟᛗ ᛗᛦ
ꝫᛟᗏᚲꝫᐃ ᛿ᛉᐃꝫꝫᛟᛟ ꝫ ꟠ᛟᛟᛖᛉᛗ ᛟᗏᛗ ᛟᛜ ᛗᛝᛉ
ᗏꝫᐃᛗᛟᗏ ᛟᛜ ᛘᐃ ᛘᛂᗏᛘᐃᛗᛗᛉᐃᛗ ꝫᐃ ᛗᛝᛉ ꝫꝫᛝᛦ
ᛟᛜ ᛉᛉ ᐃᛘᛘᛘ ᛘᐃᛗ ᗏᛈᛘᛘ ᛗꝫᛗ ꝫ ᚲᛉᛉ ᛿ᗏᛗ ᛘ
᛿ꝫᚲᛘᐃᐃᛉ ᚲᛂᛘᐃꝫᚲᛈ ᚲᛗᛦ꟠ᛉ ꝫᛈᗏᐃꝫᛈ

201

Whoa . . . sorry about that. This computer was set up to type in the Ek Naab version of Mayan hieroglyphs. It's a sort of stripped-down, high-tech version of Classic Mayan. They use it to encode all their technical stuff . . . in case something falls into The Wrong Hands.

That should read:

Here's a story I heard today from my cousin Benicio. I looked out of the window of an apartment in the city of Ek Naab. And what did I see but a bizarre, Spanish-style church?

I guess in Mexico, they really are everywhere.

"It's for the first miracle of Ek Naab," Benicio told me. "The miracle of the hibiscus."

Seems that Pedro Vallejo, the Jesuit priest who converted the Mayans of this city, chose to name his church Our Lady of the Hibiscus.

"In those days the Mayans of Ek Naab guarded the shrine really fiercely. By then it was widely known that the Spanish – they couldn't be trusted. Bishop Diego de Landa had tortured Mayan scribes in order to gain the secrets of Mayan books, which he collected and then burned. At Ek Naab they guarded the three most valuable and ancient books – the Books of Itzamna. The fourth, of course, was missing. Lost in 653 AD."

Well, I already know that – I've read the Calakmul letter. Funny to think that for the Mayans of Ek Naab, their missing codex is a fourth codex. But in the outside world, where they only know of four surviving Mayan codices, the one all the archaeologists whisper about is the "fifth".

"Even the fact that the books existed had to be guarded on pain of death. Any stranger who discovered us was forced to remain in Ek Naab. Any *European* stranger unlucky enough to stumble across Ek Naab was put to death. And not in a good way."

"Vallejo, wandering eagerly throughout Mexico in 1595, all holy and everything; he was one of those. The night before his execution, (a sacrifice of course. No way they'd waste a ready victim!), Vallejo prayed to the Virgin Mary. In the morning, everyone was astonished to discover that the entire city was filled with a rare and fragrant flower – the hibiscus. It bloomed in every nook and hollow."

Now, there's little enough light in the cavern of Ek Naab, I've seen that for myself. And that's with the high-tech mesh-thing they use for the ceiling. Centuries ago, it was all gloom and rock. There was the light from flaming torches, but you can't grow most plants in that. Let alone the hibiscus. . .

"But since that day, the hibiscus has grown here, even in the dark. Quite simply, a miracle. The Ancient Maya were a people who lived mainly by what they could grow. They really appreciated the power of Vallejo's god. For them this was an incomparable command of nature. Way beyond any demonstration of Itzamna's. And so, his life was spared. Vallejo preached and they followed, built a church, and everything."

I looked at the hibiscus flowers of Ek Naab a bit differently after I heard that.

But I mean, it's just a story. Right?

After I've had a stab at updating my blog on a laptop in a little Internet café, Benicio and I make our way around the market stalls as they're being cleared. The market is set up in the central plaza of Ek Naab, but it's still tiny compared to most Mexican *zocalos*. It's no bigger than a tennis court. The cramped feeling gets to me after a while. Ek Naab may be glitzy, clean and modern but it still feels pretty warren-like. It's claustrophobic. When I mention this to Benicio, he just gives a knowing grin.

"Hey, why do you think I became a pilot?" is all he says. "The Muwan are a great way to get out of the city."

I blanch. "You're a *what*?"

"I'm a pilot. And I'm studying aeronautical engineering."

"You must be older than you look."

Benicio shrugs. "I'm seventeen. We start our careers early here. I began flying a Muwan when I was fifteen."

"You're *never* a pilot. . . Flying one of those Muwan?

You're having a laugh."

His manner changes a little, becomes mischievous. "You think so, hey?"

I can't help but notice people staring at me curiously. I mention this to Benicio.

"Visitors are rare," he comments, "very rare."

"Why don't they ask?"

"Is not our way. But they have an idea. Everybody knows that we have no Bakab Ix. They can only hope that you are this Bakab."

"I've been wondering about that . . . why don't you just send one of the other Bakabs after the Ix Codex?"

"They would die. They can only handle their own codex."

"Oh, come on."

He seems bemused. "You think I'm kidding?"

"No, but . . . it's superstition, right?"

Benicio is wide-eyed. "No, it's real, absolutely!"

"And everyone here believes that the world's going to end on the twenty-second of December, 2012?"

"Everyone here," he agrees.

"How come no one else in the world knows?"

Benicio erupts with indignant laughter. "'No one else in the world knows'?! Josh, really, did you ever talk to anyone in Mexico? You ever talk to what's left of the Mayan people? No; I bet you walk right past them. They clean your pool, they sell you Chiclets, they wipe the floor of your hotel. But you don't talk to them, right? You don't ask them about their world, their culture?"

"They don't always speak Spanish," I say, defensive. I don't like his implication – that I'm just another rich son-of-a-conquistador who doesn't understand about Mexico's ancient customs and knowledge. In the rest of Mexico, people judge you by how European or Mexican-Indian you look. With a mostly-Spanish father and an English mother, obviously I look fairly European. Benicio's attitude suggests that those prejudices exist here too.

From everything Benicio's told me, I have plenty of Mayan heritage – enough to be one of their Bakabs. So why is he giving me a hard time?

His smile has gone now, replaced by a mixture of sadness and defiance. "If you had ever asked, if anyone ever asked them. Not everything about our Mayan culture is forgotten. But it is ignored."

"You're exaggerating," I say. "Look at you guys. You're not proper Mayan. You've got a church, right? Those Spanish priests who came here – they converted you to Christianity. You don't worship Itzamna."

"We *never* worshipped Itzamna. He was our first leader."

"Carlos Montoyo told me that they used to sacrifice people in the *cenote*."

"Yes, that was the old use of Ek Naab. By other Mayans.

We didn't always live here."

"Who's 'we'?"

"There's no name. Other Mayans have called us things like the 'Sect of Bakabs'."

I'm surprised that Benicio doesn't make more of my accusation that they aren't "proper Mayans".

Other Mayans have called us things like the "Sect of Bakabs".

Sounds to me like the people of Ek Naab have always been outsiders.

We pass under a shadow, a lengthy section of the rock ceiling with no vents to the outside. The air cools sharply. I think of Ollie and Tyler, and wonder how they're doing. They have to be out of the interrogation by now. And Mum. What will she be thinking when she hears I've gone missing? Camila's body might have been identified by now. Will they imagine that I'm dead too? It's definitely time to check in with them, let them know I'm alive.

"I really need to make those phone calls," I tell Benicio.

"OK," he says. "Let's go this way. To the surface."

I follow him into a shiny, tile-faced tower that reaches all the way to the ceiling, about ten storeys up. We ride an elevator to the roof. We emerge under a huge thatch-roofed *palapa*.

The illusion of a subterranean technological wonderland vanishes. It's like being dragged back into the everyday, tourist version of Mexico. There's a spacious tropical restaurant that appears to be at ground level but is actually on the roof of the building we entered seconds ago. The tables are filled with people sitting eating breakfast, drinking coffee, having meetings, working on their laptop computers.

I can't suppress a low chuckle. "This is just awesome! This is what you've got on the surface?"

Benicio grins. "You like?"

"You bet I do."

Through tall windows I see a garden of banana palms, lime and orange trees and what appears to be a vast landscaped swimming pool. It could be almost any Mexican resort hotel. And here too, heads turn; appraising glances sweep over me as lightly as silk.

I follow Benicio out of the restaurant, into the sunny gardens beyond. The dark horrors of the road to Becan are fading in my memory. I'm working hard to hold on to the idea that this place is in some way the legacy of the ancient Mayan civilization. Above the surface, though, there's no indication of that. Not the tiniest hint.

Under my breath I mumble, "But seriously, mate. How come no one knows about this place? People must fly over it and wonder. Don't they notice the mesh?"

"Plain view, buddy; plain view. We look just like any other eco-resort, just like any other plantation. As for the mesh, it just looks like any agricultural thing to protect seedlings. It's all legally owned. Just another of Mexico's big family businesses.

Taxes are paid; protection money is paid, you know what I'm saying. We keep a low profile. We're invisible."

We arrive at the edge of another *cenote*. A stone staircase leads down to the water. This one looks cool, refreshing and, by comparison with the "dark water" *cenote* underground, positively friendly. A slightly overcast sky gives the deep water a milky sheen. The *cenote* is open for a hundred feet or so, then goes under an overhang dripping with stalactites. The water extends far into the distance.

"Care for a swim?" Benicio says. "You've got time."

"My phone call. . .?"

He nods. "Right." Then he takes an ordinary-looking mobile phone from his pocket, presses a button on the side and hands it to me.

"Directory enquiries. . .?"

Benicio takes the phone back and dials. We get the number for Hotel Delfin. I call, ask for Tyler and Ollie. The news isn't good, but I'm prepared for the worst. They're still at the police station. That's the second day they've been questioned. The receptionist gives me the number.

I hand the phone to Benicio. "They can't know it's me. Say you're a relative of mine trying to find out where I've gone. Ask to speak to Tyler or Ollie. Try to sound worried!"

With a hint of a smile, Benicio takes the phone. He puts on a really serious, formal voice, like a kid trying to impress his elders. He does as I suggested, then puts his hand over the phone.

"They're getting one of your friends. This woman says they weren't arrested, nothing like that. They're only helping. . ."

". . .the police with their enquiries. . .?" I say with a sigh. "I'll bet."

I take the phone. Tyler's voice, sounding a bit shaky, says, "Hello? Who is this?"

"It's me, Josh. But don't let them know you're talking to me! Don't act surprised or anything! Make out I'm a friend asking after Josh."

There's a tricky silence. I guess Tyler's trying to think of something to say that doesn't give it away.

"So what do you want to know about Josh?" he asks.

"I'm OK. I can't tell you where I am exactly, but I'm safe."

Carefully, he answers, "Uh huh."

"What's your situation, Ty? Can you talk a bit?"

"We don't know where Josh is, mate. Last we saw of him was yesterday, just before we was met by these guys from the NRO. They've been looking for Josh's dad and some other people too, from what I can work out. Asked us a lot of questions about what Josh was doing here in Mexico, the Ix Codex. . ."

"What did you tell them? Did you tell them about the Calakmul letter?"

Another long pause. "Yeah. Yeah, we had to."

I can tell he's afraid to say any more. "Did you tell them what it said?"

"We didn't remember, not exactly."

"Ollie?"

"She's fine."

"Did she give anything away?"

"No, she's actually pretty chilled, considering."

"One of those NRO guys chased me and Camila, Ty. He shot at us."

I sense him tense on the other side of the line. "You're OK, though, yeah? Is she all right?"

"No . . . no. She's not. She's . . . gone."

"Mate . . . I'm sorry."

I can't speak for a second.

"We've got to get out of this place, mate," Tyler says in a whisper. "They keep on and on with the same questions. I'm not sure I stand any more of it without . . . you know . . . slipping. They know Josh went to Becan. They know why. They're not going to stop looking for Josh."

"I'm going to call my mum," I tell him. "Get her to help. She's got contacts in the British Embassy in Mexico City. Maybe they can get you out of there. You've done nothing wrong . . . they shouldn't be able to keep you locked up."

Tyler sighs heavily. "I know. Try telling them that, though."

There's a sharp voice in the background, sounds like someone's telling Tyler off. When he speaks again it's all rushed, in a strong Oxford accent, as if he doesn't want anyone to understand him. "Yeah, man, I'm . . . bloomin' give 'em what for, innit? You take care of yourself, all right, do what you can then, eh, yeah?"

And the line goes dead.

Benicio's eyeing me with interest. "Any help?"

"Not really . . . my friends are in trouble. Like I thought." I start dialling again, this time my home phone. I check my watch. It's late in England, but not alarmingly so. Miraculously, I hear my own phone at home ringing. Somehow it feels like calling a different planet. The connectedness of the world can be baffling; so near and yet so impossibly far.

Mum answers. She's happy to hear from me and doesn't seem alarmed. This is good because when we left, I wasn't sure that she'd properly cottoned on that I was actually going to Mexico.

"Have you heard from Tyler or Ollie's parents?" I ask.

"No. . ." Mum sounds anxious. "Why would I?"

"No reason . . . I just wondered, you know, what they've been saying. Of course they tell me we're having a good time but, you know."

"So everything's OK?"

I hesitate just a little too long, hear a catch in her voice as she says, "Josh. What's happened?"

"We've been called in for some questioning, Mum. By

some US agency called the NRO. It's something like the CIA, I suppose."

The line crackles with breathless horror. "What. . .?"

"I'm OK . . . I promise. I'm not with them. I ran away. But there are two things you have to know. Listen, Mum. . ."

Her voice is tense but controlled as she says, "I'm listening."

"The woman in Chetumal is not Dad's girlfriend, Mum. She's his daughter."

"What. . .?"

"His daughter," I repeat, "from way back before he met you. It's true, Mum, swear to God."

"Oh, Josh . . . what a relief."

I hesitate for a few seconds. Mum doesn't need to know about Camila's death . . . not right now, anyway So I skip that part. It's not something I'm ready to talk about.

"And there's something else. I've discovered what Dad found soon before he died. I'm going to find out why he was killed. And somehow, we'll find a way to make them pay, Mum. That's a promise."

"Where are you?"

"I'm safe."

A steely note enters her voice. "Where?"

"I don't exactly know, Mum. But I'm safe."

"That's it," she says, and I hear the panic rising. "I'm calling the police."

"That's not a bad idea. Call them, yeah. And call the

British Embassy – please, Mum. Get them to free Tyler and Ollie. They don't know anything and they're getting really freaked out by all this."

"Oh my God. . ." She chokes back a sob. "Come back to me, Josh. Now. Please."

"Mum . . . as soon as I can."

We exchange reluctant goodbyes; I hand the phone back to Benicio.

"Can they trace the call?"

"Of course not. The signal's bounced from a transmitter in Chiapas. We have our own satellite."

"A satellite. . .?"

He chuckles softly. "You have any idea what we're up against, Josh? The kind of people who want our technology?"

"Yeah, yeah, the NRO," I say.

"I've had those guys chasing me when I fly the Muwan," Benicio says casually. "Believe me, it's no picnic."

That's it – I've had enough of his boasting. "You DO NOT fly those Muwan."

He gives me this lopsided grin. "Sure I do. Don't believe me . . . you wanna see?"

I'm open-mouthed. "Do I wanna. . .?"

". . .take a trip in a Muwan with me?"

Well, yeah. Now *this* is one for the blog.

BLOG ENTRY: THE WORLD DOESN'T JUST DISAPPEAR WHEN YOU CLOSE YOUR EYES, DOES IT?

⚠3🜍⫸G3Ψ🝈✕⚕

The thing is – I could almost believe it does. Because sometimes things happen and you think, hey, what happened to the world I thought I understood? It was only when I went up in a Muwan with Benicio that I realized how much, lately, the world keeps transforming into someplace darker, a place in which I have no idea how to navigate.

Then that aircraft lifted us up over the treetops of the Campeche jungle and I felt the troubles of the past few weeks melting, dripping away like snow on a car. My spirits lifted. It was as if the sun had risen on a brand-new day in a brand-new world.

Benicio sneaked me back into the chair-lift station. This time it was a much shorter ride. After two or three minutes we arrived in a building of very obvious function – an aircraft hangar.

Even though I'd heard about the Muwan, actually seeing them just blew me away.

"Muwan means *sparrow-hawk*," Benicio explained. I could see why.

I counted five aircraft in total. Shaped like a hawk with open wings, three of them had a bronze tinge to the paintwork, a cockpit shaped like a hawk's head. They looked more like a large sculpture of a hawk than any credible version of an airplane. The other two craft were larger but sleeker, stripped-down versions of the bronze aircraft.

215

The cockpit still looked hawkish, but in a more abstract, vaguely representative way. The wings were shorter, more squat and narrower. Instead of the bronze colour, the craft were a dark bluish-grey, completely matt.

An engineer wearing a grey jumpsuit shone his torch into an open panel on one of the craft, and I noticed that the light wasn't reflected at all by the surface coating.

Benicio watched me watching the two Muwan engineers tend to their craft. There was a vaguely smug air to him, which didn't surprise me, after what I'd said.

"This is soooo cool," I whispered. "Which one's yours?"

Benicio grinned. "The chief decides all that. It's different each time. I'm going to take you out in this Mark I today. Some people really like the Mark Is. To us they have an old-fashioned style, which is totally cool. But the Mark II is a better machine."

"So my father was in a Mark I? The bronze ones?"

"Yep, your grandfather too. We wouldn't take the Mark II out for a simple mission. It's still very secret."

"My *grandfather. . .*?"

He flashed me a look then, like he'd spoken out of turn. "You'll find out soon enough. . ."

The whole "bird" was almost nine metres long – hardly any bigger than a small airplane. Judging from where the engineers were concentrating most of their efforts, the propulsion system was under the cockpit. It must be tiny. As with a fighter plane, you climb in through the top of the cockpit, a dome of bronze-tinted, one-way glass that partly retracts. The pilot's seat is planted right in the middle of the bird's neck; it's a deeply padded seat upholstered in a golden-brown suede-like fabric. Behind the pilot's station, the craft widens slightly, with space for two narrower passenger seats. The wings sit just behind the cockpit and are angled down, giving the overall impression of a bird about to make a sudden landing. The belly of the bird is chequered with clear panels.

Watching my eyes trail over the airplane, Benicio seemed to read my thoughts. "Don't bother looking for the jets. There aren't any."

"So how. . .?"

". . .does it fly? Anti-gravity," he said. "Pretty cool, huh?"

"Anti-gravity? No way."

With this self-conscious giggle, Benicio said, "Way!"

Benicio took one look into the control room and saw that it was empty. Apart from the two engineers, there was no one about. He turned to me. "OK, now. This is just between you and me, right? Just a really quick flight. A spin – and that's it."

I pointed to the engineers. "And them?"

Benicio gave them a quick glance. "They won't talk . . . they're my buddies."

With that, he leapt over some crates of equipment and swung himself on the ladder of the nearest Muwan, and clambered into the cockpit. So I followed.

By the time I joined him in the Muwan, Benicio was fitting himself with a headset: earphones and an eyepiece that settled a couple of centimetres from his left eyeball. He tapped something on the dashboard, activating a control panel. I strapped myself in and the cockpit cover slid into position. We had 360 degrees of visibility from the top of the bird.

Benicio powered up, and I felt the craft start to vibrate. In the next minute, it lifted, trembling very slightly and almost completely silently. We were hovering. In almost total silence.

We flew towards a strip of light in the ceiling. A hangar door was open to the sky outside. We whizzed right through.

And then the velvety textures of the jungle canopy stretched before us, rippling across mountains as far the eye could see. The sky was coated with a thick layer of hazy cloud that turned an ominous grey colour at the edges.

Benicio was lost in his world of piloting, concentrating hard as he flew the Muwan above the treetops. We skimmed low, almost touching the trees. We were flying over the landscape at a dizzying speed. Now and then something distant, maybe a village, appeared on the edge of our vision. Next thing I knew, we were flying over it. Trees, mountains, houses, lakes, a river, a road; we left them all behind in a matter of seconds.

"How fast are we going?"

"Just under Mach 1. That's our limit for travel close to the ground. Any faster and they hear us break the sound barrier. Next thing you know, people start reporting UFO sightings."

"So you guys are responsible for all the UFOs?"

Benicio chuckled. "Some of them, sure. But not all. We can only account for about half of the sightings."

"And the others?"

"Mostly, we guess that they're secret military aircraft tests." He seemed suddenly guarded.

"Mostly, but not all?" I was dying to know. Do the citizens of Ek Naab have some insight into one of the greatest mysteries?

Benicio wasn't giving anything away. "We're just like everyone else, Josh. We don't have all the answers."

Then the Muwan slowed down, banked hard to the right and circled. I recognized the outline of Becan's moat-enclosed structures below.

"We were miles away from Becan!" I blurted. I'd imagined Ek Naab to be right underneath.

"The *gateway* is under Becan. Remember that first ride you took with Montoyo? It took you a long way into the Depths."

"So where exactly is Ek Naab? On a map, I mean?"

He sniggered. "That's top secret, buddy."

It was the first time I'd had an aerial view of any Mayan city. Just breathtaking. There were a few tourists, so Benicio preferred not to take chances on someone getting a proper look at us. "If they just catch a glimpse, they'll assume we're a fighter plane," he muttered, concentrating on his controls. Then he swung us up into the clouds.

I peered down at Becan, watching it disappear behind the mist. Looked just like another relic of Mexico's Mayan past. Yet, who'd have thought. . .?

26

Benicio takes a call on his phone as we're walking back from the chair-lift station. It's late afternoon and people in the city look as if they're going home from work or school.

"That was Carlos Montoyo," he tells me when he's finished. "The ceremony to install you as Bakab will be this evening, with robes and everything. You're gonna eat with the Executive in the Hall of Bakabs." With a touch of envy, he adds, "I've never even seen it."

"Jeez. Sounds a bit over the top."

Benicio stares at me as though I've said something impossibly stupid.

"You're thirteen, right? Well, when you are sixteen, you have the right to take your place on the Executive as the Bakab Ix."

"When I'm sixteen?"

"That's right. Montoyo is your proxy until then. But when

you are sixteen, Montoyo will have to stand down. I hope you like government, Josh."

"That's just . . . ridiculous. Citizenship is, like, my worst school subject ever. And sixteen? Way too young!"

"If you're not born and educated for it like the other Bakabs, I think it may be. Although the truth is, I don't think they've ever actually had a Bakab from sixteen. Mostly they wait until the father dies."

"It must have happened before."

"Maybe so, but I never heard of it."

"If being the Bakab Ix means I have to join your Executive, then you can forget this whole thing."

Benicio frowns. "S'gonna be a pretty short term of office anyway. Unless you get the Ix Codex."

"Because of the end of the world thing?"

"Exactly."

Well, he may have a point. I'm finding it odd to be around people who assume the world is going to end in 2012. You'd think it would make it more scary. But no. Just the opposite – it makes it feel more like a crazy superstition.

Benicio escorts me back to the apartment I'd assumed was Montoyo's but now realize is Benicio's own. In the bedroom a clothes hanger is draped with a pair of crisply ironed, white linen trousers, a matching tunic and a poncho of pure white, finely knit wool, into which has been woven two black symbols, a glyph on the front and a jaguar's head on the back.

As I change, he watches with what looks like pride. "Now you are *Zac Cimi*, the black Bakab, the Bakab Ix."

I peer at myself in his tiny bathroom mirror. It's only now, dressed as a Maya of Ek Naab, that I see the resemblance between myself and these people. I'm painfully aware that it's just on the outside. Inside we're so, so different.

Benicio hands me a helmet shaped like a jaguar's head. It's heavy, metal coated with an enamel of matt black paint.

"Tell me you're joking."

"No, dude, you look cool!" Benicio says, giggling.

I place the helmet carefully on my shoulders. It weighs heavily, even with the padded rims. I can't see anywhere but directly ahead.

"Wouldn't be much good in a fight," I mutter.

Our evening walk through the paved alleyways is nerve-racking. Where before people had only glanced shyly or at least discreetly, now they stop in their tracks and gawp. No one says a word – they don't need to. Benicio answers their questioning looks with a bashful little shrug, as if to say, *I'm just the delivery boy*. Into my ear he rasps, "Don't worry. This is normal. In the past forty years only one man has been seen dressed as *Zac Cimi*."

"Who?"

"My uncle – your father, of course."

I try to stare directly ahead but it's impossible not to catch the occasional eye. Is it hostility? Amazement? Relief? I imagine I'm seeing all reactions. They're no more puzzling than my own. I'm wound tight as a cassette tape; snap me and I'll spool into chaos.

At the sacrificial *cenote*, we're met by two guys carrying flaming torches. Benicio whispers that it's all normal, part of the ceremony. "It's rare for all the Bakabs to dine together," he says. "They honour you."

And that's where he leaves me. Looks like the torch guys and I are headed for the main pyramid. The pyramid has no platforms, just a single staircase leading to two towers. The masonry is stuccoed, painted a deep red; the staircase inscribed with turquoise and gold-coloured glyphs. As I climb the stairs, I feel myself examined, scrutinized by the dozens of eyes. The solemnity of the moment hits me. These people – they expect something from me.

But I'm just a kid. What the heck can I do?

We enter the left tower, where the bronze door to an elevator slides open. The fire-torch guys step back. From here, I'm on my own. The lift goes down just a few metres and opens on to a wide hall, which I'm guessing occupies the entire width of the pyramid. An attendant standing by the door takes my helmet and places it on a small table with three others – one white, one red and one yellow.

The stone walls are hung with tapestries of Mayan art – ancient kings in ceremonial dress receiving prisoners of war, and other images, less obvious to interpret. The ceiling is low, giving the hall an intimate, almost claustrophobic quality. The room is lit by multiple muted lights that mimic the flicker of candlelight.

In the centre is a long table made of varnished hardwood, laid with candles, wine glasses, platters of fruit and salad, ceramic bowls filled with rice, chafing dishes containing steaming heaps of spiced chicken, fried strips of plantain and round wooden boxes for tortillas.

Standing behind their chairs, watching my entrance, are three guys dressed pretty much like I am, except for the colour of their Bakab symbols; one is white, one red, one yellow. Carlos Montoyo is there too, also dressed in some traditional clothes, without the poncho or the symbol, along with a middle-aged woman wearing a white embroidered dress and a man I'd guess to be in his sixties, his long white hair neatly plaited, deep lines drawn in his face. He looks to be a pure-blood Mayan, every bit as proud and kingly as the figures in the tapestries.

The oldest member of the group, however, isn't White Plait (who I'm guessing is the mayor) but the Bakab with the red symbol. He's completely bald, with narrow, pale eyes that don't follow me the way everyone else's do. Instead, he simply stares, almost dreamily, into the candle to his right.

They beckon me, so I approach. There's one empty place, next to the bald Bakab with the red symbol. When I'm standing close to his left, he turns to me, but his eyes won't meet mine. It's a little unnerving, and I offer Carlos Montoyo a small shrug. He replies with just the vaguest widening of his eyes in the red Bakab's direction. A quick glance around at the others, and I see they've all got the same expression.

Into the silence, the red Bakab speaks.

"They're trying to indicate to you, young Joshua, that I'm blind."

His English pronunciation is flawless.

"Oh," I say. "I'm sorry."

The red Bakab chuckles, a deep baritone laugh.

"So, young Josh. It's good to finally meet you. I knew your father, and grandfather too. Very well."

The old man seems almost moved. I don't really know what to say.

How could he have known my father well?

"In the Hall of Bakabs each of us speaks the truth of our inner self," intones the mayor in a sudden, theatrical voice that breaks the hushed atmosphere. "A truth that can only be contested with blood."

There's a long pause while the others mutter something under their breaths. My guess is it's something like "Amen".

"I am Chief Sky Mountain," he continues. "Mayor of Ek Naab."

Montoyo declares, "I am Carlos Montoyo, proxy for the Bakab Ix."

"I am Rodolfo Jaguar, the Bakab Muluc!" says a guy in his forties with white symbols.

"I am Lizard Paw, the Bakab Cauac!" says another, with yellow symbols.

The red Bakab says in a faint voice, "I am Blanco Vigores, the Bakab Kan."

"And I am Lorena Martinez, the *atanzahab*."

They all turn to me expectantly.

"I'm . . . er, Joshua Garcia," I say. Their expressions show that they're waiting for more. "The Bakab Ix."

A feeling of relief fills the room.

"Congratulations, Josh. You just became our newest Bakab Ix," says Blanco Vigores with a weak smile.

Huh! That was easy!

Chief Sky Mountain asks Blanco Vigores to say the blessing, which he does, speaking quietly, words I don't understand. I'm guessing it's a Mayan language, probably Yucatec.

Sitting down, Blanco Vigores makes slow, careful and unsteady movements; more than I'd expect on account of his blindness. He moves like a very old man, but from his looks, I'd have put him no older than seventy.

How old is the guy, really?

As I take my place amongst these people, I'm suddenly aware of how young I am. They're all trying to act as though this is an everyday matter. Well, I'm not finding it easy to play along with the act. *I'm just Josh Garcia, from Oxford*, I feel like saying. *And I think you might have the wrong guy. Books of doomsday prophecies – that's not really up my street.*

Yet everything that's happened in the past weeks and hours seems to have turned that view on its head.

Sitting in the Hall of Bakabs with the ruling Executive of Ek Naab, wearing the same ceremonial outfit that my father wore just months ago, and his father, and his father . . . it makes me feel more than a little special. Like everything fits into some cosmic plan.

Including me.

"It's a magical age for us, Josh, our modern era. They have described this as the Golden Age of Ek Naab, the Era of Wonders."

Chief Sky Mountain pours me a glass of crimson-coloured juice (pomegranate, so they tell me) and passes me a hollowed-out cactus head, chilled and filled with a cold soup of tomatoes, onions, and a cool green vegetable that I can't quite place. I'm still guessing when Montoyo butts in. "*Nopales*," he says. "Instead of cucumber, in the gazpacho. A traditional Spanish soup, yes? Adding *nopales* makes it Mexican," he says. "The colonial with the indigenous."

"Do you consider yourself an Englishman?" asks Carlos Montoyo, "Or a Mexican?"

There's an expectant silence. "Not sure, really," I reply. "My mother is half-Irish. My father was Mexican. I don't know about English, but British: yes. There's this test we have: who do you support in cricket? I'd be English by that test, I suppose."

Blanco Vigores nods, smiling. "I remember cricket. Do you still play?"

"You *remember* cricket?" I ask. "When did you see it?"

"I wasn't always blind, young Josh. This darkness, and the solitude it brings, descended slowly, generously, allowing me time to bid farewell to all the graces of a life blessed by sight."

There's an uncomfortable pause. I don't really understand what the old guy is on about. I guess he misses his sight – who wouldn't?

Montoyo says, "Blanco Vigores travelled once in the outside world, much as I do now. Before we built our aircraft, the Muwan. He travelled by the old methods."

Vigores grins, showing his almost translucent teeth. "Propeller airplane, steamboat, even an airship. Those were the heroic days of travel. When one dressed in one's best."

I want to know more about the Muwan. I promised Benicio I'd keep quiet about our joy-ride, but I can still ask questions about its history.

"It means *sparrow-hawk*," the chief tells me.

I nod *uh huh*, pretending not to know.

"We built the first one in the year you call 19 . . ." (and here he takes a moment to make the conversion from the Mayan calendar) ". . . 1952. Your grandfather and his nephew were both engineers on the project. Doubtless the source of young Benicio's own talent."

Lizard Paw watches me for a second, then tells the others, "You're making pleasantries. Isn't it obvious that Joshua wants to know why he's here?"

Something's going on between these guys, but I can't tell what. Lorena leans forward and tells Lizard Paw, "You have no manners. Let the boy eat."

I stop chewing, anxious.

"No," I say. "Tell me now. Please."

Again there's a long silence. No one seems to want to be the first to speak.

Eventually, Rodolfo Jaguar does. Conversationally, he asks, "Did you ever read the letters of Hernan Cortez to his emperor, Charles V?"

I shake my head.

Jaguar seems disappointed, even scornful. "A pity. Not to know about the world that went before, the civilization destroyed by the *conquista*, seems a shame for a young Mexican."

"Wasn't Moctezuma the Aztec Emperor," I say, "the one who surrendered Mexico City to the conquistador Cortez?"

"Indeed, yes."

"I thought the Aztecs were enemies of all the other peoples of Mexico."

"Ah, yes. But with the fall of the Aztecs, our fate, too, was sealed."

"But I thought that the Mayan empire was already in decline. Hadn't most of the Mayan cities already been deserted by 1000 AD? Hundreds of years before Cortez arrived. That's what my dad told me."

Again, silence. Since they're saying nothing, I throw in another question. "Why exactly did the Maya desert the cities?"

But no one answers. It's as though I haven't spoken. Instead, Montoyo begins to talk.

"Your cousin told you about the codices, yes? And that each codex has a guardian, the Bakab."

Nodding, I swallow my last piece of chicken taco.

Montoyo continues. "It's simple, Josh. You must complete the mission of your father and grandfather. You must find the codex, return it to us."

"Why?" I ask the question calmly, no fuss. There's been a lot of talk about how I have to find this codex. Well, I know why I want the codex – to get the NRO and Mexican police to leave my friends alone. But if this end of the world thing is real, I guess I have to face up to it, sooner or later.

"The best way to answer that, Josh, is to show you."

Montoyo takes what looks like a remote control from a drawer in the table, activates the lights. Simultaneously the wall lights fade to black. And about one metre above the table, a small point of light appears and hovers. It expands to the point where we see that the light is itself composed of thousands of even tinier pinpricks of light. Like a miniature universe expanding, the lights rush apart, swirling away from each other until the entire spectacle has expanded to fill a space almost as long as the table.

"It's the Milky Way galaxy," Montoyo says helpfully. Although that's perfectly obvious, even to me.

The image expands, zooming in on one of the spiral arms of our galaxy, presumably closing in on our own sun. One of the pinpricks of light begins to shine more intensely.

"Our sun," says Montoyo. "Situated on the inner rim of the Orion Arm. From now on we'll look at the galaxy only from this vantage point: our own. From Earth."

Rodolfo Jaguar blows out the table candles. I catch sight of Blanco Vigores staring impassively at the table. He's hardly spoken. Seems pretty rough to exclude him in this way, but I guess he's heard it all before.

"In the sky, there is a triangle of stars known as the 'summer triangle'." (A triangle is drawn slowly in the hologram above.) "Vega, Deneb and Altair."

I stare at the projection, baffled. What's this got to do with anything? I glance at Montoyo. I guess my confusion shows.

"Astronomers use it as a pointer to this dark band you see beyond, known as the Great Rift. In fact, this dark band is a distant dust cloud."

Ah . . . now I'm getting it. "The Great Rift," I say, remembering the Calakmul letter. "Xibalba be . . . the Black Road."

In the twinkling holographic light I notice that everyone at the table – except Blanco Vigores – has turned to me.

"Exactly so," Montoyo says. I detect a hint of pride, which I'm not sure I deserve.

"I didn't work it out," I say. "Camila did. My half-sister. She thought that the Great Rift crossing the sky to Polaris is some galactic event, something that the ancient Maya knew about. And some disaster will happen then."

"Well," Montoyo says, "basically, she's right."

I gasp. "How could she be?"

Lizard Paw remarks, "Seems you doubt it. Why?"

"There's going to be this massive cosmic disaster," I say, "and our scientists don't know about it? But the ancient Mayans did – how do you work that out?"

"Fundamentally," says Montoyo, "there are two ways to know that something is going to happen. One is to have scientific tools to measure things, make predictions. The other is to predict an event that happens regularly. Something that's happened before. Like knowing the equinox is coming, or a solar eclipse. The ancient Maya were capable only of the latter kind."

"So whatever this thing is that's coming . . . it's happened before?"

Montoyo nods. "That's it exactly. And the ancient Maya knew about it, because *they remembered*. From long, long before the dawn of Mayan culture. Didn't you ever wonder why an ancient civilization had the need for such big numbers? Only three things are counted in such high numbers – very small things like atoms, very big things like stars . . . and *time*. It's why the Long Count calendar ends when it does – the date beyond which they could predict or foresee . . . *nothing*."

"So the cosmic cataclysm thingy . . . what is it?"

"Did you know," begins Lorena, "that cosmologists consider that a massive gamma ray burst from the explosion of a nearby star as one of the greatest threats to life on Earth? The radiation, when it hit us, would be lethal."

I feel a ripple of energy pass through me. The hairs on my arms prickle my skin.

For the first time I'm actually a little scared.

"Wouldn't it be headline news, though," I say hopefully, "if a star nearby was going that way?"

"Correct," Lorena says. "Those are the stars we can see. But in the core of the galaxy, every so often there's a mega explosion. And the energy from that explosion can join up with interstellar magnetic fields, travelling through the galaxy at near light speed in a sort of wave-like volley."

I'm speechless. "That doesn't sound good. . ." I say.

"Physicists call it a *superwave*," Lorena continues slowly. "A burst of deadly radiation. The kind of thing that's caused extinctions in the past."

I'm aware of sweat trickling down my back. It feels icy. I

glance at Montoyo. He's just nodding, very calmly.

Montoyo says, "The Maya had records, or memory – of this kind of event. They refer to it as the Black Road meeting the Heart of Sky. This only happens once every 25,800 years – the time taken for the precession of the equinoxes. Can you guess when the next event is due to happen?"

I just stare. I haven't understood what they mean by *precession of the equinoxes*. But I can guess when the next event is due.

The twenty-second of December, 2012.

How could the guys in Ek Naab have worked this out, and no one else on Earth?

"Others *do* know," Lorena says. "It's just that at levels that count, no one listens. Think about global warming. Scientists have been warning that the earth is heating up for decades. But only now are governments actually taking it seriously."

Montoyo continues. "One physicist has predicted that a cosmic burst in the galactic core might result in a volley of wave energy gathering as it radiates across the galaxy. He's predicted that such events have occurred before. And that they have caused extinction-level events. Ice ages, for example. Another researcher has correctly interpreted the configuration of the sky at 22 December, 2012 as a time when our sun will lie at the centre of the Dark Rift."

As he speaks, the holographic image appears to melt,

shifting and changing to represent each of the positions Montoyo mentions.

Chief Sky Mountain takes over. "What the ancient Maya knew, Josh, and what we know from the three codices we have, is that this was the configuration of the sky when a massive wave of radiation from the galactic core is thought to have wreaked havoc on our planet."

"The Ix Codex tells you about the actual 2012 thing, right?" Montoyo replies. "That's right."

"But it's lost."

"It was lost to Ek Naab in 653 AD by the actions of a traitor."

"That's what the Calakmul letter is about," I say. "We worked out that much."

"Well, ever since, a Bakab from your family has sought it. Your grandfather. . ."

I interrupt Montoyo to ask, "But if the book was lost, at least the knowledge of what was in it should have been retained. Right?"

"Wrong," Lizard Paw says sharply. "The text of the codices were indecipherable until the nineteenth century. The Books of Itzamna are written in *code*. By the time this code was solved, no one alive had seen the Ix Codex."

"The knowledge in the Book of Ix," Lorena says, "can truly be said to be lost in the mists of time."

The chief continues. "Until Aureliano tracked it down. He

came across a rumour that, like other ancient Mayan books, it had made a journey across the Atlantic Ocean, and resided in the jealously-guarded collection of the reknowned British Mayan archaeologist Sir Eric Thompson."

"In Saffron Walden," I say, remembering what Montoyo told me.

I'm still concentrating on the stars above, watching as a tiny star in the galactic core begins to swell, until, glowing with dazzling intensity, it explodes. A wave of energy radiates outward, still miniscule and far from our planet. But then it seems to collect momentum, eventually passing through our own solar system as a gigantic pulse. The image of Earth is magnified as the wave hits it.

"So what happens when the wave hits?" I ask, transfixed.

The chief replies, "That's unknown."

"But probably . . . what?"

"Well, the good news is that our simulations suggest the energy levels won't be enough to deliver a lethal dose of radiation."

I can't prevent myself letting out a sigh of relief. The others are still, however, tense.

Then the chief drops his payload.

"The bad news is that the energy may be enough *and of the correct nature* to deliver a massive electromagnetic pulse."

From his tone, I guess that this is a Very Bad Thing.

"A pulse of energy that will erase and eradicate all known computer systems. Every computer on the planet will cease to function, simultaneously."

Lorena says, "Think just for a minute about the implications, Josh."

"If this electromagnetic pulse hits Earth," she continues, "it will be as though the 'world memory' were erased."

"People on life support machines will die," says Montoyo, looking me straight in the eye. "Airplanes will fall out of the sky, or crash. Hospital records, social security and employee records, bank accounts details; all erased. Overnight, everyone will become non-persons, as far as the state goes. Non-persons, owning nothing, earning nothing, with no rights to anything provided by the state. And the state? What state? Food companies won't be able to make deliveries. Money supplies will go to hell. People will kill each other for food and fuel. Cities will become bloodbaths."

I feel like leaving right there and then. What can I do about a massive event like that? What can anyone do? If this galactic superwave is real, seems to me that we're all goners.

I guess my expression gives me away, because Chief Sky
Mountain tells me, "It's not hopeless. Itzamna made provision
for this in his four codices. Each one teaches of advanced
technologies. We've used this knowledge to build and conceal
the city around you. The fourth – the Ix Codex, as you've
already guessed – deals exclusively with the technology to
protect the 'world memory' from the event of 2012."

"And that's where I come in?"

Montoyo and the chief seem relieved that I'm starting to
buy into this.

"We know exactly where your grandfather, Aureliano,
went," the chief admits. "He was in England, meeting with
Thompson, a British archaeologist whom he believed
possessed the codex. Then he flew back. It's our
understanding that Aureliano had the Ix Codex at that time.
We lost contact with him when his Muwan was somewhere
over the state of Veracruz in Mexico, near the mountain

range of Orizaba. We think that his craft experienced difficulties. He must have landed it, or tried to."

"Then what?" I ask.

Montoyo shrugs. "One theory is that he was shot down, crashed maybe, somewhere in the mountains."

"For forty years we sent people to the surrounding villages in Orizaba," the chief says, "trying to piece together the truth from witnesses. The Muwan was seen, in the air and in chunks on the ground. Where the wreckage was moved to – and by whom – that's where we lost the trail."

As I'm trying to picture my grandfather's final journey, it strikes me that both he and my father were last seen flying a Muwan. The crash, wherever it happened, was not the end of Aureliano.

"And my grandfather?"

"He simply vanished," says Montoyo.

Like mist.

At the back of my mind, something's not quite right. In my dream, my grandfather died near water. Choking, surrounded by a swirl of fragrant smoke. The dream told me about the Bakab Ix long before I heard about it in Ek Naab.

The dream must mean something.

"My grandfather died near water," I tell them. "I dreamt it."

They're silent for a moment. "Montoyo told us," Lorena says in a kind voice. "And it's interesting that your father had the same dream."

"The dream is real," says Vigores, not looking up from his food.

I turn to the old man. "How do you know?"

"Sometimes we receive information through dreams. I've lived long enough to learn the truth of this."

"Is there water in Veracruz?" I ask.

"Lots of it," says Lorena. "There are rivers, lakes and the ocean."

"Then that's where he died," I say. "In Veracruz."

There's a long pause. "Veracruz. . ." says Lorena, "is rather large. And we've always suspected that Aureliano died there. As for the wreckage of his Muwan, we may have a precise location. Recently, one of our scientists developed a machine to detect the remaining pieces of the downed Muwan. The core of the engine contains a device that emits a type of radiation," Lorena says. "We sent our pilots to look for it."

"Your grandfather had the Ix Codex with him when he crashed. We think there's a good chance that it's with the wreckage," says the chief.

"The wreckage is in a museum in the state of Veracruz. Not on display," says Lorena. "Of course – it's covered with Mayan symbols but clearly, it's modern. The story was even leaked into the papers recently – maybe you saw? But the Mexican government intervened and made the witnesses say that it was a hoax."

"Here's what we need you to do, Josh," the chief tells me. "You have to get into the room where the wreckage is stored, see what else they've recovered from the site. If the Ix Codex is there, only you can touch it. To anyone else, it is certain death."

"Death . . . how?" I ask.

"We don't know. Each codex has its own unique protection. As your father's son, you will be immune."

I nod, slowly. "And . . . I just have to believe this?"

"There's no way to prove it to you," admits Montoyo.

"What is required is an act of faith," says Blanco Vigores. I'm surprised to hear him speak after his long silence. He looks in my direction. "And I warn you, hesitation will cost you everything."

The chief explains how I'm to get into the museum. He places a small aluminium briefcase on the table. Inside, a collection of devices are encased in granite-coloured foam to keep them in position. I can't help thinking it's just like *Mission: Impossible*.

My mission (should I choose to accept), is to break into the museum at night (using a lock-dissolving device), to avoid the laser security by spraying a dry mist that will light up the beams, then use a blueprint of the museum to get into the locked storeroom where they keep the Muwan wreckage.

Obviously they've mistaken me for Secret Agent Ethan Hunt.

"And if I'm caught? Then what?"

The chief's eyes hold mine in a rock-steady glare. From a small case he picks out what looks like a small ballpoint pen. "Then you use this. It's a spring-loaded hypodermic syringe," he says. "One dose will knock you out within seconds."

"Suicide. . .?"

"Relax!" Lorena says, with a rare smile. "It's a drug I've developed. From information we found in the Muluc Codex. It has an amnesiac effect. All your memories from the past six to ten days will be erased."

I look around at the gathered group. What they're suggesting – it's unbelievable. "I'd forget all this?"

Lorena nods.

My thoughts race ahead, then backwards, recalling the past few days. "And Camila, and even arriving in Mexico?"

"Yes," says Lorena. "It's a blanket effect. There can be damage to some older memories too, but we're less certain how that works."

I'm shocked into silence, weighing up the risks. Losing the memory of Camila's death – that's something I could handle, even welcome, but to lose even the brief memory of knowing her? Of the incredible sights of Ek Naab, and the knowledge about my dad's fate? It's just unacceptable.

The chief pushes the briefcase towards me. "It contains everything you need to bring back the codex. And a cell phone we've adapted to call into our network. When you've

243

completed the mission, you simply call us and we'll send a
Muwan."

I reach for the case, hesitate. They notice. I remember
what Vigores said about hesitation.

Is this it? Or is that still to come?

"The boy is anxious," remarks Blanco Vigores. "He must
have time to think."

One by one, the members of the Executive say goodbye,
leaving me staring, dazed, practically punch-drunk. They
leave via the elevator, the two Bakabs holding their helmets
in the crook of their arms.

Bad enough for me if I don't find the codex – but where
would it leave the Mayans of Ek Naab? Are they really the last
hope of all the technologically advanced civilizations of the
planet? Can it really be that without the knowledge in the Ix
Codex, the world will be helpless, facing a global computer
wipe-out?

They say that any civilized society is no more than three
days away from total breakdown. I'd never really worried
about it before; never believed it was possible. Until now.

And me – can I really be part of this? I can't decide what's
more mind-boggling – the idea that there's a secret group of
Mayans guarding ancient knowledge of advanced
technology, or that I'm one of them.

This is light-years from what I set out to find. And I'm still
not much closer to knowing what really happened to Dad.

Montoyo told me that Dad took their "Bracelet of Itzamna". Why? What does the Bracelet of Itzamna do? Why hadn't any of the Executive mentioned it tonight?

The sheer amount I still don't understand about Ek Naab and my father's trip here, threatens to swamp me. I feel as though they're feeding me just enough to get me to find the Ix Codex. When I think about it, I actually start to tremble. It doesn't help that my father and my grandfather both died trying to complete the same mission.

How can I succeed where they failed? I'm only thirteen! I've got nothing special going for me.

Blanco Vigores said, *What is required is an act of faith.*

But in what? God? Destiny? Myself?

Only Vigores is still at the table. He doesn't move. Montoyo hovers. He asks Vigores whether he "might have the honour of escorting you to your city apartments". Vigores nods, humming slightly under his breath, seemingly lost in his thoughts. Then, "I'd like the boy to return me to the Garden," he says. "Alone."

I glance at Montoyo for guidance. With the tiniest nod, he indicates that I should stay by Vigores. I do. Montoyo leaves. Vigores doesn't move. And then he stands, and so do I.

I have no idea where we are going. Almost literally, the blind leading the blind.

"My home, the Garden, exists as an eternal foundation," Vigores tells me as we begin to walk. "The very basis of Ek Naab. Volcanic activity produced lava tubes, then came the perpetual drip-drip-drip of water."

We take the elevator not *up* but *down*. The descent takes us deeper than the pyramid. I remember the dizzying journey

I made through the tunnels with Carlos Montoyo. I'm returning to those tunnels, I'm sure of it.

"There is the Garden, with its forking paths and delicately aromatic blooms. And then there are the Depths. Did Carlos Montoyo tell you of the Depths?"

"He told me about the booby-traps. To guard against invaders."

Vigores nods, smiles. "No sane person would enter the Depths without an excellent guide. And of these, there are few. In fact," he smiles, "I'm the only one you should trust. And as you see, I'm blind."

The elevator opens in front of a long tunnel, lined with a flower bed in which only one plant grows: hibiscus. The passageway is illuminated at intervals by the same five-globed lamps I've seen in the main cavern of the city. Aside from this, no effort has been made to tame the tunnels. They look rough, natural, made of a black, porous rock.

"The flowers really do grow without natural light. . ." I say in wonder.

"You didn't believe in our miracle of the hibiscus?"

I blush. "Not really. I assumed there was some trick with artifical light."

"No trick," Vigores says. "Everything you see here is quite real. Although sometimes, it may seem otherwise. Don't assume that our ancestors would have been convinced by a lesser miracle. And it's not the only miracle of Ek Naab."

"There are others? Like what?"

"Miracles, mysteries. One transforms into the other. But who's to see them? Travellers to these parts are rare. I myself travelled, once. Travelling, one becomes aware that differences are lost. One city comes to resemble all others. Places exchange their form, order, distances. One way or another, we're all destined for the dust cloud – the Great Dark Rift."

Sounds to me like he's rambling, but his way of talking draws me in, like quicksand. I try to struggle but it's useless; I'm sucked under.

Faced by a sudden crossroads, we take another left.

"When navigating a labyrinth, one should turn always *left*," mutters Vigores to himself, nodding all the while.

We walk for several moments in silence. That's when I realize that there are sounds down here if you listen carefully enough. Not the crickle-crackle insect sounds of above but a hollow yawning, like a whispered sigh. Air circulates down here. Where does it go?

"Back there," I begin nervously, "you said that what you need from me is an act of faith."

Vigores just nods.

"Well, see, I'm a bit worried about that."

"You lack faith?"

"I kind of like proof."

Vigores shakes his head. "Not always possible."

"It usually is."

"Do you love your mother?"

I'm taken aback. "Well, yeah."

"Prove it."

"I'm here . . . I'm here for her, so that she stops worrying about my dad and why he died."

Vigores stops, and turns to look at me. I could swear, for a minute, that he sees me staring back at him in astonishment.

"That's not proof of love," he says. "Scientifically, there's no such thing. You're here for reasons you can't possibly begin to comprehend. But you do love your mother, and your father too. You know that to be true. And I accept your love for them. On faith, because of what I know of you."

"But you don't know me," I point out.

He smiles. "I have faith in you, Josh. We all do. Now you must have faith in yourself, too."

"This codex curse, though . . . it's not real, is it?"

Vigores detects the scepticism in my voice, answers it with a wry, flat statement. "Oh, it's real enough. There are still stories of the day the Ix Codex was stolen from Ek Naab. In the middle of what you know as the seventh century, the Snake Kingdom – Calakmul – was on the rise. It seemed as though none could resist their power. In those days, the 'Sect of Bakabs' was a tiny group, the secret well-protected. Or so we thought. But the Bakab Ix betrayed us. His name was K'inich K'ane Ajk, but we know him as the *Traitor Bakab*. He left Ek Naab, took the codex to the Ruler of Calakmul, Yuknoom Ch'een."

"I've heard of those two," I say. "They're mentioned in the Calakmul letter."

"Yuknoom, like many Mayans, believed that any of the four books of Itzamna would make him all-powerful. He conquered Cancuen and invited the Traitor Bakab to join him in his court at Calakmul. At first, Yuknoom simply asked for the Ix Codex. And the Bakab refused. It is said that twenty of Yuknoom's guards died trying to take the codex. Twenty! The 'curse', it was said. Each death as bloody and painful as the next. And when the Traitor Bakab failed to help him find the other three books, or to decipher the Ix Codex, that's how Yuknoom decided that he would die; a bloody, painful death. A death that lasted days."

"Jeez. Why'd this guy betray Ek Naab in the first place?"

"Love. Power. Jealousy. Maybe none, maybe all three."

It sounds as if the Calakmul letter conceals a pretty grisly tale!

Unprompted, he starts up again, his voice lilting.

"There was a storm, once, that destroyed an unfortunate city by the sea. Perhaps you know it? Tulum, they call it. A Caribbean nightmare: the devastation of the hurricane. Nothing survived. Trees were torn out by their roots, thatched temple roofs flew into the air, houses were stripped of walls. Crops even: blasted by the force of the storm. The sky filled with leaves, crops, palm fronds: the night of the leaf storm. The citizens of Tulum never did recover. Some events can shake a person so badly that it's as though a tornado ripped them apart from inside."

I stop walking, turn towards Vigores.

Why is he telling me this?

Without warning, something's changed. I've lost all sense of guiding a harmless old man to his mysterious home. Now it's me who feels lost. Vigores looks directly into my eyes. And once again, I have the weirdest sensation that he sees me as clearly as I see him.

"The world around us, it changes so fast. Ripples in the air become violent currents; before you know it, there's a storm. You feel it, I know – you've carried a storm in your heart for some time now."

I almost stop breathing.

Is he talking about my dream?

Vigores only nods, shushing me as if to soothe my nerves. "This storm . . . will carry more of us with it than just you, mark my words."

I want to ask Vigores to be clearer, more specific. There's something about his eyes, though: they've glazed over. He seems lost in some interior world. With every passing second, I have a growing impression that he's forgotten I'm here. Finally, he stops taking those slow, measured steps along the tunnel.

"This is far enough."

He extracts a folding white stick from his sleeve.

"The universal tool of the blind," he says with a sad smile. "Goodbye, Josh. We'll meet again, no doubt. Remember what the poet said: *Any life is made up of a single moment: the moment in which a man finds out, once and for all, who he is*. It is your great fortune to have discovered this so early in life."

"You think?"

For some reason, my doubtful answer makes him laugh, showing all the teeth of his upper jaw. "Share our faith in you, Josh. Embrace your adventure. Because it will, above all, be that."

With that he turns away from me and continues down the dimly lit floral path.

I'm confused. After a second or two I call out after him, "How do I get back?"

"By turning right, naturally! Always right!"

Another left turn, tap-tapping along. Then he's gone, leaving me wondering what's just happened.

How could Vigores know about the leaf storm of my dream? It's as though, for just a moment, he stared deep into my soul and reflected it back to me. I feel a sudden chill; the hairs on the back of my neck bristle.

The dream is my connection with Aureliano and my father. The dream is the key.

In the Hall of Bakabs, Carlos Montoyo is alone, waiting for me. The table has been cleared, the lights dimmed. I almost miss him in the gloom.

"You've been honoured, Josh."

I don't know what to say. He stands, walks towards the elevator to meet me.

"In the past five years, I've seen Blanco Vigores, oh, maybe five times. Three of them in the past six months. Those last three meetings have concerned your father, or you."

I'm mystified. Doesn't the Executive meet regularly?

"Yes. But Vigores doesn't attend all meetings. We send a message, telling him what we will discuss. And his messenger returns with news of whether or not he will join us. Concerning the succession of the Bakab Ix, he hasn't missed a meeting."

"Why?"

Montoyo shrugs. "Who knows? Time must become very

253

precious when one is so old. All in all, sightings of him are exceedingly rare."

"What does he do down there, all alone?"

"The only one who knows – his servant and messenger – is sworn to secrecy. And that guy – he's pretty old too. There are rumours, naturally. That he has a great library of books, a collection from the entire world. That he studies at length, and is more knowledgeable than any living being. And then there's the story that he lives in what used to be Itzamna's chambers."

"Itzamna really lived here? And he really brought the four codices?"

Montoyo nods. "He inscribed them. Himself!"

"Thousands of years ago?"

"Approximately two thousand years ago."

"Wouldn't that have to make him, you know, a visiting extraterrestrial from an advanced civilization?"

I'm only half-joking, but Montoyo doesn't laugh or even smile.

"Well, there's always speculation. Itzamna was a technological prophet of some kind. Where he gained his knowledge – that's unknown."

"The answer's down there, though, isn't it? In the Garden? In the Depths? Why don't you send out search parties, find where Vigores lives, see what's going on?"

Montoyo seems irritated. "There are great dangers in the

Depths, as I've already told you. As for Vigores, we respect his privacy. He's only brought good things to Ek Naab."

I don't ask again. But I have the strong feeling that Montoyo is holding back. Big time.

Montoyo says, "We need your decision, Josh. Take the night, sleep on it. And let us know tomorrow. OK?"

Walking back to Benicio's apartment, I glimpse what passes for nightlife in Ek Naab. The plaza has been cleared of the market stalls. Round tables and chairs have taken their place. Couples and groups huddle around them, faces intimately lit with blue and red flickers from candles set in thick slabs of coloured glass.

Montoyo insists that I wear the Bakab helmet all the way back. It's for my own good, he says: "You need to learn to separate *yourself* from the *role*." I try to imagine myself as a kind of superhero paraded through the streets. It works – I feel better. I even manage to work up a little strut.

There's no sign of Benicio at the apartment. "He flies patrol most weeknights," says Montoyo. Patrolling what, I wonder? And why? These are just two of the ten million questions I want to ask about Ek Naab and all its workings. I'm on the verge of information overload, but my mind won't stop buzzing.

"You're not tired?" Montoyo asks. I shake my head. Jet-lagged is what I am, after staying up most of last night.

Montoyo searches through Benicio's kitchen cupboards.

With a murmur of satisfaction, he finds a canister and gets busy making a cafetière of coffee. A few minutes later we're sitting on the couch slurping sweet milky coffee.

"OK, Josh," he says with a smack of his lips. "Now's your time. I promised you I would answer your questions. Yes? So, go ahead."

Answer my questions? Wow. If only this happened every day. Or if he could deal with the questions I really needed to have answered. Why did my father have to die? How do I get rid of the image of my sister's head sinking underwater? Why can't my mum be one of those totally together, *I've-got-it-all-covered-no-problem* mothers? Please, can I have my ordinary life back?

Maybe he senses my line of thinking, because watching me search silently for something to ask, he says, "Things are confusing for you right now, yes?"

"Yes. Very."

"What's your biggest problem?"

"I suppose . . . thinking that you really can't get anyone else to do this. That it's all down to me. And the feeling that this is really not my job. If anyone's, it should be my dad's."

"He's let you down, yes? By not staying alive? By making this 'cup pass to you'?"

I nod slowly. He's right. At the heart of everything, that's my problem.

"I would have to say, I agree with you. Andres let us

256

down. Not only in allowing himself to be shot down or captured. But in taking the Bracelet of Itzamna."

I stare blankly into my coffee. "Why didn't the Executive mention that?"

Montoyo doesn't miss a beat. "They don't know, except for Vigores. And you'd better not tell anyone else."

"What. . .?"

"I'm serious. It would *severely* complicate matters."

I gaze at Montoyo, amazed. He's a dark horse, that guy!

"Please tell me what it is. I won't tell anyone that Dad took it, I promise."

Montoyo nods, rocking slightly, his tone grave. "There is a collection of artefacts said to have been owned originally by Itzamna himself."

"Extraterrestrial artefacts?"

He's irritated. "Not extraterrestrial, Josh. Itzamna was human, we know that. He had human children. You are one of his descendents."

"Maybe humans came from space. You know, originally?"

"Don't you learn anything in school? Humans evolved on Earth. That's proven, completely."

Deflated, I say, "Oh." Then, "So what is the Bracelet?"

"We don't know its function. Another thing we hope to learn from the Ix Codex. Each of the four books of Itzamna details a different kind of technology. We've learned much from the three we already have. Over two hundred of our engineers and scientists are working right now trying to figure them out."

"I thought they were decoded in the nineteenth century. What's taken so long?"

"Let me ask you this: if Isaac Newton had come across a modern manual of schematics for building a nuclear power plant, would he have known how to use it?"

"I guess not. The world didn't understand physics in the same way back then."

"There's your answer. In the nineteenth century our scholars learned how to read the Books of Itzamna. Understanding what they meant – we had to wait for Einstein's help there."

"Seriously?"

"Yes – 1905 and the Theory of Special Relativity. None of those books made any sense to us. Until we read Einstein. Then we could understand the Kan Codex. As scientific knowledge advanced, we gained sudden understanding of the contents of the books."

"But that doesn't help with the Bracelet of Itzamna?"

"No."

"Where did he get it?"

"That's just it," says Montoyo. "I can only think that either Blanco Vigores gave it to him – or else he stole it from Vigores."

"My dad went down to the Garden with Vigores?"

"Just like you."

"Vigores and I, we just talked. I didn't see any chambers of Itzamna. I didn't see any artefacts."

"All the same. I think Vigores and your father were involved in something. I think maybe it went wrong."

My coffee's finished now. I stand, pull off the woollen poncho and replace it on the hanger.

"So this Bracelet of Itzamna – it's important?"

Montoyo stands up too. "I have no clue what it does. But I doubt that it's just a piece of jewellery. Blanco Vigores is a somewhat eccentric old man. All the same, I've never known him do anything without good reason. If he gave the Bracelet to your father, it's because he had a plan. I want to know what that plan was, what became of it."

For a second or two I catch a whiff of Montoyo's sheer determination, maybe even ambition to be in control. Seems that he doesn't like it when he's not at the centre of things.

"You want me to find this Bracelet?"

"Yes, Josh. That's your very secret mission, for me alone."

I nod. "OK. How?"

"As next-of-kin, sooner or later, they must return to you your father's remains and any possessions they rescued from the wreckage. I simply ask that you look out for anything unusual."

"You said my dad left here in a Muwan. Was he flying it himself?"

Montoyo nods. "Yes. It can be flown in a basic fashion with little training."

"If it was captured, where would the Muwan be now?"

Montoyo laughs, apparently surprised. "Area 51, of course."

"Area 51?! As in Roswell, that Area 51? You think they took my dad there?"

"At first."

"And that's where they strangled him?"

"That's my guess."

I sit down, brooding quietly. There's no getting away from it – someone deliberately murdered my father. The Mayans may have sent him on a dangerous mission, but at least it was a mission even I could understand. Whoever killed him – they did it for their own purposes. They didn't stop to think for a second what that would mean to Dad's family.

I think about the weapons and technology that might now be put at my disposal. Deep inside me, anger squirms uneasily for the very first time.

"There's no point in revenge," Montoyo says, "if that's what you're thinking."

Deliberately, I reply, "That's up to me, isn't it?"

"You will not even think about revenge! Like it or not, you are the heir of the Bakab Ix; you *will* carry out your duties; you *will not* allow personal vendettas to interfere!"

I just stand there, livid, returning his intense stare. "I do not have to live by your rules."

"You think I care where you were born? You are a Bakab: it's that simple. So, yes, you do have to live by our rules." Montoyo grabs my arm, his fingers digging hard into the bicep. "Ignore your anger," he implores. "Put aside your personal feelings. This agency: with them it's not personal. OK? It's their living. Until you have the same professional outlook, you are no match for them."

It takes all my self-control not to struggle against him. I must know seven different ways to get out of a simple hold like this. Yet, somewhere along the line, Montoyo's won my respect.

Still gripping my arm, he adds, "You want justice, yes? That's beyond your control. What you *can* do is bring back the Ix Codex and maybe the Bracelet of Itzamna too. This must be your revenge. Understand?"

Cold fury envelops me. "Let go of me," I tell him quietly.

"You're not a member of the Executive yet, Josh. When you turn sixteen, take my place, then you make your own orders."

Finally he lets me pull myself free. Without giving him another look, I storm into the bedroom, throw myself into the hammock.

"Get some sleep," I hear him say, his voice tired and dull.

"Tomorrow, Josh, you must take your first action as the Bakab we have awaited these past forty years."

I wait for Montoyo to leave before I let myself fall asleep. Just like the night before, it takes me ages to get to sleep. The occasional shiver runs through me. My past, my future; it all brims with possibility.

When I wake up, the place is totally quiet, totally dark. I roll out of the hammock, pad around the apartment looking for signs of life. It's deserted. I gravitate to the kitchen, open the fridge. I find some sliced cheese and ham, fold them inside two flour tortillas and warm them on the griddle.

It hits me then that I haven't thought of Ollie and Tyler for ages . . . back when I tried to phone them, near the *cenote*. In fact, I haven't thought of anything much, except what's happening to me, and Ek Naab. I stare around the living room.

Can it really be so easy to step into another world, another life?

I've heard people say you can get used to anything. But it scares me how quickly I'm getting used to this. I don't want to forget about everything else – I want to get this mission over with and get back to my life in Oxford.

Yet it's hard not to forget. This is all so foreign and at the same time, eerily familiar. Part of the strangeness is the lack of ordinary things, like advertising posters and television and stuff. I'm sitting on the sofa, eating and wondering how the people of Ek Naab survive without television, when the front door opens. Benicio strolls in wearing a navy flightsuit. There's no insignia, badge or anything. He might as well be a window cleaner for all his clothes tell.

Benicio doesn't seem surprised to see that I'm awake, but he doesn't look too pleased either. In fact, he's got a face like thunder.

I take a guess. "Bet you're fed up with babysitting me."

"No," he answers shortly. "It's fine."

But pretty obviously, it's not. The sudden difference in Benicio really throws me.

I don't really know any of these people.

I'm still wondering what to say when he breaks in, all business-like. "Have you made your decision yet?"

"Yes. Don't see that I really have a choice."

"Well, that sounds real committed," he says with a hint of sarcasm.

"I didn't mean it like that. Well, maybe a bit. No, I'm in. I can do this."

"Excellent," he says without expression. What the heck is wrong with him? "Let's go through your instructions again."

"You know what I have to do?" I ask, a bit surprised that he's in on it.

"I was part of the team that proposed and planned the

mission," he says, giving me a sharp look. "So let's go over it again."

I return my plate to the kitchen, hesitating on the way.

"Benicio. Is something wrong?"

He seems slightly irked. "No."

I've never been much good at pressuring people to "open up". Normally I'm only too pleased to ask once and then leave it at that. In this case, though, I'm too anxious.

"Sorry, mate, but I think there is."

Now he looks really irritated. "There's stuff going on in my life that's . . . complex."

"Uh huh?"

"Yeah," he says. "And I prefer not to talk about it."

"Have I done something?"

"You?" His show of surprise seems just a tad insincere. "No. It concerns Ixchel, if you must know."

"Pumas Girl?"

"I'm the one who helped her run away from home," he admits. "Catching some flak for it now."

"Why'd she go?"

"A difference of opinion."

"She told me to say it was a 'matter of principle'," I say.

"You could say that," he agreed.

"A row with her parents?"

He nods. "That's one way to see it."

"You're not gonna tell me?"

"Not possible," he says. "I'm sworn to secrecy in so many ways, you can't believe it."

"So you and me, we're cool?"

Benicio shrugs. "Sure. Why wouldn't we be?"

I pull what I hope is my most vacant expression. "No reason."

Who knows whether he's convinced or not. Either way, he doesn't pursue it further. He joins me on the couch and draws the occasional table closer. My *Mission: Impossible* case – the aluminium briefcase from Chief Sky Mountain – sits on top of the table.

"First," says Benicio, "the lock combination."

We spend the next hour going over the details of the mission to find the codex. When I'm word perfect, Benicio escorts me across the city and back to the aircraft hangar.

I keep a tight grip on to the mission briefcase. There are things in there that they don't want falling into the wrong hands. The responsibility of keeping all those secrets is beginning to weigh pretty heavily.

When we arrive, the place is lit up by giant arc lamps. A Mark I Muwan is being checked over by two jumpsuited engineers. From behind the Muwan, Chief Sky Mountain appears. He plants his hands on his hips and watches us approach, beaming widely. When we reach him, he puts a wide, heavy palm on each of our shoulders, gives us a proud smile.

"Josh, you are all prepared?"

I give a quick, hopefully competent-looking nod.

"That's good." He grins and tips his head slightly at the Muwan with pride. "You like our aircraft?"

I remember that I'm supposed to be seeing them for the first time. I widen my eyes, nod vigorously. "Yeah. Wow!"

"Any questions?"

Mentally I run quickly through Benicio's instructions and the various gadgets in the case that he showed me how to use.

"Can I get the mobile phone out of the case?"

The pockets of my jeans are packed with the cash I salvaged from Camila's backpack in the jungle two nights ago. My UK mobile phone is somewhere amongst the cash – but it doesn't work right now. I figure that in an emergency, I'll need one that does. The chief decides that for extra security, he'll handcuff the case to me. I take out the little mobile phone and pocket it while he cuffs the case to my left wrist.

If I'd been expecting any grand ceremony – the big send-off – I'd have been disappointed. The chief and a few engineers loiter, watching as Benicio leads me to a Mark I Muwan, climbs a ladder and disappears inside the hawk's head. He doesn't invite me to follow, so I make to climb the ladder, glancing at the chief for confirmation. As his eyes meet mine, the chief appears to make a decision of some sort. He waves me to come back. Benicio is already strapping himself in as I climb back down.

"I talked to Montoyo this morning," begins the chief. "You know about what?"

It's obvious from his searching expression that he means business. I restrict myself to a short nod.

"So we're agreed, yes? No revenge. You go to the museum in Jalapa, you break into the room with the wreckage fragments, find the codex if it's there, bring it right back. OK? Just stick to your orders."

Orders.

I nod again.

He pauses; I wait, itching to pull away, to join Benicio in a Muwan once again.

"You don't know a lot about us yet. Then again, we don't know a lot about you. But we do know this: you're family. And there are some things you don't do with family. You understand? You don't cheat and lie to your family. That is something we do not forgive."

He speaks casually, almost avuncular in his manner. But who does he think he's kidding?

"Are you threatening me?"

The chief gives a mild shrug. "Just telling you how it is. If you'd grown up here, this wouldn't be necessary. But frankly, I don't know how you've been raised, or with what values. So I'm telling you the way things are with us."

"I'm for my family. *That's* how I've been raised. You needn't worry."

"Good."

"But if I find the people who killed my dad, or my sister, I want my chance," I add. "Today, tomorrow, next year; it's all the same to me."

We stare each other out until my eyes almost water. The chief nods slowly, considering. "If that's so," he eventually says, "better wait. See how you feel next year."

I can't imagine that it's ever going to change. How could it? Dad and Camila – they're never coming back.

And part of me can't help wondering . . . will I?

It feels amazing to be back in a Muwan. The minute we lift out of the underground hangar, my spirits soar. The sun hasn't risen yet; there's a pinkish sky. I'm hoping that Benicio will fly back over the ruins of Becan, but he takes some other route, flying straight towards the sea, which fills our field of vision quite suddenly: immense, flat, grey.

Finally I see a proper chance to check in with my mates. I'm desperate to know what's happened to them. "Is there any way we can drop by Hotel Delfin?"

Benicio sounds doubtful. "It's kinda risky."

"I need to know. Please. It's really important. I can't relax until I know if they're OK."

"We don't need you relaxed. We need you focused."

But I'm adamant. "Relaxed, focused. Whatever you want to call it."

I can hear him sighing. "I can't get anywhere near Chetumal. We'll be noticed."

"There has to be a secluded spot somewhere. Maybe up the beach?"

My watch says 5.30 a.m. The beaches will be deserted.

"OK," he says after a long pause. "About a mile north. There's a place I know, trees on both sides of the inlet. I'll drop you and wait an hour. You walk to Chetumal, make a call from a payphone in the doughnut place across the road from the Delfin. Whatever they tell you, you don't go into the hotel. If you speak to your friends, you tell them to walk out, to meet you in the pizza place next door. Got that? Not the doughnut place. You watch to check that they come alone. If not, you wait until they leave. If they come alone, you follow them into the pizza shop. Take a few minutes with them – no more than five. Tell them you're safe, you'll be back soon, not to follow you. *Not to follow you!* But if you hear that your friends are still with the NRO guys, you hang up. Right away. And you come back to the Muwan. If you don't return in one hour, I'll raise the alarm. Believe me, you don't come back in one hour, the chief will give me hell. And then I'll hand it over to you."

Benicio makes me repeat his instructions back to him three times. When he's convinced I know them, he takes the Muwan down. As we drop through the clouds, the sea sweeps into view, rapidly filling our entire field of vision. I see the landing spot that Benicio's aiming for – it's a small cove surrounded by trees.

He lands the craft with a rapid vertical descent that reminds me the Tower of Terror ride at Disney Studios in Orlando. It's just fast enough to be thrilling, but I don't quite lose my stomach. Which is what I think he may have been hoping for, judging by the mischievous look Benicio flashes me as he leans over his seat once we've landed.

"This plane . . . seriously, it's incredible."

"You think this is good," he remarks, removing his headset, "you wanna see the Mark II."

Three rungs spring from the body of the craft just under the cockpit. They're enough to bring me within jumping distance of the sandy beach. The metal briefcase swings down, dealing me a slap to the thigh.

Benicio waves as I start a slow jog back towards Chetumal's main beach. I don't even hear the Muwan take off, but I do hear it humming as it flies overhead. The sound seems vaguely familiar – like a cloud of swarming honeybees.

I check my watch: 5.40. As I round the outline of palm trees on the beach, Chetumal comes into view. It's further than I'd guessed. Time to pick up some speed. The briefcase doesn't help. Before long I'm cursing the irritating way the handcuff cuts into my wrist.

It's 5.51 as I cross the seafront boulevard and stroll down Chetumal's main road. Hotel Delfin is about a hundred metres away; the pizza and doughnut places slightly further.

Three minutes later I'm calling from the doughnut place.

The first batch of doughnuts is just being dropped on to cinnamon sugar – an unbelievably delicious smell. In a corner there's a slot machine and a payphone to entertain customers while they wait. The reception desk at Hotel Delfin takes their sweet time answering the phone. It's Paco. Yes, of course he remembers me. They hadn't given the game away to the *gringos*, no way. The hotel's owner wouldn't hear of it – the Professor was one heck of a guy. Lying to the *gringos* to protect the Professor's son? Paco considered it a privilege.

Tyler and Ollie, though, that couldn't be helped. The *gringo* agents had caught the hotel staff napping as far as that went. Poor kids – they'd spent a whole night in the cells down with Detective Rojas and those agents. Who knew what they'd been through. So, where was I? Come on, I could tell Paco! Was Andres really a secret agent or something? They'd suspected something like that all along.

Paco talks at me like it's going out of fashion. Eventually I manage to squeeze in a question of my own: "Can you bring them to the phone?"

At 6.11, just as I'm pacing the tiny doughnut place and checking my watch for the millionth time, Tyler and Ollie appear at the door of Hotel Delfin, dressed in pyjamas. They're headed my way. I duck behind the slot machine and watch them run towards the pizza place to the left. As it happens, the shop is still shut. Who knows where Benicio gets his fast-food-store intelligence, but on this occasion it's unreliable. Tyler and Ollie press their noses up against the glass of the pizza shop, looking frantic. I check back towards the hotel. No sign of anyone following. So, I risk it. I break from Benicio's instructions: I step into the street, beckon them round the corner.

"Where did you go?" *"God, what a nightmare!"* *"The NRO, Josh, the NRO!"*

And of course, *"What's in the case?"*

I want to listen to everything that spills out of them, but I can't listen, answer questions and ask them all at the same time. At least, not in less than five minutes.

"Guys, listen, listen, *listen*, dammit!"

That gets their attention.

"I'm leaving, OK? In three minutes. So, just listen."

I tell them how Camila died. How I escaped, got lost in the jungle, wandered. Someone helped me, brought me back. "Now I need to get back into hiding. Until I know it's safe to be around here. So I'm going. I've found a place to stay. I'm safe there."

"Josh, what the hell's going on?" Tyler says, eyes full of doubt and anxiety.

"With these US agents? I'm not sure. But I think they're the ones who killed my dad. I don't trust them for a second."

"It's true," says Ollie. "This has to do with your father. They asked hundreds of questions about him. And about your sister. Josh, it's awful about Camila."

"Yeah. She was really cool."

I want to hug them both just for being there. They feel real, concrete. They make me feel real again, plugged into the world. But I'm already splitting in two; fifteen minutes down the beach, the legacy of an ancient world waits for me.

"So, I'll be seeing you," I tell them both, giving Ollie a grin. They're still protesting as I open the door. And I'm jogging down the street before I remember to shout my final instruction to them.

Don't follow me.

In another four minutes I'm down the avenue, turning left on to the seafront boulevard, vaulting the low wall and into the beach car park at Chetumal. I check my watch: 6.15.

With timing this perfect, the mission to fetch the codex seems like a simple errand.

I dash across the car park.

I notice it but don't notice it.

Well, I have a lot on my mind.

It's a common enough car in Mexico. In hindsight, it's as obvious as a lonely fishing boat on a fine, windless day.

A blue Nissan.

And that's the last thing that goes through my mind before I hit the ground with my face, mouth open in a yelp of pain and surprise.

33

I was terrified when the car carrying Camila and me hit the swamp in the dark and bubbled under. That was a wild panic. Not a patch on the desperate sensation of feeling alone, helpless, tiny, insignificant; all the forces of nature and evil ranged against me, slowly becoming aware that all options have run out and that death looms, inevitable, just minutes away.

I wake up in the dark, the back of my head violently throbbing. In my mouth there's the taste of the sea and the hard, salty crunch of sand.

How did I miss seeing that blue Nissan?

I had better things to dream about: Benicio waiting for me up the coast in the Muwan, the amazed and admiring gazes of my two friends.

I can't deny it. That had felt *great*.

Result? I was attacked, surprised from behind – by Blue Nissan. The blow was clean enough – I can feel a lump now but no blood. The hand attached to the briefcase is chafed and raw. I have vague memories of someone repeatedly trying to pull the cuff free.

I'm in the trunk of a car. Moving. I check my pockets. I still have my soaked UK mobile phone and the wad of cash. But the mobile phone from Ek Naab is gone.

There is no way to call the Mayans to rescue me.

After about thirty minutes, the motion sickness gets the better of me. The inevitable happens – I throw up. Then I get tumbled around in it. Which makes me throw up some more. I finally figure a way to brace myself in the trunk so that I don't move about too much. That, and working hard on keeping my stomach muscles tight, helps stop the vicious cycle of nausea.

All pretty grim. But as a prelude of what's to come, it's no big deal.

I lose track of time. The car slows to a stop. The driver's door opens. Someone pops the boot. I blink, dazzled by the sunlight. The driver is just a dark silhouette. I still can't see his face and have no idea where we are.

I hear him say, "Get out." American, definitely.

Reluctantly, I climb out. We're alone on a beach; totally isolated. On the coast, cliffs rise to the left, rocks to the right. After a few seconds my eyes adjust. I get my first proper look at the guy – Simon Madison – whom I still think of as "Blue Nissan".

My mouth falls open. "You!"

It's him – the burglar, the guy who bought that book from under me back in Oxford.

The NRO – they've been on to me from the beginning!

He doesn't smile – too busy making faces. He's just figured out that the nauseating smell is coming from me. He holds his nose, calls me a variety of disgusting insults.

"Now look what you've done, you stupid jerk. You messed up my trunk. Do you know what rental companies charge for cleaning that? I should make you do it yourself."

"You broke into my house . . . you stole my bloody book. . ." I say, my voice getting louder. "Why? Why take the book?"

Now he does smile; a nasty, self-satisfied grin. "If you don't know the answer to that, then there's no way I'm telling you."

Simon Madison sounds pretty American, but now that I see him properly, there's a definite Hispanic touch. I pick up the same whiff of cologne that I first noticed when he burgled my house. Unlike his two Hawaiian-shirted counterparts who came calling for me at Hotel Delfin, there's something vaguely refined about his accent, clothes and grooming.

· I scan the surroundings for any hint of other people. It's no use; we're alone and not far from the coast road; that much I can hear. Unless a passerby were to actually stop and walk right to the edge of the road, I doubt they'd see anything.

This is the sort of beach you'd search for hours to find and be tickled pink to discover you had all to yourself on a clear, perfect morning like this. But I see it another way. This could be the last place I ever see.

Madison slaps me hard across the face. The attack takes me by surprise; I'm still woozy from the car trip. But the burning pain from my cheek does wonders for my state of alertness.

He uses his right fist the second time. I sidestep easily enough, moving in to trip him up with a wide arcing swipe at his legs. I don't wait around to watch him hit the ground; I'm already running back towards the road.

I don't get far. There's a loud crack of gunfire. I throw myself to the ground, head tucked under my arms.

He calls out, "Hey, scumbag, think I enjoy chasing you? Now, stand, slowly."

I get to my feet, turn to see him about ten metres away. There's an automatic pistol in his hand pointed straight at me. They say it's tricky to shoot a moving target, but once I hear that bullet whiz past me, I stop being able to think rationally. I've never faced a guy with a gun before. And I've no idea what to do.

Walking towards me and still pointing the weapon, he says, "Undo the handcuff. I want that briefcase."

I shake my head. There's no way he can remove it without my help.

Madison cocks his head and a nasty smile turns the corners of his mouth. "No? Oh well, I had to try." He turns away, then whirls around. This time, he hits me for real; this time, it's with the gun. I'm toppled, clutching my ear. It rings with pain.

When I open my eyes, I see nothing but stars. I stay on the ground, trying to protect my head from the blows I'm sure are about to rain down on me. He takes something out of his pocket, holds it up to show me. It's the mobile phone from Ek Naab.

"It's from Ek Naab, correct? You've been there, I know it. Well, I promise you, before I'm done with you, you're going to tell me every goddamn thing you know about that place."

He leans over me, sticks the gun in my face and speaks very clearly.

"Josh. I want you to listen to me real careful. You're, what, thirteen, fourteen? This thing you're involved in is way beyond you. Doesn't end with me; I answer to a boss."

I say nothing. Madison sighs and then kicks me in the ribs. I crumple once again, gasping in agony. He waits for my groans to subside. "I need to know if we understand each other. Do we?"

I nod and in a tired voice reply, "Yeah."

"That's good. That's excellent. Because the people I report

to, they don't play nice and reasonable like me. I don't enjoy hitting kids, but in this regard, well hell, you don't qualify."

By now I'm springing tears, terrified, sick with my own fear.

This guy killed Camila. And unless I do something soon, he's going to kill me too.

He pulls me to my feet, leans me against the car.

"OK, Josh. The combination for the case."

I shake my head. I don't dare to speak in case my voice cracks. He waits, biting his lip.

With his left hand, he begins to hunt around in his pockets. "If that's your final answer, Josh, then I'm gonna have to *cut* you out of it. I don't think you'll have to lose your whole hand. If I take your thumb, I'm pretty sure I can slip the case off. Course, I'll have to tie you down. That bone takes some sawing through. It's none too quick." He chuckles, adding, "And there's gonna be some blood."

I'm frozen to the spot, just like in those dreams where you're being chased but your legs won't move. I try to flex my fingers, testing to see if I'm really paralysed or what. Madison looks annoyed. What the hell is he doing? He smiles suddenly. I peer over his shoulder, catch a glimpse of steel through the glass. A hunting knife, on a bed of coiled climbing rope. I can hardly breathe.

"Listen, kid. With or without your help, I'm taking that case. Then me and my associates, kid, we're going to

Ek Naab. And we'll do something that should have been done five hundred years ago: we'll destroy them. Superior little smart-aleck half-breeds, they think they can keep all those secrets to themselves? We're gonna teach them a lesson. And, kid – that's starting with you."

I struggle to take in what he's saying.

Madison knows all about Ek Naab. How?

As Madison opens the car door, I make my decision. When his attention is momentarily distracted, I throw myself forward into a handstand spin, knocking the mobile phone out of his hand with my kick. The phone flies into the air and lands a couple of feet away. When I land, I run for it. But this time, I head down towards the sea, ducking to pick up the phone on the way.

I sprint down the sands, holding the briefcase behind my head as a shield. A second or two later, I leap into the surf. A couple of bullets zoom past my ear, one even hits the briefcase, and I'm zig-zagging, hoping that it's true what they say about hitting a moving target. By the time he decides to swim after me, I'm already underwater.

I hear him shout things like, "Where do you think you're gonna go, punk?"

I dive under the first line of waves, put my head down and keep going. I swim hard until I'm disoriented, tossed around by the waves, pulled under by the riptide. The bigger waves come in on the third line. Each wave picks me up and slams me down. I hit the sand, roll, but I keep swimming.

By the time I surface and turn to look around, I can see that the sea has dragged me out beyond the fourth wave. Madison has stopped behind the third, which I guess is where the undercurrent hits him. He's treading water, shouting, "Come back, dumbass. You're gonna drown. Get back here and we'll cut a deal for the case."

I'm fighting to stay put, resisting the pull of the waves that threaten to tug me further out. I stare at him defiantly, daring him to come out further, risk his own life to grab me.

I see him spit mouthfuls of water before eventually he yells, "All right, jerk. We'll do this your way. I'll wait for you to drown, then I'll come in and cut the case from your freakin' dead body. It's all the same to me."

And he turns, swimming back to shore.

In the relative calm of the outer waves, I think through my options. Up the coast, tall grey limestone cliffs block access to the road for several hundred metres. In the far distance I can see the clifftop ruins of Tulum. Even if I could make it to an inaccessible beach, I'd be trapped. There'd be no guarantee that he wouldn't be able to follow.

In the other direction there's a tiny chink of hope; jagged rocks rise from the sand out into the sea, but only for a short distance. If I can make it out beyond, I'll maybe have a chance to swim round the rocks to the next beach. That beach also seems inaccessible from the road. If Madison tries following me, he'll definitely be risking his life. And we might both be trapped.

Either option looks grim. The briefcase bobs in the water next to me. Luckily, it's very slightly buoyant, from the trapped air in the packing foam, I guess. I'm still clutching the mobile phone from Ek Naab in my right fist. It's probably ruined by the sea, but I open it up anyway, hoping that their technology can make phones waterproof. It can't – the phone is dead. I drop it into my front pocket and work on treading water.

Taking the decision to ditch the case is tough, but I know that to stay alive that little bit longer, I'll have to sacrifice it. I dial the combination on the handcuff and release it. I try to use it as a float in front of me, but it just sinks immediately under my weight. Slowly, I open the case and remove all the gadgets, dropping them one by one into the sea. They're safely destroyed. The only thing that can be useful now is the phone – if it can ever be made to work again.

I study the rocks to the left. Looks as if they stretch about a hundred metres into the sea. I know that once I set out to go round the rocks, there's no turning back. If I hit exhaustion too soon, that'll be it. I have to make it around the rocks and in as far as the third wave. After that, I should be able to ride the waves on to the shore. I'll be beached, bedraggled, but hopefully still breathing.

I gaze back towards the beach. Then I see something that almost paralyses me. Madison is walking back from the car, carrying what looks like scuba-diving equipment. Up on the beach, he's suiting up.

That's when I know I have to get moving. Stay where I am and he'll find my body – and the phone – no problem. If I move out beyond the rocks, the constant pull of the open water might take my body out too far for him to ever find me. If I do drown, at least I'll be taking the secrets of Ek Naab with me.

So, I turn round, face the horizon and begin to swim.

I'm already tired when it occurs to me that the rocks actually stretch more than a hundred metres out to sea. I'm sure I've swum much more than a hundred metres, but the rocks appear to be just as distant as before. The waves hadn't looked significant from where I started the swim.

After another exhausting few minutes, I'm feeling the first real sense of being defeated. Plan A is not going to work. There's no way I can swim back, either. The tide is pulling me hard into the rocks. Clearing them has to be the priority. I need a Plan B.

I ease into a slower rhythm, not trying to go over the choppy waves but letting them pass over me. It's closer to drowning but I feel more in control; less like I'm fighting a losing battle against the sea. I'm about ten metres from the rocks, another ten from the end point, the head. I know I'll have to swim at least another ten metres past the end or risk being pulled into the rocks and injured, probably fatally.

I count every metre, think about nothing else. My muscles already know the truth. I don't let my brain go there. Not yet. I have to keep moving.

I stop hearing any sound except the waves and my own breathing. When finally I clear the rock head safely, I turn around. I'm shocked to see that I'm probably two hundred metres out to sea. At least Madison and his car are almost too far away to see.

I can't see what he's doing, but I'm guessing that he's livid. I manage a tiny chuckle. Leaning my head back, I rest for a few minutes. I wonder what might be going through his head, watching the prize slip through his fingers. I hope then that the people Madison works for show him no mercy. I hope they'll get medieval on him.

I try to persuade myself that I'll just rest here awhile and then start the swim back to shore. Part of me believes it. But in my arms and legs and lungs I know that it's over. The sea is too rough. Staying away from the rocks is just too much work. The minute I turn in towards the shore, I'll be battling the currents forcing my body against the rocks. I need to swim a lot further away; so far that I'll probably never make it back to shore.

Luckily my brain is still in charge. It orders the lazybones muscles to take me further out, at least thirty metres beyond the rocks. But then the body takes over. And I stop swimming. I float up on to my back, my eyes closed. Rest – that's what I need. Every fibre of my body screams out for it.

I know now that I'll go under very soon. The power of the sea to sap my energy so quickly comes as an abysmal shock. I become aware, floating on my back, of a sense of intense unease at the depths of water underneath me. Most people simply aren't dumb enough to put themselves at this kind of risk. In the open water of the Caribbean, I might as well be a tasty shark biscuit. One thing I know about shark attacks – you don't see them coming. The fish swim deep below and launch a speedy attack from directly underneath. Watching out for a fin is pointless. The first thing I'd know about it, my legs would already have been ripped off.

I'd rather drown. I've heard that the lack of oxygen to the brain gives you an ecstatic rush. I wonder how that first lungful of water will feel; think about the grief that's heading straight for my mother; about all the things I'll never do, and the stupid fact that this happened because I wanted to see my friends.

I resort to a bargain with the God I stopped believing in two years ago.

Save me and I'll save your precious world.

I promise: I'll do everything in my power to find the Ix

Codex. Then it occurs to me that maybe He doesn't want to save us. Maybe the disaster of 2012 is His way of wiping the slate clean and starting over: Flood 2.0.

Finally, I wonder if there really is an afterlife and if I'll ever see my father again. In waters of the deepest turquoise blue I've ever seen, I prepare to drown.

35

Someone must have been listening to my last few thoughts before I slip under the waves. I glimpse arms reaching down to pull me out of the water. They drag me over the edge of a boat. Even without looking, I can tell that it's Tyler and Ollie. Opening my eyes, I see Ollie standing behind us as Tyler holds me upright.

Ollie stares at me.

"Why? Why did you swim so far out? Where's your case?"

I start to answer, but can't speak. I collapse then, I think.

Some time later, I come around, still lying in the bottom of a small speedboat that is beached under the shade of a palm. Tyler opens a cooler and passes me a bottle of Orange Crush that's already sweating on the glass. Fingers trembling, I clutch it.

Ollie leans on the side of the boat. For the first time I notice that they are both dressed in pyjamas.

"We knew something was wrong, you know. Right from

the start. Camila wasn't entirely straight with us, was she? She knew that those men from the NRO were following her. And she didn't warn us."

Tyler and Ollie are furious about what had happened to them. My disappearance made it worse for them; they were held for questioning even longer, precisely because of it. When they were released, it came as something of a surprise.

"Thought they'd never let up," Tyler says. "But then, they let us go. Something to do with a phone call from the British Embassy."

I'm relieved to hear that – my advice to Mum must have worked.

Earlier this morning, Tyler and Ollie woke to my phone call.

"Somehow, I knew you'd be back. And that you'd be in trouble," Ollie tells me, grinning.

Our meeting in the doughnut shop only increased their suspicion. So, they followed me down to the beach car park. They arrived just in time to see Madison shoving me into the boot of his car and disappearing down the coastal road. A taxi driver was just picking up his morning doughnuts and coffee when they pounced on him and begged him to hightail it down the coast with them in search of Madison.

Luckily for them, he was a sport.

"This is a first for me," the driver told them. "I've never actually done 'follow that cab'."

Tyler held his coffee and doughnuts while he broke the

speed limit to catch up with Madison. Once they had the car comfortably within sight, the taxi settled at a discreet distance, always just out of sight.

"Don't think he didn't complain, though," Tyler comments. "Givin' it, 'I don't take credit cards' and 'We should have agreed a price' and 'Where are we going, all the freakin' way to Cancun?'"

When they saw the car come off the road, they stopped too, arrived in time to see Madison shooting at me as I escaped into the sea. If I'd decided to head for the road – and them – instead of the sea, maybe they'd have been able to stop everything then and there.

Instead, they watched in horror as I turned out to sea, swimming into what was obviously a deadly situation. From up high they saw more accurately than I that the rocks went out way further than anyone could swim in high waves and ebb tides.

From that moment, they knew that every second would count.

"Your pal is going to drown," said the taxi driver. "Unless we can find a boat."

Then the driver really stepped on it. He raced to the next village. It was one of those places with nothing but a fish restaurant and snorkel-hire stall on the beach.

But they did have a boat.

Ollie threw money at the speedboat's owner until he agreed

to sail them down the coast to look for me. By the time they'd both piled into the boat, twenty minutes had gone by. Down south, I was now approaching the end of the rocks, turning round and realizing what a ghastly mistake I'd made.

It took another fifteen minutes for them to get to the beach where they'd last seen me. They scanned the sea for any sign of me. Luckily, they knew more or less where to look. Even so, the waves were choppy enough to hide me until they were almost on top of me. By then I really didn't have much fight left.

I'm itching to check the mobile phone from Ek Naab. How dry would it have to be to work again? Or has sea water shorted the circuitry beyond repair? Afraid that my frustration will show, I concentrate on sipping Orange Crush and watch as two Mexican guys stand chatting nearby.

Again Ollie asks me: what happened to the case – the one I had strapped to my wrist when they met me at the doughnut shop?

Tyler says "Yeah, mate, where'd you get that anyhow?"

I don't answer. I can't betray the secrets of Ek Naab. And anyway, why are Tyler and Ollie suddenly so interested in the case?

Every now and then the two Mexican guys throw our little group a glance. Tyler notices me looking. "Hope you got some dosh, mate. Speed Boat Guy and *el taxiste*. In case you hadn't guessed, you owe them big-time."

As we drive back down the coast to Chetumal, Tyler and Ollie tell me about their interrogation session.

Those NRO guys already know quite a bit. They know that Becan hides a secret entrance to some hideout. From what Tyler tells me, they've got it into their heads that there's some underground, Bond-villain-type set-up down there.

It actually makes me smile, remembering my first impression of Carlos Montoyo.

"Where is the secret entrance to Ek Naab?" they asked, and, "Who has been feeding you information?" All they managed to get out of Tyler and Ollie was some vague memory of the inscription on the Calakmul letter. Luckily, it was very vague, infuriatingly so. When they couldn't agree on the text, the NRO guys gave them a long rant. "We'll find out who you're protecting and put them in jail", "We'll extradite you to Guantanamo, you jerks, all we have to do is call you terrorists and then we can do what the hell we like."

"So is it true?" Ollie asks, looking deep into my eyes. "Is there a secret hideout under Becan?"

I hesitate for just a second before saying, "Yes." Well – I always said I'd be loyal to my family. These guys are like my family. I can't deal with lying to them, but I can limit what I tell them.

They both gasp. "Aw . . . you lie!" Tyler says, giving me a shove. But he can tell I'm serious.

"Mate, if this is for real, then you've gotter come clean with it," he says. "Them NRO idiots – they'll never leave us alone. They've got our names, addresses; they've copied our passports, our tickets. We can't leave the country without them knowing."

"They said that?"

Ollie gives a reluctant nod. "Actually, they did."

"I can't tell them anything," I say. "Not a thing."

Tyler looks astounded. "Well, I've had enough of this! We come out here for a bit of a laugh and to support you with your *emotional* problems, and what happens? We end up spending the night in a Mexican slammer – with toilets that would make you actually spew, mind you – with some bloody scary American agents who think we're involved in some big drug-lord operation. . ."

"They said that?" I interrupt. "'Drug-lord'?"

"They mentioned drugs, they mentioned arms dealing, I dunno what they think is going on."

Ollie is uncharacteristically quiet. "They think this is about gangsters?" I ask her. She looks away without replying.

"Why would the NRO care about gangsters, Tyler?" I say, raising my voice. "They're a joint operation of the CIA and US Air Force! How is a bit of weed-smuggling going to upset them?"

"I think they were trying to confuse us," Ollie says in a soothing voice.

"I think they succeeded," I reply angrily.

There's a long, deeply uncomfortable silence.

"Where did you go, Josh?" Ollie asks. "Who gave you the case? And what did you do with it?"

Ignoring her questions, I say, "That guy in the blue Nissan, he was going to kill me, you know. After he'd tortured me to find out what I knew. He shot Camila, drove her car off the road. I almost drowned, and she died. These NRO people are dangerous. And you want me to go back and tell them?"

"They weren't like that with us," Tyler says. "They were all talk, no trousers."

"Because they could see you didn't know any more than them," I yell in frustration. "With me, it's a different story."

"With you, they know they can get real information," agrees Ollie.

"The blue Nissan guy is called 'Simon Madison'. Whether that's his real name or not, I don't know, but that's what his passport says."

Very curious, Ollie asks, "How do you know that?"

"I just do." I can see she's not satisfied with that but I don't care. "He wanted the case. And to know how to get into Ek Naab. But I'm not sure I could get in again. They were waiting for me. They led me there."

Tyler and Ollie stare at me. "*They?*"

I sigh. "I've already said too much."

Tyler scratches the stubble on his chin. "Now you're scarin' me. Josh, you're in danger so long as you keep this to yourself. Just tell 'em. They're on our side, right – the Yanks? What harm can it do?"

"I'm not sure I agree with you there," Ollie says carefully.

The taxi driver interrupts to tell us he has to stop for petrol at the next service station. Do we want to grab some snacks? He pulls in at the crowded service station, where half a dozen tourist coaches have stopped to refuel. Tyler and Ollie go for the drinks whilst I visit the bathrooms. Washing my hands with pink liquid soap, I watch them on the other side of the concourse, talking to local people selling home-made cookies, crisps and fresh juice. There's something too cosy, too familiar about the way they are together. He even feeds her a crisp, while she laughs at something he's said. I'm suddenly jealous.

"*Who gave you the case?*" "*Just tell them!*"

If I didn't know better, I'd wonder if I could even afford to trust my two friends. But they did save me.

Or did they?

What if the NRO somehow got to them – made a deal?

Maybe they just saved me from drowning so that they could make sure I delivered myself into the hands of the NRO again.

A sudden feeling of desperation sweeps through me. I have to grip the washbasin to stay upright.

What if the NRO got to them?

I can hardly breathe. Standing over there they look so calm, relaxed. I watch them smile, choose bags of fresh potato crisps sprinkled with lime and chilli, watch them wait as a woman cuts green-skinned oranges, lining them up to be squeezed for juice.

Between us, an aging yellow bus prepares to pull out of the station, blocking my view of Tyler and Ollie. I make my decision. I race out of the washroom and jump on to the bus just before its door closes. The driver isn't unduly surprised, just asks me how far I'm going. I ask, "Where are you headed?"

"Valladolid," he replies. "Via everywhere."

I'm not sure where Valladolid is, but it sounds fine. Not on the beaten track, that's for sure. And I like the sound of "via everywhere". For what I'm planning, that sounds perfect. I peel off a fifty-peso note and wait for change. There's nowhere to sit on the bus, which is full of tired-eyed workers coming home from night shifts at the tourist resorts and plantations hereabouts. I check my watch – it's almost 9 a.m. I'm pretty conspicuous at this time of day. Backpackers carry backpacks and they don't show up anywhere before 10 a.m.

I catch a final glimpse of Tyler and Ollie as the bus drives off. They're tasting the juice. It looks good. I wish I'd thought to bring something to drink. How long, I wonder, until they work out that I've gone? Another bus pulls out almost at the same time, the destination listed as Cancun.

They must have chosen to chase the Cancun bus, because my bus takes a leisurely journey through villages from Felipe Carrillo Puerto to Valladolid without ever being followed by a taxi containing two curious British teenagers.

The minute we're away from the bus station, I take out the Ek Naab phone, give it a hard shake and try the power switch again. Absolutely nothing. I'm not surprised, but my heart sinks. I stand, legs still aching from exhaustion, hanging on to my leather bus strap. I stare out of the window. Like the road to Becan, this road cuts directly into the jungle. The sides of the road are littered with black patches that, when we draw closer, I realize are made up of big tarantulas warming themselves on the early morning heat of the tarmac. They rear up as we rush past.

I disembark at every bus stop to keep an eye out. At one stop I buy a map to keep track of our route. I get a drink from the omnipresent street vendor who'll sell you a fizzy drink cheap if you chug it straight down and return him the bottle. The bus isn't air-conditioned, and by eleven in the morning, the temperature inside is forty degrees, with almost a hundred per cent humidity. The sweat pours off my head and down my sides.

If they think I've run, where do they think I'd run to? I figure that I'll stay hidden better by taking short trips on local buses, avoiding the main cities.

I could try to go after my grandfather's Muwan in the museum in Veracruz. But without the contents of the case – how will I break in? It's not as though I have a natural talent for thievery. I could aim for Mexico City, hide out with some colleagues of my father's, maybe find a way to contact the Mayans of Ek Naab. I even toy with the idea of trying to find my way back into Ek Naab, but I don't dare be seen anywhere near Becan. I could be leading Simon Madison and the NRO right to the city they seem so keen to destroy.

My plan to aim for Mexico City has a tricky flaw, though. I'm assuming that I can find a colleague of Dad's just by walking into the archaeology faculty of the university. Picking a name to trust, that's another matter. But Carlos Montoyo didn't turn out to be who he claimed to be. What if there are other secret agents posing as Mayanists? If any of them have connections with the NRO, I'm sunk.

So, it has to be the museum. I check the map again – it's in Jalapa. If I manage to dry out the mobile phone from Ek Naab, get it working again, I could call Benicio up to Jalapa. With another case of equipment, we'd be back in business. If the Ix Codex is there, I'll do my job and then leave the Mayans to it.

I smooth out my road map until I can only see the states along the rest of my route: Tabasco to Veracruz.

Via everywhere.

In this part of Mexico every town looks the same: rough buildings covered with political graffiti on the outskirts of town; cramped roads that can hardly fit a bus and yet seem to be the main thoroughfare into town; street vendors with their boxes of roses, phone cards, Chiclets, trays of pink meringues or whatever they happen to be selling.

I never step out of the bus without taking a good look around the station. I'm on a constant watch for police, smartly-dressed men in sunglasses, people who carry nothing. In almost every station there's something to set me off. A guy in a sleeveless T-shirt who stares openly at me. The helmeted guy on a Harley who, I'm almost certain, has been behind my last two buses. A guy in a shirt and tie who makes urgent-sounding calls on a payphone, casting nervous looks around. Could any of these people be grassing me up?

When I'm hungry, I buy potato crisps or cupcakes. Even though I've spent the whole day sweating uselessly in muggy, blistering heat, by early evening I'm dying to eat something hot.

I'm staring out of the window, watching the endless jungle scroll by. The light is beginning to fade. It's on my mind that I've been on the go since 5 a.m. As we cross into the state of Veracruz, the vegetation turns into banana and coffee plantations, orange groves with fruit at the bullet-hard, shiny green phase. The surroundings become mountainous. Volcanic peaks with coatings of mossy green frame the distant landscape like mouldy shark's teeth.

Somewhere around here, my eyes close.

I wake to find myself the last passenger on the bus. The driver is shouting at me, "Hey, dude, get off my bus!" I stagger to my feet and stumble to the front. Through the window, at the end of a street, there's water stretching as far and wide as the eye can see. Somewhere along the way, there's been a big mistake. The bus I'd taken was supposed to go deep inland.

In Spanish I say, "What the heck . . . is that the sea?"

"The lagoon," replies the driver. "Catemaco."

Catemaco. He pronounces it to rhyme with *taco*. I've never heard of the place. I grab my map, baffled. "I thought your last stop was Acayucan."

"It was. You missed it. I started on my next route and abracadabra, we're off to Catemaco. Shouldn't be such a sleepy-head, should you?"

I study my map and groan loudly. Catemaco turns out to be a big detour on the way to nowhere.

For some reason the frustration hits me massively hard. On my own, I can't do anything right. What am I thinking? How can I possibly live up to all these people's expectations?

I can't hold back the tears. I put my hand across my face to try to hide them, but it's no use. I stumble off the bus, sniffling like a little kid.

37

The bus driver locks the ignition, staring at me. "Hey, kid, don't take it so hard! I just need to park the bus for the night, I'm not mad at you. . ."

I shake my head, wiping my nose. "No . . . it's just that I really needed to get to Jalapa."

"Well, Catemaco's nice too. Why not take a rest? You look like you could use it. Buy a charm or a cure. Swim in the lake, visit the waterfall. It's really beautiful."

I take a look around. Catemaco feels unlike anywhere I've ever been in Mexico. There's a claustrophobic feel to the town, on the banks of a mysterious sea that goes nowhere, hemmed in by an intense mist. The lake and town are surrounded by thick jungle, and you know about it from the constant din of birds, insects and the occasional screech of howler monkeys.

The bus driver follows me to the gift-stand near to the bus stop, where a huge display of postcards catches my eye. It stops me in my tracks, dries my tears in an instant.

Again and again, I see images of statues, a Buddha-like stone figure; old boats moored on water; the lake in the morning, blanketed with mist.

There's something very, very familiar about them. Is it possible that I've been here before. . .with my parents? I begin to feel disoriented.

In a complete daze, I stumble down to the lakeside, where a deep ochre sunset silhouettes the low volcanoes and cliff edges around the lake. Mist rolls slowly towards the town, enveloping tiny islands that are just visible within the swirling fog. There's a mystical feel to the place.

Out of the corner of my eye, I notice that the bus driver is still behind me. I try to avoid his eye. What's wrong with the guy? Can't he leave me be?

In the distance I see something else that jolts my memory. A light-blue-painted boat carries a load of passengers under a canopy, towards a twin pair of straw huts. The huts seem to be suspended in the middle of the lake until I notice; a trick of the early evening light hides a long pier. But something doesn't look quite right. I hurry to the edge of the pier. When I look straight down the pier, see the two huts framed symmetrically on either side, the image looks right.

Finally it makes sense. I've seen these places, these images – in a dream. It's the scene of my grandfather's death.

The bus driver is right next to me now, by the water's edge. He stares at me, long and hard. "Something wrong, friend? Maybe I can help you out? A little charm, a cure for what ails you? I'm as good as any of the *brujos* you'll meet down on the Malecon, you know."

Confused, I turn to him. "What are you on about?"

"Well, don't get mad, but ever since you got off the bus, you look like you've seen a ghost." He grins. "In Catemaco, that means you probably have."

"What. . .?"

He folds his arms. "Come on, pal. Maybe I can help?"

"I've seen this place before," I mutter, half to myself. "In a dream."

"A dream, you say? What good luck – Catemaco is the perfect place to explain your dreams!"

"Catemaco? I've never heard of it."

He laughs, incredulous. "Come on now. You've never heard of the *brujos* of Catemaco?"

I stare at him. *Brujos?* He's talking about witches?

"I've never heard of it," I repeat, with a straight face.

Suddenly he stops laughing. "Your being here is no accident, friend. You've been led here by the spirits. They must know about your dream."

"Sounds like crazy talk to me."

He looks insulted. "Hey – don't be saying things like that. You'll offend the spirits!"

I start to back away from him. The guy is beginning to unnerve me.

"The spirits have led you here, pal," he says, chasing after me. "There must be a reason. Why don't you tell me your dream? Maybe I can help you out?"

I look at him. "You're a bus driver. What do you know about dreams?"

"I was born and raised here. The witchcraft, it's in my blood. But you know how it is. The town is full of charlatans, con artists trying to cash in on the fame of the *brujos*. They're bad for trade, push the prices down. Driving my bus – it pays better."

He comes closer and lays a hand on my shoulder. "I'm not messing you around here. Tell me your dream."

I hesitate. "You want money?"

He blushes and shrugs. "Well, sure, boss. But only when you're satisfied with the result."

"How much?"

"Five hundred."

I gasp. "You're crazy."

"Dreams are about destiny. And destiny costs."

I hesitate again. Five hundred pesos – that's almost forty quid!

"You don't like what you hear, you don't pay."

I sigh. What could it hurt? In a way, I'm itching to tell someone.

In the fading sunlight, under tall palms whose fronds rustle in the cooling air, I tell this *brujo* who moonlights as a bus driver about my dream. He listens without saying a single word, his face blank. When I'm done, I throw him an expectant look.

He's quiet for a very long time, staring past me, into the lake.

"Well, you got me," he says. "Could mean anything."

"What. . .? But you said. . .?"

The bus driver takes a few steps away. He shrugs. "What can I say? I was wrong. I don't have a thing to say to you. Sorry for wasting your time. OK?"

And with that, he just walks away, leaving me even more puzzled and confused than before.

The unbearable heat of the day has dropped off. There's a sudden chill. It feels as though a storm might be coming. In the last half hour, the sky has filled with heavy grey clouds. With a sigh, I start walking down the pier, looking for somewhere to stay the night.

Hotel Los Balcones is just a little further along. The rooms are arranged in a modern, long, two-storey building around landscaped gardens. Deep balconies filled with flowers separate the layers. One look is enough to tell me that it's the fanciest joint in town. I wonder how I'm going to persuade them to let a thirteen-year-old boy check in all alone.

I only know I need to sleep. To call Ek Naab, then maybe the museum.

But talking to that bus driver has unsettled me. Catemaco is where my grandfather died. That's what the dream is telling me, it has to be. Why did the bus driver go cold on me?

I find I can't focus on finding the Ix Codex any more. The threads of my life have become wrapped around me in a messy tangle. I feel their blood run hot inside me; my grandfather's and my dad's. I sense the call of a destiny I can't and don't want to understand.

In the end, it isn't too hard to persuade someone to give me a room at Hotel Balcones. "You here with your parents?" the receptionist asks, obviously suspicious. "Of course," I reply, all innocence.

"Where are they?"

"They're taking a boat ride. They wanted to be alone. You know, romantic. So they sent me to check in by myself."

She's immediately sympathetic. "How selfish of them! You poor lad! I'll give them a good ticking off when they get here."

The receptionist gives me a first-floor room with a lakeside view. The sudden change in weather hasn't taken the people of Catemaco by surprise – a tropical storm is picking up in the Gulf of Mexico. I ask her how bad it gets, this far from the coast. "We'll survive," she tells me with a friendly grin. "But by the end of the night it's going to rain, and how!"

In the room, I hunt for a hairdryer and turn it on, blowing

warm air over both of my useless mobile phones. I take my time, being careful not to let the metal heat up too much, forcing myself to be patient, turning the phones over periodically. And finally, the moment of truth: I hit the power switches.

Both phones power up. I'm ecstatic, breathless with the excitement of sudden hope. It strikes me that Catemaco is an even better place for the Mayans to pick me up. Plenty of cover in the countryside nearby for a Muwan to land.

My British mobile phone lights up for a few seconds and then bleeps with the flat-battery signal. The Ek Naab phone remains lit. The problem is, there's no signal. Not a single bar.

I step out on to my balcony. There's no improvement. I walk up and down the entire corridor, holding the phone out to try to reach a phantom signal. Zero.

I notice that the lakeside lights are already burning. Boats too have turned on the rows of white lights around their canopies. Night is drawing in, but there's no sign that I'll be able to phone for help anytime soon.

There's nothing for it but to try the phone further away from the hotel. So I go outside again, begin to stroll. On the busy part of the promenade, I notice that some tourists are negotiating with local men dressed in *indigeno* – Indian – garb. From the sounds of it, they're discussing medical matters; back pains, frozen shoulders, tumours. I guess these are the *brujos* I've heard about.

A crowd of tourists has assembled to listen to a trio of musicians. They play guitar-like instruments and strike up the popular tune "La Bamba", a *jarocho* song I've often heard my dad sing. I watch for a few seconds, check my mobile phone for a signal.

When I don't detect one, I give up and turn back to the hotel. The sky's looking really threatening now. At a hot food stall I buy a barbequed corn on the cob and munch it all the way back to the hotel.

By the time I reach my room, the rain has started. Heavy from the outset, within minutes it's a spectacular downpour. Not the gentle type of rain we get in England; a proper soaking. The balcony floor floods with water and overflows. The next floor up does the same, because suddenly there's a torrent of water coming down from the balcony above. Engulfed in sheets of rain, Catemaco seems even more isolated from the rest of the world.

In my bedroom, I pull aside the polyester bed cover and slide under the sheets. There doesn't seem to be any point undressing – it's already uncomfortably cool. Before long, I'm on the brink of sleep.

I find myself thinking back to something Camila said about the dream. The dream that she, my dad and I had all shared. She'd mentioned the Olmec Indians, how they know techniques to enter other people's dreams. *It all connects*, she'd said. But how does it all connect? Is it really possible that my being here is no accident? Is there someone in Catemaco who knows what happened to my grandfather? Can it really be possible to enter the dream of someone you've never met, never seen?

The sound of the rain continues into my dreams. I dream that I'm in my bed, at home in Oxford. My mum is knocking on my door. Have I finished my homework? Have I done my revision? I'm trying to ignore her, but she turns the doorknob. I must have a new kind of lock because she can't get in. She fiddles with the door. I have a little laugh to myself. She can't get in. But then the door gives way and she does.

The next few moments are confused. My eyes open, and after a second or two I remember where I am. It's dark, but I sense that someone else is in the room with me. I reach out for the bedside lamp when they grab my arms, pin them both behind me. I'm trying to leverage myself up with my legs when another hand grips my jaw, forces my mouth open. A warm, acrid liquid burns its way down my throat; I try to spit it out but the hand closes up my jaw, pinches my nose until I have to swallow. There's alcohol in the drink, and a strong flavour of herbs. When it hits my stomach, I start to convulse. My entire body tries to reject the fluid, panic surging through me: I'm certain I'm being poisoned. I'm gagging, I taste stomach acid, but nothing quite comes out. When I open my mouth to protest, a hand clamps over my face, cutting off the scream.

312

They hold me down as the poison takes effect. Within minutes whatever they've given me hits my brain. There's an explosion of sensation within, as though my head has been lit up from inside. I feel my muscles relax and the hands release me. There's no need for restraint now – I can barely move. I try to speak but can't. They pull me to my feet, support me with their shoulders and walk me out of the room. My vision seems blurry. I could swear that the room, corridor and the rest of the hotel rotates as we pass through.

They take me down some stairs and into the car park. I'm vaguely aware of being thrown into the back seat of a car and driven. Wherever we go, it is dark, the roads simple dirt tracks. Rain drums hard against the car. We stop amongst some trees and they carry me out. My legs don't seem to work any more. I'm conscious but almost totally out of it.

I'm pushed through a door. I'm suddenly aware of a familiar smell, a musky perfume of deep notes, so strong that it triggers a memory – another wave of déjà vu. The room is filled with a thin film of smoke, the walls lined with what look like hundreds of bottles filled with coloured liquids. Dust-covered objects hang from the ceiling; rag dolls, bones, ribbons. Candles are everywhere, all different sizes. The walls are dotted with postcards showing images of saints. In the centre of the room there's a circle of small candles set in glass tumblers; they look like the tumblers we use at school. In the middle of the circle is an old pine chair. They drag me to the

313

chair, pull off my shirt, bind my legs and arms to the chair. I can't protest; I can hardly make a sound.

My limbs may be frozen, I may have lost the power of speech, but all my other senses are heightened beyond anything I've ever known. Sounds echo loudly, reverberate inside my head. I hear whispers from people I can't see, a low thrum of music. I'm begging them to release me but I can't form the words.

When they've tied me and stripped me to the waist, they begin to smear my back and shoulders with some kind of foul-smelling ointment. I flinch from their hands at first. For a second, they stop.

"*No pasa nada*," a voice says, almost soothing. "It's nothing bad."

It's thick and greasy, like goose fat. Then, very gently, a hand lifts my head up by the chin and paints two stripes of something on to my face. All the while, the whispers and low beat of a drum fill me with dread.

I don't even know what I'm afraid of. Torture? Violence? They haven't hurt me so far, but they've drugged me, forced me to come to this place, to be part of this ceremony. The fear feels more primitive. As if I were close to something malevolent, something that just intends to use me for its own ends.

The whispers become a slow chant. From the shadows beyond, an old man emerges, dressed in white robes. A *brujo*. I know instinctively that this is not one of those street charlatans. This is the real thing.

His eyes are wide, seeming to roll around in his head. He sips from a glass of blue liquid, which he gargles, then spits into my face. The chanting gets louder. I gasp. My eyes sting from the burning juice. Now I really can't see. But I sense him approach. He begins to shout at me, moving all around the circle, yelling and barking out strange words in a language I don't understand. The sounds mingle with the incessant drone of the rain on the roof.

For the first time I have some inkling of what may be taking place. This is a purification ceremony – a casting out of evil spirits. I don't believe in evil spirits – never have – and yet between the candles and the chanting and the ointment, I feel wretched, dizzy and scared. There's something evil in this room, that's for sure.

Could there be something evil inside me?

The white-robed *brujo* finishes his shouting. He stands in front of me, speaks very loudly and clearly.

"Close your eyes, boy. See me with your inner eye."

For some reason, I obey without hesitation. It's like I'm programmed. I screw my eyes closed. I see nothing.

"Concentrate," he tells me. "Search deep within. It will come."

Then, amazingly, an image starts to form behind my eyes. It's the white-robed *brujo*. I see him clearly; clearer than if I were to open my eyes. In my mind, he's standing in a room with a thatched roof. If I concentrate hard, I can almost screen out the sounds of rain, chanting and drums. It's the room from my dream, but the vision has none of the qualities of a dream. It's harsh, stark and violent in its accuracy.

Amazed, I blurt out, "This is my dream!"

"Empty your mind of everything," the *brujo* tells me. "Let the image within consume you. Enter it. Become one with it."

I concentrate on the sound of the waves, feeling a sensation of disconnection. It's as though my consciousness slowly separates from my body, leaves it and hovers somewhere above. I'm slowly materializing in the hut. There's water all around us. We're surrounded by a wide range of bottles, candles and images of saints.

I watch as the *brujo* sits in his chair, meditating. The door swings open. A man dressed in a tattered navy jumpsuit tumbles inside. He falls to the floor. His backpack slides around, falling next to him. I see enough of his face to recognize my grandfather. In the dream I'd never noticed his clothes. But now it's clear. For the first time I see that he's dressed in the same flying uniform I've seen Benicio wear.

"Help me."

The *brujo* leaps to his feet. The next thing I'm aware of is the *brujo* feeding my grandfather a potion. There's a bout of appalling coughing, and then my grandfather seems to regain control.

"It is asthma, damn you, asthma. Haven't you got something for that?"

The choking begins once again. He collapses, coughing. The *brujo* rushes to his bottles, mixes another potion. My grandfather can barely raise his head. The *brujo* tips the bottle to my grandfather's mouth. He tastes it, protesting between splutters, "Not alcohol, you imbecile. What kind of doctor are you?"

"A medic of the spirits," says the *brujo*. "I fear your demons are too powerful."

The rest of is all too familiar. The *brujo* stands watching as my grandfather slowly chokes to death. He turns purple, his eyes bug out, flecks of spit and vomit appear at the edges of his mouth. His final words are virtually ripped out of him: "Summon the Bakab Ix."

The *brujo* places a finger on my grandfather's neck, feeling for a pulse. Then he calls out, "Roberto." A darkly tanned boy in his late teens appears at the door. Sunlight momentarily floods the gloomy surroundings. "He's dead. Fetch your brother to carry the body. We'll make an announcement in the town. He looks like a stranger, but maybe someone knows who he is."

Roberto looks down at the body, says, "What's in the backpack? Can I take it?"

He doesn't wait for the *brujo*'s reply. The boy picks up the sisal-weave backpack and opens it. I catch sight of a large volume. It looks like a book. The vision explodes with pain and confusion. I watch the boy gasp, begin to scream in agony. His mouth fills with blood, he retches, blood streams from his nose, even his eyeballs begin to bleed. He staggers around the hut, backing away from the volume in the backpack. The boy collapses face-down; his whole body convulses for a few minutes, then stops. The *brujo* finally moves slowly, touches the body of his son and rolls the body over. When he sees the boy's face, he lets out a howl of pain and distress. "My son, my son," he cries, again and again.

The images of bloody death in the hut fade. I open my eyes, pull myself up and look directly into the eyes of the old *brujo*.

Deep within me something shifts; it's as though I sense cogs that move, rotate, adjust. On the horizon of my mind there's an explosion of nuclear proportions as finally, I recognize the truth.

My grandfather had the codex with him when he died. The Ix Codex is here.

The old man speaks. "You are the 'Bakab Ix'?"

I nod. "His grandson."

"But you're just a child," he says in wonder. "And a foreigner. How can this be?"

"I don't know, sir."

"Yet it is truth. The dream cannot lie. You will take the Cursed Book far from here," he says in a flat voice. "It is possessed of tremendous evil. All who touch it die."

"I'll take it." I swallow hard, think of that poor kid Roberto. What if there's been a mistake and I'm not really the Bakab Ix?

Perhaps the *brujo* detects my fear, because he places a hand on my shoulder, saying, "Consider yourself already dead and there is nothing to lose. Take heart, son. You've shown bravery here. We shall take you to the book."

In the back seat of the car, I use my shirt to wipe away most of the ointment. We drive to a jungle clearing. The trees are so thick overhead that the canopy blocks out most of the rain. A rattlesnake slithers across our path. The *brujo* leans over, grabs it in one deft movement, and snaps the neck as if it were no tougher than a twig.

I become aware that this is no ordinary clearing – it's some kind of shrine. There's an inner ring of fat bamboo canes and at one end, a small collection of stone statues on the ground, at the wide base of a tree. The statues are of the same Buddha-like figure I remember from my dream; a cross-looking, chubby, child-like creature.

The men light two flame torches and place them inside two hollowed-out bamboo shoots which have been sliced open at the right height.

"*Chaneques*," murmurs the *brujo*, noticing me stare at the stone statues. "A changeling spirit of these forests. These live off the evil that lurks within the Cursed Book. If the Curse of the Book doesn't destroy you, the *chaneques* may terrify the very soul from of your body." He takes a few steps back. "We cannot remain. You must complete this task alone."

One of the two men who brought me steps forward. I recognize him for the first time – it's the bus driver. He just nods. "I'm sorry. But it had to be this way." He hands me a shovel. "Dig. At the base of the *ceiba*, beneath the statues of the *chaneques*. If the curse can't harm you, neither shall the chaneques. Find the Cursed Book, take it away with you."

They all back away, watch as I begin my work. Once they see I've started to dig, I notice they're leaving. "How do I get back?" I yell.

"Follow the road," answers the bus driver. "It goes to all the way to the lagoon."

I take the shovel and dig. Above me I can hear the canopy of the *ceiba* tree rattling its leaves as the storm picks up. The rain, already falling at a fierce rate, seems to redouble its effort, as if to say: *Now let's really drop some water*. And me, I'm shaking from a mixture of excitement and terror. This is it: the Ix Codex is just a few inches of dirt away.

40

I dig like a maniac, toss shovelfuls of leaves and soil over my shoulder. My skin crawls at the thought of being left alone in this place; my ears roar with the sounds of the living jungle. The stone *chaneques* stare at me, their angry little eyes brimming with accusation. I think I imagine them moving. I can hardly bear to stay. I have visions of them coming to life, swarming over me, scratching at my face, stone fingers digging mercilessly into my flesh. It doesn't matter how much I tell myself that the ceremonial drug is still in my system. I'm hallucinating, but it seems pretty darn real.

Sometime after I start digging, I find myself gazing into a pit about two feet deep. I have no sense of how much time has passed. I can't lean over far enough any more. I jump in, begin digging some more. From nearby I hear the sound of a car, tyres crunching along a gravel track. The headlamps have been switched off to allow a stealthy approach. But there's no hiding such a mechanical sound in the jungle.

I pause in my digging, look up and listen. Doors open and slam shut.

"Mr Garcia. Nice to finally catch up with you."

It's the two NRO agents – the ones who arrested Tyler and Ollie.

"So, that's gotta be the lost codex under there, right? Hey, buddy, don't let me stop you."

"That's right," says the other. "Dig."

It doesn't take much longer, just long enough for me to wonder how I've managed to screw up so badly. Where did I go wrong?

"How? How did you find me?"

"A cop called in your description from a bus station in Tabasco. Someone reported a kid who looked like he'd run away from his family. People can be neighbourly that way."

I return to my digging, numb with shock and disappointment. I try not to think about what's going to happen to me now.

I reach the buried package a few minutes later. It is still wrapped in what are now rotting threads of sisal fibre. I pick them off, hold the dense volume in my hands. It's a solid box; not exactly a book, more a case. The box is covered with a soft, dry-yet-spongy material that yields to the slightest touch. Incredibly, it is perfectly clean; dust won't even to stick to it. I'm about to give it a few more prods when one agent shouts, "Cut that out. We'll take it from here." He reaches down, snatching the box.

I try to warn him. "I don't think you should. . ."

He ignores me, of course.

Pandemonium.

At first I can't tear my eyes away as one, then the other, agent falls to his knees, clutching first his throat, then his chest, stomach, all the while screaming, a sound so terrible I want to cover my ears to stop listening to the sheer agony. The bleeding starts seconds after. Their screams become muffled as blood bubbles up inside their throats, choking them. They try spitting it out, but more spews up. Into the warm, peaty smell of the forest mingles the rusty odour of fresh blood.

They're dying, just as I'd seen the *brujo*'s son die, in the most agonizing way I can imagine, their insides liquefying, organs rupturing, screaming to the bitter end.

I feel my legs weaken. I turn away. There's nothing I can do to help them. I have a feeling those terrible cries of anguish will haunt me for a long time yet.

Trembling from the horror of what I've seen, I climb out of the ditch. I grab the codex. I haven't even made it out of the jungle clearing when another car pulls up behind the first. Another door slams. And into view comes the back-up plan: Simon Madison.

"OK, Josh, nice job, now drop the codex, nice and slow."

I hesitate. "I would, but . . . you really want to end up like your mates?"

Madison glances at the two guys who lie squirming on the floor, still retching and groaning as blood spurts from their mouths, noses and eyes. He seems genuinely shocked.

"What in hell did you do to them?"

I shake my head. "Nothing. The codex. It's cursed."

To my surprise, he doesn't laugh or show any sign of disdain. He just waves his pistol at me. "How come you're not like them?"

"Immunity?"

"So you really are one of them. . ." is all he says, with bitterness.

While I'm wondering what he means, tense seconds pass. He seems to be frozen with indecision, keeps looking at the codex, his eyes full of apprehension.

"Know what I'm thinking, Madison?" I say, stalling for more time. "I'm wondering how close I need to get to you, to make you die like them."

41

I lunge towards him, hoping desperately that he won't fire the gun. My gamble pays off. As I approach, Madison lurches backwards in instinctive fear. He trips, falls and lands on his back. His gun goes off, the bullet zinging through the leaves. I lob the codex as far away as possible, vault over his body, clear him with my legs and arms safely out of reach and land with a handstand flip. I stop only to lean over and pick up the codex. I head straight for the blue Nissan, parked behind the first car, a Taurus.

I have absolutely no idea to drive, but luckily it's an automatic. I feel as though I'm in one of those dreams where you want to run but your limbs feel heavy and numb. I want to turn the blue Nissan round, but for the life of me I can't think how. Driving always looks so easy!

In a narrow trail between the trees, I try frantically to get a three-point turn out of the car. All that happens is that the car backs up, lurches forward, backs up again until I'm cursing out loud. My hands are so slick with sweat, they barely grip the steering wheel. I finally give up when I see Madison jumping into the other car up ahead. I shift into reverse and slam my foot on to the accelerator.

The rain has stopped almost as abruptly as it began, like a tap being closed. The downpour has already turned the ground into a mud bath, and for a heart-stopping second, the car doesn't budge an inch, its wheels spinning like crazy. And then the tyres get some grip and I'm moving, zooming backwards out of the jungle.

The reversing lights cast a beam deep into the trees. I can't remember how long it took to get here, but reversing out seems to be painfully slow. Madison is only metres behind me, making exactly the same manouevre. *Straight down to the lake*, the bus driver told me. Twisted round in the car, peering into the darkness of the jungle, I pray that he's right.

The lake springs on me almost too late to avoid it. There are no buildings around, no lights of any kind. Only the sudden absence of trees and the fathomless black ahead give me any warning that the road is about to run out. I stop the car with a violent lunge. I throw myself out, clutching the codex. I'm just in time to see Madison's car tumble down the same slope out of the jungle, crashing into the Nissan. I don't stop to see whether he's survived. There's a momentary silence. It crosses my mind that I'm free.

I'm already running along the lakeside, searching the water for any sign of a boat. Back near the town there were craft of all different types moored on the water. In the distance I hear a car door open – Madison is alive. Even running in the dark, I know I'll never be safe from him – he has a gun. On water I might have a chance to evade him.

Madison's bullets must be numbered because he doesn't waste any shooting at me in the dark. There is just enough starlight to see the water. It's my only guide to where I'm going. I hear him giving chase – he isn't far behind. His footsteps sound disturbingly light and fast. After a few minutes I see what I've been hoping for – a small rowing boat. And more importantly – only one.

I jump in, drop the codex on to the hull with a heavy thud. I spend a few seconds untying the mooring knot before Madison catches up. He comes into view at the very last second, about twenty metres behind. Triumph and disappointment combine in one sudden glance when he sees that I've found a boat. Seeing him lift his pistol arm, I give the shore a hefty push and hurl myself into the bottom of the boat. He shoots; I hear a bullet crack noisily, splintering wood at the stern.

I row in small, rapid strokes with no break until the shore recedes. When Madison is as close as he's going to get, I duck down again. This time there's no gunshot. I guess that a lucky shot might get me now. Then again, it might just waste another bullet. Plus, I have the feeling I'm worth more to him alive. Whatever Madison knows about Ek Naab, he's certain that I know much more. He's desperate for that information.

Then he disappears, continuing down the shore. My muscles relax automatically. I rest for the first time since digging under the shrine. Only now do I realize how hard my heart is pumping, the blood pounding in my ears. I double over, gasping, trying to catch my breath. I know I shouldn't stop but it's impossible not to feel a tiny sense of relief.

I gaze across the shiny black depths, where thick mist looms ahead. Will the islands be somewhere inside? I don't see that I have any other option than to aim directly for the heart of that fog. Lying about halfway across the lake, the mist rises like a smoky wall, concealing the lake's interior.

I've rowed almost four hundred metres across the water. Then I hear the approach of a motor boat. I hold my breath, listening. It's obvious within seconds that the boat is headed my way. I grab both oars and row hard, pulling the boat closer to the mist. As Madison's boat approaches, I notice that he's found a torch. Its long beam reaches out over the water, seeking me out. Just as we disappear before each other's eyes, a thick column of mist between us, his torchlight locks for one second on to my face. For that brief instant, I'm blind.

Under dense swirls of grey mist, I change direction. I row

to the right, away from the interior, towards the secretive eastern bank of the lake.

Inside that cloud, sounds seem muffled. The world outside disappears, with all its whirring insect life and distant echoes of howler monkeys. Within, the sounds of my boat are amplified. The splashes of my oars sound riotously loud. Silence is my greatest ally now – Madison's torch will penetrate less than a few feet inside this mist.

When his motorboat enters the mist, I know about it. He cuts the engine, keen to gain the element of surprise through stealth. I don't know for how long we float around, perhaps only a few metres apart.

Finally, he calls into the gloom, "Josh. It's the end of the road. Give yourself up."

When I don't reply, he shouts louder, "I'm gonna wait here until morning. You can't escape, you know it."

Making only tiny movements now, I propel the boat forward. I'm inching along now, but it's still progress. I hear him start up the engine once more.

"You ever hear of a search grid, Josh? I'm gonna find you, kid. And when I do, you're gonna tell me everything there is to tell about Ek Naab. Oh, you might hold out a little while, but not for long."

From behind the mist, land looms abruptly. An island appears before me, the gnarled branches of its trees close enough to touch. I steer the boat into a snug, tiny cove, jam it into place with the oars. Land stretches in all directions ahead. This is no speck of beach, but a major island – big enough to hide on.

Taking the codex with me, I climb on to the shore. I pull out the mobile phone. It may be useless as a communication device, but it works as a torch. Fog and darkness have combined to make this a treacherous place to walk at night. And all those poisonous creatures I worried about in the Yucatan jungle – they'll be here too.

Madison hovers close by, enough to hear his boat. Any second now he's going to discover the island. I find a path and break into a run. I'm vaguely thinking of caves, or a tree; anything that might hide me until morning, when the tourists are sure to arrive on those pale blue launches.

I pass an area of mounds that could be some archaeological remains – stone platforms and terraces. I'm running so fast now that I almost skid headlong into a swamp. I'm about to turn around when I notice a dark shape moving in the water. I freeze. It couldn't be. . . Ahead, to my left, another shadow shifts, then another next to it. Soon the whole swamp is a heaving mass of slithering bodies.

Crocodiles. They've picked up my scent. I'm being hunted.

I'm faced with a killer on one side and crocodiles on the other. Icy terror grabs hold of me. I feel the same dread I experienced in the sea, fearing a shark would appear, that I would be consumed, alive and screaming, by the razor-like teeth of a wild beast. Now, this is no figment of my imagination; it's completely real.

I slowly back up the slope towards drier land. Only steps away there's a mangrove tree, the roots spread wide around the base. I hurl myself at the tree, manage to land a good distance up the roots and scramble higher. I hear the crocodiles' teeth scrape at the wood under my feet. For one hideous second I even feel their rancid breath against my ankles. Even from up the tree, I can smell fish rotting in their guts. When I've clambered far enough out of reach, I turn my phone light on to them. Hopelessly, I look for an escape route.

There's no possible escape. The light seems to make them even crazier, lashing their tails and snarling themselves into a frenzy. The beady, evil eyes of a dozen crocodiles gleam back at me from the ground. I find myself wondering about Madison, and if he has the nerve to tackle the whole crew of crocs.

As I move to turn off the mobile phone, I notice that there's one bar of signal showing. It's such an amazing sight that for a minute I wonder if I'm imagining things. I climb higher into the tree. I graze my legs and arms but I don't care. A second bar appears on the phone's display. Relief cascades through me. Almost laughing, I dial Benicio, just as he showed me.

He picks up without a single ring.

"Where the hell are you?!" he screams, furious.

"In a lake . . . Catemaco," I tell him. "On an island."

I sense his relief, too. Benicio's voice becomes calmer, serious. "East or west of the town?"

"Er . . . east, I think."

"Are there howler monkeys?"

"I think I heard some, yeah."

He pauses as if to catch his breath. "Are there ruins?"

"Yes," I say. "Definitely."

"OK. Good. Thank God! You're on Isla Agaltepec. Don't move. I'm coming for you."

"I'm not moving."

"Good."

"Benicio . . . I'm up a tree."

"Is probably a good idea. There is *crocodilos* in that lake."

"And . . . Simon Madison is looking for me."

Benicio swears softly under his breath.

"And . . . Benicio . . . I've got the codex."

Benicio's Muwan drops vertically, coming to a halt several metres above my head. From the outline I see immediately that it's a Mark II – much larger than the Mark I. It's like a gigantic bat's shadow, blocking the rain, and creating a faint glow of cloud particles that reflect the Muwan's lights. I wait for a few seconds, wondering what kind of high-tech tool Benicio will use to get me inside the craft without landing. A sisal-weave bag like the one Ixchel had been carrying lands on my upturned face, attached to a climbing rope. Above, I hear Benicio say, "Put the codex in the bag!"

Once he's taken the codex safely on board, he lowers the rope for me. A rope ladder would have been even better, but at least this one has a series of thick knots on which I'm able to stand. The Muwan hovers unsteadily, swings lightly with my weight.

I clamber over the cockpit, startled to catch sight of Benicio's face behind what looks like a gas mask. We stare at each other through the windscreen for a second. He beams a big smile, gives me a thumbs-up. When I climb into the passenger seat, he turns around.

"Nice going, cousin!"

"What's with the mask?"

"With that thing around," he says, indicating the bag containing the codex, "only you are safe within a metre of it."

"So it's . . . a gas?"

"Sure," he says, his voice distinctly cheery even when muffled. "What did you think? Magic?" And he bursts out laughing. "Josh, dude. This is incredible news!"

The window through which I climbed begins to retract. I strap myself into the seat. The humming noise alters; a subtle harmonic shift. The Muwan lifts. I clutch my seat, almost gag at the next – sudden and violent – lurch; a crazy right-hand spin. The Muwan banks left, flips by 180 degrees within less than a second. Just as being in a Cessna feels more like you're actually flying than when you ride a commercial jet, this sensation has an essence to it that's totally new. Maybe you get that in those really advanced fighter jets – I wouldn't know. At this moment, however, I'm certain I've experienced something beyond what I've imagined is possible inside a machine. The Muwan Mark II feels like a bird – simple as that.

"All four codices are kept in the original casings," Benicio shouts. "That's thousands of years old! The coating is made of some material we still don't understand. A matrix of some kind; partly organic, partly synthetic. It's resistant to destruction by anything except a strong denaturing acid, which would destroy the contents too, obviously."

"But gas?"

"Released when someone activates the matrix," he replies. "By simple touch."

"Gas did *that* to those guys?"

Benicio seems alarmed. "It killed people?"

"Yeah," I confirm sadly. "I watched it. Horrible."

It's clear from his silence – this is a setback.

"Tell me it didn't kill anyone important."

"They were agents," I tell him. "From the NRO. The guys who captured me in Chetumal."

Benicio seems to go berserk. He drags hard at the controls of the Muwan. We accelerate forward, the sudden G-force pressing me back hard into the seat.

"Josh, I need to know how those agents found you. Did they lead you to the codex? Or was it the other way around?"

"They followed me. They're the three guys who've been following me since I got to Mexico. One of them captured me when you dropped me off."

"I knew it! Was a *stupid* thing to do! Didn't I tell you? And I took the blame, just so you know. So all three are dead?"

"No, Simon Madison isn't. He chased me all the way on to the island."

Benicio groans. "So he saw me pick you up."

"Well, yeah. Him and anyone else who might have been looking out over Lake Catemaco."

"That's nothing. There is always UFO sightings out here. No one takes it seriously."

"Madison will."

"Yeah, he will."

But our conversation is cut short. As we fly low over the mountainous terrain, I grasp the fact that we're not alone in the sky. Three spherical lights appear in the distant sky ahead, crossing our path.

"Those aren't our planes . . . are they?"

"No," Benicio replies grimly. "They are not."

And one look is enough to tell me that they aren't your everyday fighter planes either.

Benicio curses softly when those three lights appear on the horizon.

"Three," he mutters. "Caray! I've never outrun three."

"You've seen these before?"

"Yeah," he breathes. "Sometimes I'll see one. And it'll chase me. Never seen three."

"What are they?"

"You can't tell? They're Muwan. That's how they look from outside, when the anti-gravity drive is fully engaged."

"We glow?"

"Yeah. When you get in the mood for a physics lesson, let me know; I'll give you all the details."

"I'll live without, thanks."

Wait a minute. . .

"It's the NRO, isn't it?"

"We've never been certain of it. But, yeah, I think we can put two and two together here."

"Are they armed?"

"You bet."

"Are *we* armed?"

"Not like them. And if we fire on them, we start the war. So, we run."

"This is how it happened with my dad, isn't it? This is how they got him."

Benicio doesn't reply. He points the nose of the Muwan upwards and accelerates so fast that for a second or two I literally can't breathe. Underneath us, the three glowing lights stop in midair and swoop upwards, following.

"Let's show these guys what they're missing in their Mark Is."

The Muwan shoots up; slams us back into our seats for what seems an unreasonable length of time. Where are we going – the moon? My legs and arms are pinned into position; the urge to move becomes unbearable. If I could make my voice heard, I'd beg Benicio to stop. Outside, the sky turns from a star-speckled, deep navy blue to pitch-black, and a star field so thick, it's as though the lights just came on. We've reached the stratosphere, I guess. At the very least.

The craft decelerates and levels off. I can't see the spherical lights anywhere now.

"They still on our tail?"

"They are," comes his terse reply.

"Where?"

"Seven o'clock," he says, angling the craft so that I can watch their approach.

"What are you waiting for?"

"Them. The Mark I is like a slug at terminal velocity. When we hit rock bottom, they won't have any idea which direction I'm pulling out."

"Terminal velocity. . .?"

"That's it. Hey, Josh, you like roller coasters?"

And then we drop, just like a stone.

If the gravity was bad on the way up, it's pure insanity on the descent. My guts smash into my diaphragm and stay there jammed against it. It's impossible to believe that Benicio's still in control. Every sense is telling me that we're hurtling to our deaths. I can't stop thinking about those people who jumped from the Twin Towers. I badly don't want to think about that, I don't want those images in my head while I feel this appalling, deadly rush. Eventually I stop holding back. I scream.

Benicio joins in, but he's not screaming with fear.

"*Wooooooooooo hoooooo!*" he yelps as the Muwan brakes sharply and pulls out into a horizontal swoop. "Yabadaba doo!"

Yabadaba doo? Who actually *says* that?

And then it's back to all his favourite Mexican curse words, this time belted out with a gusto that I've never seen from him before.

"Dude, I am a GOD!" he roars, laughing. "Just watch them try to do that without blowing apart."

"Did we lose them?"

"Nope. They're on our six."

"What?"

"It's cool. They can't catch us now. And their weapons are out of range."

"But they'll see where we land."

"Don't think so."

I look down to see we're flying low above the ground again. There are mountains everywhere, sparsely covered by trees. Ahead is the sea, by the second growing larger in the screen.

"The Gulf?"

"The Pacific Ocean," says Benicio. "We're flying over Chiapas. Tapachula."

We drop still lower, change direction as we fly over a huge installation underneath. Seconds later, behind us I see the three Mark Is swing around the same collection of buildings, still following us.

We're heading straight for a huge, conical volcano. It looms, dominating the entire screen. Benicio takes us so low that we're practically hugging the terrain. As we fly over the crater, the Muwan swerves suddenly to the left, around the cone and then flips up, looping backwards. Straight into the jagged opening of the crater, only metres above the rocks.

I'm bracing for impact when the rock wall ahead parts and we fly into a wide tunnel.

"We're in the volcano?"

I hear his smile. "You got it, coz."

The tunnel leads vertically through the heart of the extinct volcano, into a huge, empty magma chamber beneath.

And it's lit. Four powerful arc lights beam like little suns, lighting up the vast space. It's at least the size of the chamber of Ek Naab. Benicio skims the Muwan around the perimeter at a sedate pace. At intervals the walls of the chamber give way to plunging tunnels that lead who knows where, their lights disappearing into the far distance. Eventually Benicio finds what he's looking for and turns into one of these tunnels.

We fly along in silence for a few seconds. I'm so astounded that I can't think of anything but dumb questions. I've just about had enough of being the wide-eyed kid around Benicio, and I'm beginning to wish I were the one yelling, *Dude – I am a GOD!* After all, I brought the codex back. . .

So, I wait for him to speak. Which, of course, he eventually does.

"Pretty cool, no?"

"Oh yeah."

The tunnel emerges on a mountainside miles away. The Muwan bursts free of the rock and into the cool air of a misty early dawn. We fly out, low, coasting under the lip of a small canyon with a river at the bottom. After a few miles of following the river, Benicio changes direction. We jump out of the canyon, back over fields and hills. Then we're over the jungle, heading straight for the blue line on the horizon – the Caribbean Sea. Twenty minutes later the craft slows to a complete stop, hovers and lowers on to a deserted beach.

So – Chetumal again.

I can scarcely believe this is happening: I'm back, with the Ix Codex. And I did it all by myself. Well, practically.

BLOG ENTRY: VIGORES AND ME

ᛌＯ◫ＷᛇᛎＡᛜ◁᛭Ƨ

It was about five in the morning. Still gloomy; the sun was still over the horizon. I walked with Benicio through the deserted streets of Chetumal, to the banks of a river. Benicio pointed and I saw right away what he wanted me to do.

"There he is," he said. "He's waiting for you."

I stared at the figure sitting on the bench by the river. Blanco Vigores, dressed in a loose-fitting, cream-coloured linen suit and a panama hat. He hadn't heard us approach, or if he had, he was ignoring us. It looked like he was deep in thought. Or something.

Not exactly what I was expecting, to be honest. For some reason, I'd assumed that Carlos Montoyo would be the one to greet me. But no. I guess this codex business – it's between us Bakabs.

Benicio left me with the old guy, and even left his own gas mask, because we both noticed that Vigores hadn't brought his own. *Forgetful*, Benicio said, tutting. Benicio went back to the Muwan, I guess. To wait.

When he'd gone, I walked over to the bench. Vigores didn't move, even when I was right there. I cleared my throat. "It's me, sir. Josh."

He looked up slowly. It struck me then how lonely he looked.

"Hello again, young Josh."

"I've got the codex," I said, a bit pointlessly.

He smiled. "I know."

"You need the gas mask."

Vigores just patted the empty space on the bench beside him. "Sit at the end of the bench. I'll be fine."

So there we sat in silence for a few seconds. Me, nervous about the deadly poison gas that was released from the codex every time something nudged its case. Vigores, sitting there as calm as you like.

He asked after my mother, which threw me completely.

"Umm ... better than she was. She got my friends out of jail. So, that was good."

He nodded. "Will she let you come to live with us in Ek Naab?"

I shrugged. "Would she have to come too?"

"Of course."

"I can't see that happening."

"Why not?"

"Cos she has a life. Even without my dad, she's got her friends and her job."

And she's not going to fit in at Ek Naab, I wanted to say. *Nor me.* But it might have sounded rude.

"Josh, it may not be safe for you in Oxford now. Simon Madison knows about you now. He knows what you are. What he knows, *they* will know."

"But he knows that I've already found the codex. He'll work out pretty quick that it's gone back to Ek Naab."

"Even so, the knowledge you have is dangerous. To you, Josh. And to anyone you choose to tell."

I guessed he was talking about Tyler and Ollie. So I made a decision. "I won't tell. Not my friends, not my mum. I'll be like a vault."

The old man turned to me, but this time his eyes didn't meet mine. "You still have the phone we gave you. Use it to call us whenever you are in danger. Or even if you just suspect."

I waited for him to say something else, but that seemed to be it.

"So . . . now what?"

"You can go back to your friends in the hotel."

"That's it?"

Mildly, he replied, "What did you expect? A hero's welcome?"

Well, yeah, actually . . . why not?

What Blanco Vigores tells me is way too secret to blog.

I swallow. "Some answers would be good."

Vigores nods, leans on his stick and gazes into the river. "Go ahead."

"Well . . . I want to know about the codex, of course! Can I see it?"

He doesn't take his eyes off the river. "You want to see it? Very well. Open the codex casing by holding both sides at once, locate the dimple studs with your fingers, press them in and hold for ten seconds."

I do as he says. The dimple studs are tiny depressions on the left and right sides of the box, inside which are tiny hidden buttons. These yield only to hard pressure, enough to mark my fingertips after holding them in for ten seconds. Nothing happens until the tenth second. Then I hear a hissing sound, like a vacuum being released. Around the edges of the top of the case, a crease appears. Until then, the volume looked impossible to open. I run my fingers along the crease and dig a fingernail underneath. The hissing sound grows louder for a second. Then there's was a final little *pop*. The lid springs open.

Inside there's a pile of thick parchment pages, tanned with age, folded concertina-fashion, just like Mayan codices I've seen in museums. The hieroglyphs are rendered in faded colours. The pages are thick, densely covered with glyphic writing.

"Pick it up," Vigores says with pride. "Your ancestors' work."

"Itzamna wrote this?"

"Not this actual codex. You'll see no codex this old – almost fifteen hundred years! It's almost a shame to destroy it, but destroy it we must."

"What?" I can barely hide my indignation. After everything I've been through to bring it back?

"You misunderstand. Parchment doesn't preserve well; even in a hermetic environment like this case, its days are numbered. Therefore, a Bakab must make a faithful transcription at least every fifty years. Only when the reproduction has been passed as a faithful and authentic transcription by the other three Bakabs, do we destroy the former version."

"Why?"

"Such was Itzamna's instruction."

"But why? You could copy it, scan it, distribute it. . ."

Vigores interrupts gently, "This knowledge isn't for general consumption, Josh."

"You want to keep all this knowledge to yourselves?" I say. "You think that's right?"

Vigores says, "So have we been instructed."

"That's what Madison has against you all, you know."

Vigores just nods calmly.

"That's what he said. 'We're gonna do what the *conquista* should have done. We're gonna finish off Ek Naab.' Something on those lines."

"The information in the Ix Codex will lead to a powerful technology. Perhaps the most powerful yet – the technology to counteract the electromagnetic pulse of the superwave. That power mustn't fall into the wrong hands, Josh."

"But *how will it do that*?"

"Well," he says with a bashful grin, "we haven't read the codex yet. We need to transcribe, then decipher it. Now," he says, tapping the space beside us with his white stick, "seal the case again. The sea air is highly damaging to parchment."

I take a final glance at the parchment pages. It's incredible to think they can hold such a secret. And to anyone but the people in Ek Naab, the writing is total gobbledygook. Written in a code, using Mayan glyphs. Then I close the codex case and return it to the sisal backpack, safely at the other end of the bench.

"But this amazing power . . . it's safe in your hands?"

"We're not interested in world domination, Josh. We're guardians of an ancient secret, something that will preserve civilization on the planet. Every member of Ek Naab's community is dedicated to that end."

"And what happens after 2012?"

Vigores sighs. "Well, that's another matter."

"So it could be that everything Itzamna did was to save civilization from the 2012 thing?"

"Yes."

"And after 2012, you're free. Ek Naab will have this amazing technology. What will they do with it?"

Vigores looks thoughtful. "By then you'll be part of the Executive. You can shape the destiny of Ek Naab. In fact, young Josh, I'm sure that you will. As for the technology being safe in our hands, the alternative is rather more dangerous. Josh, if we don't develop this technology, at the end of 2012, the world will be propelled back into the nineteenth century. With the population problems of the twenty-first. Oh, without computers there won't be any machinery of war. But as we've seen, if people want to kill each other badly enough, they'll use knives, axes, clubs. And millions can die."

I struggle to grasp the implications of the vast responsibility they've suddenly loaded on to me. If I choose to help them, to follow the destiny that's been laid out for me, I might save civilization, sure: whilst equipping Ek Naab with the kind of power that would corrupt anyone. If I don't, then I can take a ticket for the line of "people who destroyed civilization".

"You hesitate only because you don't believe in your heart that a civilization can end," Vigores remarks. "You've lived your whole life in a thriving civilization that can see its direct, unbroken origins in the Middle Ages. But remember for one minute what you've seen of fallen empires – the ancient Greeks, Romans. Of us, here in Mexico. Just as you've walked in the ruined streets of our Mayan cities, don't imagine that one day people won't stroll through the ruins of Manhattan, of Trafalgar Square. This has happened to every other civilization on the planet so far. It will happen again. We all exist in the shadow of tomorrow."

"What will you do with the codex now?"

"I'll take it back to Ek Naab and we'll begin the transcription. A pilot will pick me up shortly."

"Not Benicio?"

"Benicio has other orders. You should go to him now. Say your goodbyes."

I stare at Vigores again. I feel as though I'm missing something here. Like there's something between us, something unsaid. He seems sad and resigned and I don't understand why.

All I can manage to say is, "So, you and me. Think we'll ever meet again?"

He nods. "I'm sure of it. But not for a while. I suspect you'll grow up a great deal before we do."

"Well . . . yeah, of course. I'm not a little kid any more."

Almost wistfully, he replies, "That's true. I wish it didn't have to happen so quickly. But there it is, things are what they are."

His manner suddenly changes. "Now, go. Benicio will be waiting for you."

"Don't forget the gas mask," I say. Vigores nods absentmindedly. I'm worried that he hasn't heard me, so I push the gas mask into his hands. I picture the codex being received in Ek Naab. By a bunch of Mayans wearing full-on protective clothing, I'd guess.

Still staring into the water, Vigores tells me, "Josh, you've made us prouder than you can know."

I don't know what to say other than, "Thanks!"

"Goodbye, young Josh."

"Goodbye," I tell him, standing up, trying to think of something else to say. "I'll keep in touch."

And then his face turns up, looks in my direction. "One more thing, Josh. The storm."

"Yeah, it hit, big time," I say. "In Catemaco."

Vigores shakes his head. "No," he replies. "It's yet to come."

"Uh . . . OK," I tell him. Why is he telling me about a storm? "I'll warn Benicio. . ."

Vigores just looks right past me as I walk away. Well, I

guess he *is* blind. I leave him sitting on the riverbank and catch up with Benicio in front of Hotel Delfin.

Benicio turns to me, arms outstretched. "Give me a hug, cousin. This is goodbye."

"So you're not going back to Ek Naab?"

"Not me, not right now. I've got something else to do."

I hover, curious. "Yeah, Vigores said. What's up?"

When he answers, Benicio seems almost reluctant to speak. "Well, it's about Ixchel. She didn't come back yet, which is kind of strange. We've lost touch with her."

"She's done this before?"

Benicio looks glum. "Uh huh."

"She keeps running away from home?"

"Well . . . she is kinda angry with the decision of the *atanzahab*."

"The matchmaker?"

Suddenly it all makes sense. The arranged marriages for the Bakabs. The sudden appearance in her life of the last guy in the world she wanted to see.

"It's me, isn't it?" I say slowly. "She's supposed to marry *me*. And she doesn't want to."

Benicio says nothing, flashing me a look that's somewhere between sympathy and annoyance.

It's nothing personal, Ixchel had said. *A matter of principle*.

Now it's pretty clear – those words were really intended for me. I don't want an arranged marriage either. Well, of course not. But I don't much like the feeling I'm getting right now.

"She 'usually comes back'," I say. "But now that she's actually met me, she's gone for good?"

"It's not personal," murmurs Benicio.

"Why are *you* going? Shouldn't it be me?"

"You?" Benicio laughs. "You're a kid! You don't know your way around Mexico."

Angrily, I say, "I did OK. Found the codex, didn't I?"

"Hey, you already knew where it was. Montoyo told us about your dream. That's why I let you go."

I'm stunned. "You . . . let me go?"

"I saw what happened on the beach with Madison, saw your friends rescue you."

I stare at him, dumbstruck.

Benicio continues. "I saw you leave your friends at the service station. So I called to Carlos. And he ordered me not to pick you up. To let you wander. You had a journey to complete, Josh. You carried the location of the codex in your subconscious."

"You let me go. . .?" I repeat, reeling.

"I lost you in Acayucan," he comments. "Looked for you in the bus station. Guess you didn't get off the bus."

"You were tailing me?"

"On a motorbike. We carry one in the belly of the Muwan."

"A Harley?"

"Yeah."

I stare at him. "I saw you," I tell him.

"When I lost you," Benicio says, "I went back to the Muwan, back to Ek Naab."

"Good thing for me I got that mobile phone working."

"They can survive almost anything, those phones."

I'm silent, chewing my lip. It's tough to deal with the fact that the Mayans were prepared to leave me in situations of potential violence, of real danger.

Benicio touches my arm. "We didn't hang you out to dry, Josh."

He looks uncomfortable, though. Like he's itching to leave. He pats my back again. "We'll see each other again, I'm sure."

Will we? But when? Now that they've got their precious codex, seems to me that the Mayans of Ek Naab are only too keen to get back to business.

"Oh, I almost forgot," Benicio says, "Carlos sent you something." He hands me a pen-sized syringe. "For when the NRO talk to you. Which they will want to do, and soon. This will make it possible not to give away the secrets of Ek Naab."

"The amnesia juice? Oh . . . now I get it. You want me to forget everything?"

"Don't worry!" laughs Benicio. "This just works to

354

suppress your nervous system. A tranquillizer. You'll be as cool as a cucumber for several hours. Even a polygraph test won't crack this."

I look at the syringe. "The NRO. . .? What should I tell them?"

"Just tell them what they want to hear."

"Which is. . .?"

Benicio shrugs. "Hey, who better than you to invent something, Blog Boy? Just tell them what they already believe."

"Have you been drinking, son?" asks the first agent, the one who calls himself Jack.

It's the first time I truly appreciate that evil doesn't have to dress in black, wear gothic clothes, have fangs, horns or red eyes, doesn't have to burn incense. Evil wears a suit and tie, a friendly smile, smells of after-shave. Makes deadly decisions. Kills people who get in the way of its plans as if they were ants. And then calls you *son*.

With bleary eyes, I look up at this cold-blooded murderer. And try to hide my hatred.

"I'm just tired," I admit. "Been awake for almost two days. Least, it feels like that."

"It's just that . . . this story . . . it's kind of incredible."

"You've heard stuff like this before," I say. "You must have."

"I'm not saying it's unprecedented," he acknowledges. "But this thing about the aliens having a base under the volcano. . ."

"They have more than one," I say. "There are bases under other volcanoes."

"You went to other bases?"

"I did. We flew in through one and came out through another."

"Son . . . most of the volcanoes around here are still active."

I just shrug.

"What did the aliens look like?"

"I already told you. Standard Greys."

"Like in *The X-Files*?" he asks, making no attempt to hide his scepticism.

I nod. "Like the *Greys* in *X-Files*."

"Why were you in Catemaco?"

"I don't remember why. They gave me mind-control drugs. Everything that happened there is hazy."

"How did our agents die?"

"I've no idea. Maybe a poisonous gas?"

"And then this ship that picked you up . . . that was them again?"

"Yes. And then others chased us. Three other ships. Dunno who they were. Didn't understand what they were saying."

"How do they talk?"

"It's sort of clicky."

"Jack" and his colleague "Steve". They say they're both

with the NRO, but the badges they show me are CIA. They keep staring at the polygraph trace, which is as clean as a whistle. They look pretty nonplussed. After taking my statement for over two hours, they put their heads together.

"Let's talk about this guy, the one you called 'Blue Nissan'."

"That was back then."

"What?"

"That's what I called him. Back then when those things were happening to me. Before I was abducted for the first time."

"You're referring to your abduction in the jungle, on the way to Becan?"

"Yeah. I called him 'Blue Nissan' then, but it's not his name."

"His name is Simon Madison?"

"That's what I said."

They both nod, whisper to each other, then continue. "Can you pick him out? From a few photos?"

"Sure."

They bring up a collection of photographs on their laptop computer. Madison's face is the fourth one to appear. "It's him," I tell them.

"Now, you say you assumed he was with us?"

"He'd been tailing Camila for ages. I heard one of the NRO guys tell the hotel guy at Delfin that he was NRO. We just assumed."

"Mm-hmm."

"So he isn't?"

They take a long time deciding how to phrase their next statement. Finally they admit, "Simon Madison is wanted by the FBI in connection with several serious charges."

"What charges?"

"Data theft, identity theft, fraud. Unlicensed weapons: the list goes on."

"Doesn't sound so bad."

"It's the combination that's dangerous. Highly characteristic of a deeply embedded terrorist cell. And from what you've told us, he's violent too."

"What's he up to?"

"Well, lately he's interested in stealing ancient Mayan artefacts that have tremendous importance to extra-terrestrial visitors, according to you."

"He threatened to torture and kill me," I say. "Even shot at me. That part I remember pretty vividly."

"Why do you think the 'Greys' want this Mayan codex?"

"No idea," I reply.

"Why did they use *you* to get to it?"

"Because of the dream. The one the *brujo* planted in my head."

They look disappointed, consult their interview record. "You already said that."

It goes on for another four hours. I stick to the truth as

much as possible, but say nothing about Ek Naab. Where I don't have a good answer prepared, I claim amnesia. I tell the NRO that I'd been contacted by Greys – alien visitors here to check up on the civilization they'd helped to start back in 3000 BC. That they had bases on the moon and under several extinct volcanoes. I spin a story so rich in detail, so complex, that it takes six hours to complete. I could have done it in two, but they insist on hearing it over and over.

Without the tranquillizer, I'd probably have broken. It would have been impossible to hide my fury with the NRO about what happened to my dad.

Which one of you bastards killed him? The drug gives me little option other than to be calm, polite and genial throughout. And just a bit spacey.

In the end, they're the ones who sweat with exasperation. Couldn't have dreamt up a better result.

"How about this identity theft?" I say. "If he isn't Simon Madison, then what's his real name?"

"There's a long trail of identities," Jack tells me. He sounds drained. "The earliest one we can find is Simon Martineau."

Martineau. I know that name. From where?

They release me after that. Waiting outside the police station with Tyler and Ollie is Camila's husband, Saul. After over a month in jail, he's lean and gaunt. He says nothing, but when he sees me, he gives me a hug and his eyes fill with tears.

I can hardly bear to look at Saul. He reminds me of my part in Camila's death. I keep thinking that if only Camila hadn't got involved, she'd still be alive. She died because she wanted to help. Without Camila, I'd never have made the connection with Ek Naab.

But something tells me that the Mayans would have come for me anyway. Eventually.

BLOG ENTRY: IN THE SHADOW OF TOMORROW

ᴏ⳩ᴀꙂᴐᴍᴏꓘᴎ

Tomorrow, Mum will arrive and we'll have the funeral mass. We'll bury Dad's ashes and Camila. I'll be able to visit them both at the same time: very efficient.

I'm dreading it. I've never been to a funeral. Pretty worried that I might cry.

Tonight, Camila's husband, Saul, took me, Tyler and Ollie out for dinner. We were kind of subdued. Part of me is still amazed at what I've achieved. Yet I can't talk about it to anyone. It's a nightmare to think I'm going to have to lie to my friends. Even if they did wimp out and try to make me hand myself in.

Ollie mentioned that I seemed different. *Older*, she said. Tyler said it was understandable. On account of my seeing my sister drown.

They think that I "went off on one", that Camila's death, then Madison chasing me, almost drowning me, pushed me over some sort of edge. That's not quite the whole picture, of course. I reckon deep down, they know it.

Tyler and Ollie must be curious about what happened to me. But they don't ask – not any more. In the silence of their unasked questions, I sense a distance between us that wasn't there before. I can't tell if I caused it, or they did.

Near the restaurant, a group of young musicians congregated; a jazz combo. A tall, dark, very thin girl wearing a sarong with a sleeveless top stepped up to the microphone.

My eyes met Ollie's over our drinks. There was something new about the way she looked at me – a really searching look. Like she knew I was hiding something. And was curious.

But I'll never tell her. After what happened to Camila, I'm not telling anyone.

The band struck up their first number. I felt a stab at my heart the minute I heard the first line.

"A cigarette that bears a lipstick's traces."

I thought I felt my UK mobile phone buzzing. I checked – for a second I imagined I'd seen the words "Camila Call Me" flash on to the screen. But that's all it was; my imagination. I kept pushing buttons until Camila's number came up on the display. And for seconds, I stared at it.

In the distance I heard the flutter of windblown leaves; a tiny whirlwind. My mind went back to my dream, the leaf storm. I felt a sudden chill. Camila was like one of those leaves. Connected one day, gone the next.

362

The singer crooned the lines I was waiting to hear.

"A telephone that rings, but who's to answer?
Oh, how the ghost of you clings.
These foolish things remind me of you."

My finger hovered above the call button. After everything I've seen, I couldn't help wondering: is it possible that there's somewhere in the universe where Camila's number will ring, somewhere it might be heard?

Josh's Guide to Pronunciation

In my everyday life I have to speak three different languages – English, Spanish and even a little Portuguese (for my Brazilian martial arts class). Added to that, I sometimes have to use words from the home-grown Mexican languages like Mayan and Aztec. So here's a guide to how to say some of these words. Out loud, I mean. In case you ever need to.

A Guide to the Guide

1) There is no *oh* sound in Spanish. No tac-*oh*, no Catemac-*oh*. It's a shorter *o*, like in *hot* or *cot*.

2) In Spanish, the emphasis is usually on the second-to-last syllable (e.g., Benicio is *Ben-EES-yo*).

3) In Spanish, words starting with *v* have a sort of soft *b* sound. Not a hard popping *b* like you'd have in *bicycle* . . . try for something between a *b* and a *v* (e.g., Vigores is *Bee-GOR-rez*).

4) The *x* sound in Mexican words is often (but not always) soft, like *sh*.

5) I'm going to bundle all the Mexican-origin words, like Mayan or Aztec words, and call them all "Mexican". So there.

Atanzahab	Atans-ah-hab	Mexican
Au malandrau	Or-malan-draw	Portuguese
Agaltepec	Agal-teh-pec	Mexican
Bakab	Bak-ahb	Mexican
Becan	Beh-can	Mexican
Benicio	Ben-ees-yo	Spanish
Brujos	Broo-hos	Spanish
Calakmul	Calak-mool	Mexican
Cancuen	Can-cwen	Mexican
Capoeira	Capoo-wera	Portuguese
Catemaco	Cateh-mah-cor	Spanish
Cauac	Ca-wac	Mexican
Ceiba	Say-bah	Spanish
Cenote	Seh-not-eh	Mexican
Chaneque	Chan-eh-kweh	Mexican
Chechan Naab	Cheh-chan-nahb	Mexican
Chetumal	Chetoo-mal	Mexican
Chiapas	Chee-apas	Mexican
Cocorinha	Cor-cor-rinia	Portuguese
Delfin	Del-feen	Spanish
Ek Naab	Ek-nahb	Mexican
Ginga	Jeen-gah	Portuguese
Indigeno	Indee-heno	Spanish
Itzamna	Eets-am-nah	Mexican
Ix	Eesh	Mexican
Ixchel	Eesh-el	Mexican

Jalapa	Hal-ah-pa	Spanish
Jarocho	Ha-roh-cho	Spanish
Mayan	My-ann	Mexican
Muluc	Mool-ook	Mexican
Muwan	Moo-ann	Mexican
Nopales	Nor-pal-ez	Mexican
Orizaba	Oree-sah-ba	Spanish
Tapachula	Tapa-choola	Spanish
Tikal	Tee-kahl	Spanish
Tulum	Tool-oom	Mexican
Tuxtla	Toox-lah	Mexican
Queixada	Kay-shada	Portuguese
Valladolid	Bay-add-ol-eed	Spanish
Veracruz	Beh-rah-crooz	Spanish
Vigores	Beeg-or-ez	Spanish
Xibalba be	Shee-bahl-bah beh	Mexican
Yucatan	Yoo-cat-an	Mexican
Yuknoom ch'een	Yook-noom ch'-ehn	Mexican

Acknowledgements

To all the authors who've ever inspired me; to James, Lucy and Celia Catchpole for encouragement and reading early drafts; to my husband, David, for taking care of everything when I broke my leg and expressing such passion for my writing; to my daughter, Josie, for making an exception to her rule of not reading adventure stories and giving me so much great feedback; to my gifted editor Elv Moody at Scholastic for her enthusiasm and razor-sharp ability to improve the manuscript; to Georgia, Alyx, Jessica and Elaine at Scholastic for their excitement and support for *Joshua*; to my inspirational and brilliant agent, Peter Cox, without whom, quite simply, this book would never have happened; to all of you, eternally, THANK YOU!

Desperate to know what happens next? Read

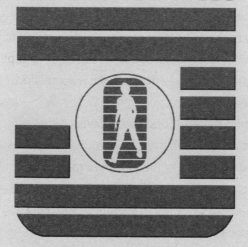

THE INTERNATIONAL BEST-SELLER

M.G. HARRIS

THE JOSHUA FILES

ICE SHOCK

*And now, a sneak preview
from Josh's next adventure...*

Minutes later, standing in the bus shelter, Tyler says breath-lessly, "Wow … what do you reckon to that story? Thompson's Mayan curse could be linked to the Ix Codex, innit? Didn't those blokes who emailed you say it was dangerous or cursed or summat?"

"It is cursed," I say, shortly. "But the codex isn't there any more. Someone got there already, years ago. And my dad would have known that too. What I want to know is, why did he go to the trouble of coming back here? With those NRO men?"

Tyler stares at me. "What are you talking about? How do you know all that?"

"My grandfather found the Ix Codex," I tell him. "And I think I know how – he must have found the stories about Eric Thompson's assistant in the local newspapers. Something must have put him on to Thompson – I guess we'll never know what. But once my grandfather realized that Thompson had some sort of cursed Mayan relic, he must have decided there was a chance it was the Ix Codex."

That's the thing about mysterious disappearances – one way or another, they pull in the curious.

Tyler isn't entirely satisfied with my answer, I can tell.

**Need to read even more of Josh's adventures?
Pick up**

Turn the page to read an extract

*Hungry for more action? Here's a sneak
preview of Josh's third adventure...*

"This whole Bracelet thing ... it's taken over you. Hasn't it?"

I can hardly believe what I'm hearing. Has she only just worked that out?

Ixchel continues, "Because maybe ... maybe you should be thinking more carefully about what you'll do ... if you fix it."

But I've never really talked about that in detail, not with anyone.

"You're going to use it to go back and save your father ... right?"

"Yes."

"But what if that changes things?"

I gaze at Ixchel in disbelief. "I want it to change things!"

"If your father isn't there on the volcano when we climb it – how do you know that you won't die? Or me?"

Exasperated, I say, "No one will die! I'll bring Dad back in the past. None of that mountain stuff will have happened. Dad can find the Ix Codex. Then everything will go on like before. Except that Dad will be the Bakab and I'll be back to my normal life."

Looking right into my eyes, with what I'm sure is a hint of a blush, Ixchel says, "So if this works ... you and me ... we might never meet?"

I mumble, "I'm sure Dad will introduce us one day ... he's

the one who agreed to us being fixed up, after all."

Softly she says, "And you're so sure that your father will find the Ix Codex?"

"Yeah … course … he had the same dream as me, the one with the brujo who says 'Summon the Bakab Ix'…"

Ixchel shakes her head. "You're taking a big risk. Your father had that same dream since he was a child. But even so, it never occurred to him to search for a Mayan codex in Catemaco."

"Me neither."

"No, Josh – you were led there."

I laugh. "It was a coincidence. I took a bus. Never planned it. I just wound up in Catemaco."

Ixchel sighs. "After everything that's happened to you … after the ghosts of Chan and Abita saved us in the caves … you still believe that it's all been a coincidence?"

"Yes," I say firmly. "A coincidence! They happen all the time. My dad could have found the Ix Codex in Catemaco, just the same as me!"

I stop talking. Why is she trying to talk me out of this? It's not so complicated. This isn't a Chosen One-type situation. Anyone with the Bakab Ix gene could do what I did.

Even Madison – and all those other guys in the Sect of Huracan who happen to have the Bakab genes.

I move away from Ixchel, let her see the anger that's rising within me. "I just want things back the way they're supposed to be."

Then I turn and walk away. And from behind I hear Ixchel's firm, quiet voice following me.

"But, Josh … how can you know what that is?"

BLOG ENTRY: JOSH NEEDS YOU!

Help Josh solve a murder!
Enter **www.thejoshuafiles.com** to join the
Alternate Reality Game
Plus:
Watch exclusive trailers
Enter competitions
Win cool prizes

BLOG ENTRY: THE COUNTDOWN HAS BEGUN!

Is the world really going to end in 2012?
Where did this all come from?
Is there any truth in the stories we're hearing?
Find out more at **www.mayan2012kids.com**

Keep up with M.G. Harris at:

www.themgharris.com – M.G.'s website
www.mgharris.net – M.G.'s blog
www.facebook.com – join the official *Joshua Files*
Facebook group
www.youtube.com/user/mgharrisauthor – visit
M.G.'s author channel on YouTube

Q&A with Maria Harris

Tell us a bit about your background.

I was born in Mexico City and came to live in Manchester, England via Germany when my parents split up and my air-stewardess mother met and married a British cellist who played for the Halle orchestra.

What inspired you to write *The Joshua Files*?

The Joshua Files is partly an idea I've had since I was fifteen and first visited the Mayan ruins of Yucatan and heard the more outlandish theories about the Maya. The idea of a boy hero searching for a lost Mayan codex spun out of a thriller I was writing as my first attempt at a novel when I broke my leg.

Is Josh or any of the other characters based on people you know?

Four of the characters are based on people in my family, but not Josh. I'll tell you about just one . . . my cousin Oscar Raul, an engineering student at uni, is the inspiration for Benicio. At least one character is based on a figure from Latin American literature, also, but that's one way I'm leaving clues to what is going on . . . so I won't tell.

What made you choose capoeira as the sport Josh is into?

I love the way capoeira looks and sounds, with all that singing and flying around. There actually is a local team who perform in Summertown during our annual street festival and I really enjoy watching them.

So far, *The Joshua Files* has had several plot twists, and it seems like there are more to come. Do you think of them before you write the story, or do they come to you as you're writing?

There are more to come . . . we've barely gotten started! I plot about 90% of every manuscript I write beforehand, so most of them are there from the beginning.

Describe your typical day.

I wake around seven a.m., go straight to the computer, fool around on my blog and Facebook, maybe chat with my cousin in Mexico if he's up late, then write until around nine a.m., shower and write some more, then stroll into Summertown for lunch. Then I write some more, waste more time on the Web, pick up my youngest daughter from school and wait for the eldest one to wander home. After that I TRY to be a good wife and mummy, doing family things, baking cupcakes, etc. . .